SEMI-SCRIPTED

A WANDERLOVE NOVEL

AMANDA HEGER

DIVERSIONBOOKS

Also by Amanda Heger

Wanderlove Novels
Without Borders

Diversion Books
A Division of Diversion Publishing Corp.
443 Park Avenue South, Suite 1008
New York, New York 10016
www.DiversionBooks.com

For more information, email info@diversionbooks.com

First Diversion Books edition November 2016.
Print ISBN: 978-1-68230-303-0
eBook ISBN: 978-1-68230-302-3

For Jamie,
my favorite sister.

DAY ONE

From a distance, Marisol could only make out a shaggy gorilla, giant yellow bird, and diapered adult baby. But by the time she reached the game show studio, the line of would-be contestants snaked from the door, down the sidewalk, and out into the parking lot. In front of her, a man in a purple unicorn suit swished his tail against her kneecaps. Behind her, a group of middle-aged women in florescent pink and green shirts clumped together, fanning themselves with handwritten signs and checking their bright green lipstick in a compact passed from person to person.

"I promise it is not too revealing." Marisol looked toward the white-blue California sky as she held the phone to her ear.

"Just promise you won't have a wardrobe malfunction onstage." Even from across the Pacific, her mother's voice carried more than a hint of desperation. And two hints of anxiety. Marisol still couldn't understand why this—a few hours on the set of her favorite game show—seemed to worry her mother more than anything else.

"I promise. I am being very responsible." And she was. She'd traded in her long-held plan of wearing a red and green bikini and a string of multicolored Christmas lights for a costume. Instead, she'd opted for a boring black T-shirt, snooze-worthy black jeans, and a pair of insomnia-curing cat ears. She'd even left the tail behind in her hotel room.

"I know you are, Mari. I'm so proud of you."

Marisol felt a million things about this trip, but not one of them was pride.

"I have to go now. They're here." She closed the tiny flip phone––a pay-as-you-go she'd bought when she'd stepped off the plane at LAX only a handful of hours before—and jammed it into her bag.

An army of women with clipboards marched through the crowd. The *Who's Got the Coconut* staff. Their tennis shoes clomped against the blacktop of the parking lot, and a murmur trickled through the crowd behind them. Each wore a stark white T-shirt with a drawing of a coconut across the front. Smiling from the center of each coconut—and directly between each woman's breasts—was the host of *Who's Got the Coconut*, Sammy Samuelson.

One of the women pushed her way along the edge of the crowd, her gaze shifting steadily between the clipboard and the salivating game show hopefuls. Marisol pulled her sign from between her knees, ignoring the fact that she smacked the unicorn's ass on the way up.

BIRTHDAY QUEEN. She'd written the words in the same bubble letters she'd drawn for years, ever since she was thirteen and watching reruns of the show in her doctor's office.

"Hello? *Hola.* Today is my birthday." She flipped her hair over one shoulder and put on her brightest smile.

The woman remained expressionless and marched on, stopping in the sparse shade of a palm tree at the edge of the lot.

"Is this your first time?" the purple unicorn asked. His horn was covered in silver glitter that rained down on the pavement in front of them.

"Yes. I should have gotten here earlier."

"Naw. If you don't have a ticket, it doesn't matter when you show up. They pick from the crowd at random to fill the extra seats. All those suckers been here for three hours already, but they probably won't get in." More glitter showered them both as he shook out his mane. "I keep telling Ted that—he's the one up there in the diaper—but he never listens."

"How many times have you been here?" she asked.

"Every Monday and Wednesday for the last year." His grin was wide and proud, and the perfect circles of purple blush on his cheeks crinkled with the movement.

Marisol imagined the prizes he must have stored somewhere in the back room of his house. A treadmill with a dozen settings no one could figure out, three sets of golf clubs, fourteen washer and dryer combos.

"Even got in once," he said. "About three months ago."

"Once?"

He nodded. "Maybe today will make two, huh?"

The *Who's Got the Coconut* woman made her way toward them again, eyes narrowed as she stared down at her clipboard. Marisol exhaled. This was it. The show's website said they tried to let in contestants who were celebrating special occasions. A birthday *had* to qualify. Marisol crossed her fingers and prayed this woman with the sweaty face and magical clipboard would let her in. Then she would have one big, mind-bending adventure as a contestant before she had to buckle down and focus on why she was in California in the first place.

"You. Unicorn. You're in." The woman blew her bangs from her forehead and took the mythical creature by the elbow.

"Excuse me," Marisol called after her. "Excuse me, today is my birthday."

"Sorry. The unicorn was my last spot. Try a more unique costume next time."

The last of her hope circled the smoggy Los Angeles drain as the crowd began to dissipate. Scowls marked the faces of fuzzy dragons, and the man dressed as a baby pulled a flask from his diaper. For a moment, Marisol considered asking him for a swig to wash away her sorrows.

Instead, she followed the crowd down a wide alley and then along a fenced-in parking lot. Mercedes after shiny Mercedes filled the spots, and she tried to imagine which television star belonged to which vehicle.

That one is Sammy Samuelson's. No, that one? Maybe that one with the funny—

"Watch it!"

Her right foot slipped out from under her. Then her left. Her butt smacked the pavement, and everything became a mess of feathers and expletives—some Spanish, some English. When they stopped, she lay on the ground beside a man dressed as a peacock.

A very large, very angry peacock.

"I said watch it." He sneered at her through the cutout below his beak. "Dumb bitches never look where they're going."

Marisol stood and dusted off her pants. "Excuse me?" This was too much. Being turned away from the show. Falling on her butt in front of all of these people. Then being verbally assaulted by a man dressed as a peacock. *On her birthday.* "It was an accident."

A small crowd had gathered around them, a mix of pedestrians and game show rejects staring at the tiny Latina and the fallen bird—who was still rolling on his back, unable to stand because of the weight of his tail feather display.

"Can somebody give me a hand?" He looked at the crowd.

She waited, arms crossed against her chest. No way she was going to help. In fact, she quite enjoyed watching him roll and grunt on the ground, the beak flopping over his face each time he moved.

"*Buenas dias.*" She stepped around him in long, quick strides, determined to make it back to the hotel without another man-bird related incident.

Footsteps scrambled up beside her, and Marisol whipped around. "You are a grown man in a leotard. Leave me alone."

"I am?" An unfamiliar face—human, definitely not animal—looked back at her. "I knew I was a little color-blind, but—"

"Sorry." She shook her head. "I thought you were someone else."

"Happy birthday, by the way." His brown eyes were a bit sleepy and framed by dark glasses. He had a bit of stubble along his jaw. Like he'd crawled out of bed ten minutes ago, with no time for coffee or shaving.

"How did you know?"

"I assume you're the queen?" He held up her hand-painted BIRTHDAY QUEEN sign in one hand and her cat ears in the other. "And this is your crown? Personally, I would have gone with jewels, but to each their own."

"Oh." She took her props and stuffed them into a nearby garbage can. Her mother had been right. Trying to cram a visit to *Who's Got the Coconut* into the first day of her trip was an irresponsible thing to do. She needed to be settled into her hotel room and practicing for tomorrow's interviews. With a twenty thousand dollar grant on the line, Marisol knew she had to be at the top of her nursing game. And her volunteer coordinator game. And her don't-let-my-family-down game.

"Wait. How about a birthday present?" With three long steps, the guy was beside her. He held out a green wristband. "A free ticket to see *So Late It's Early*."

"So late what?" Maybe it was a new game show. Maybe she'd walk out of the studio with a new car. Or a boat.

"*So Late It's Early*." He pointed at his gray T-shirt, where a cartoon sun poked over a jagged horizon. "A talk show."

"No prizes?"

"Sorry, no prizes. But the warm-up comedian sometimes gives out candy." He slipped the band onto her wrist before she could say "yes" or "no". "Make a right here and someone will scan your band at the holding area," the guy said.

The mid-afternoon sun reflected off the pavement, and sweat beaded along her hairline. The conference hotel was at least an hour-long bus ride from the studio. Plus, she still had to unpack, iron the wrinkles from her suit, and try to get some sleep before her interview tomorrow. The voice of panic settled into the back of her mind, filling it with words like responsibility. Restraint. Face of the organization. Bankruptcy. Sitting in the studio audience of a television show she'd never even heard of would be an epically stupid decision.

"This way? Through those gates?" she asked.

"Yep. Enjoy the show. And happy birthday."

With every step Marisol took, she intended to veer away from the studio and toward the bus stop. But she walked on, winding her way through the velvet ropes and picturing a set full of overstuffed furniture. There'd be air conditioning and candy. And maybe an up close and personal experience with a celebrity. On the plane, she'd spent two hours watching Delta Airlines' *Patriot Ninja Fighter* special. In her dream world, she'd end up sitting primly on a couch, surrounded by shirtless game show ninjas as they fed her birthday cake.

She stared at the line of people on the other side of the gate. This was not her dream world.

A man and woman in beige shorts stared into space while the teenagers beside them stared at the phones in their hands. Twin girls who looked about Marisol's age hooked their arms around an elderly woman. The woman's walker was covered in streamers, and a balloon floated from a string attached to one of the handles. BIRTHDAY GIRL! it read.

"Wristband?" a brunette with too much eyeliner asked.

"Oh. Sorry. I think I have made a wrong turn."

"*So Late*? This is the right line." The girl scanned her wristband. "They'll send someone to get you in a few minutes."

Marisol barely heard her. Her mind was occupied not with the old woman or the surly teenagers, but with the group of people at the very front of the line. Their obnoxious pink and green T-shirts hurt her eyes, and she would have recognized them even if there wasn't a grown man in a diaper and bonnet standing directly behind them.

"I am in the wrong place."

The elderly woman in front of her turned, her walker clomping with every tiny movement. "They always let in the freaks that didn't get into the game show next door. Back when Jimmy was here you had to be classy to get into the studio. None of this"—she waved her hand at the over-excited teenagers and the teetering baby— "disgustingness."

"Now, Gran. We talked about this." The girls turned their grandmother forward, the walker making everything happen in slow motion. *Sorry*, one of them mouthed.

"Welcome to the *So Late It's Early Show*. My name is Evan," a voice boomed from the front of the line. Marisol stood on tiptoe and craned her neck. It was him. Wristband Guy. Standing on a chair and holding a megaphone to his lips. "We're trying to fill the audience, so stick with us for a few more minutes and then we'll let everyone into the studio. In the meantime, I'll be around with some sticky notes and a bin for all your cell phones. They are not allowed in the studio. Thanks for your patience."

Three minutes later, Marisol's mind was still spinning as he stood in front of her.

"Hi, Betty." He waved to the elderly woman. "I guess you left all your electronic devices at home today."

"Sure did," the woman answered.

"Hey, the birthday girls found each other." He leaned in closer to Marisol. "It's not really her birthday, but she thinks it is. Phone?"

She stared at the sticky note and pen in his hand. "I am not going to stay."

"Why not?"

Because she'd never seen this show? Because she had other things to do? Because what kind of television show couldn't even fill its studio audience without pilfering from the game show next door?

"Look Gran!" One of the twins pointed over the other's shoulder. "There they are."

Marisol turned in the direction of the woman's wide-eyed excitement. A long white van pulled into the nearest fire lane. A giant bald eagle in a ninja mask graced the side, flapping its wings around the gargantuan letters. PATRIOT NINJA FIGHTER. The door slid open, and two brawny, muscle-bound ninja hopefuls walked straight into the studio.

"They are the guests?" she asked.

Wristband Guy nodded.

When was she ever going to get another chance to see the inside of a television studio? And an hour or two of fun before she had to buckle down wouldn't hurt anything, right?

Marisol dropped her cell phone into the container. "Happy birthday to me."

• • •

When the congratulatory "You've Been Selected for an Internship at the *So Late It's Early Show*" email showed up in his inbox a few months ago, Evan had been granted the prestigious title of script intern. For the first two weeks, he put in a few hours at the copy machine and a few more hours running scripts all over the studio, getting lost among the maze of nondescript rooms and closets. Every time he dropped a thick stack of papers in the writers' room, a buzz ran through him.

If he played his cards right, one day that could be him. After all, *So Late It's Early* was slated to be a pioneer in the late-night arena. No real competition. A witty host with a cult-like following. A slew of brilliant writers, poached from some of the best network comedy had to offer. Rumor was that James had never been asked to audition for the show. His legion of unrelenting fans had uncovered the location of the auditions—a comedy club down a back alley in Santa Monica—and begged James to show up uninvited.

Apparently it had worked.

Kind of. Until the ratings hit.

The show began to drown. They were probably still number one in the eighteen to twenty-five stoner demographic. But the critics hit hard and fast, and each article was like a wave of icy saltwater filling the show's collective lungs.

James January: The Biggest Flop Since Donald Trump's Comb-Over.

So Late It's Early? More Like So Late It's Over.

And Evan's personal favorite, *Patty Duke Spanks James January Every Night: Affiliates Choose Reruns Over* So Late It's Early.

The other interns started jumping ship. Then the writers. A mess of production assistants. A month into his internship and the show was being renewed on a week-to-week basis. Which was why today's celebrity guests were a couple of "ninjas" with IQ scores lower than their body fat percentages. It was also why Evan's duties had expanded to luring audience members into the studio, scouring the Internet for old videos of celebrity guests, and setting out food in the green room.

And today, he found himself dropping off a tray of protein shakes for tonight's esteemed guests, Tim and Tony. They'd requested three flavors: chocolate, banana, and chocolate banana. In frosted glasses with green twisty straws.

"Do you guys need anything else?" he asked.

"When do we go on?" one of them grunted.

"After the monologue and the main comedy piece. It's like…" He glanced at the monitor, which gave a live feed of the show. Currently, James was mid-monologue, and the guys' glazed stares said they weren't following. "Don't worry about it. Someone will come get you when it's time." He unmuted the volume on the television.

"Did you hear about the truck that overturned in South Dakota this afternoon?" Onscreen, James leaned in to address the camera directly. "Hold on. Do people really live in South Dakota? Where is that anyway? Shite. Can I say that one? Probably not." He shoved his bony middle finger up at the camera. "Anyway, truck overturns in South Dakota and spills five hundred pounds of McDonald's french fries all over the highway. Cops arrested the driver for driving under the influence. Said he'd been dipping into the *Special Sauce*."

Evan groaned.

"I don't get it," one of the *Patriot Ninja Fighter* guys said, producing a white powder from a bag and dumping it into a bottle of water. "Protein powder. Don't worry."

The door swung open, and Julia bolted in with her usual air of crisis and caffeine. She'd been promoted three times in the last two weeks, from writer to head writer to producer. Evan wasn't sure if she was a genius or on the verge of a nervous breakdown. Maybe both.

"We need to replace the *Facts of Life* parody." Her short brown hair stood up in fourteen different directions, and the circles under her eyes said she hadn't slept in days. "Couldn't get it past the network with James dropping the f-bomb every ten seconds."

"What do you need?" Evan asked.

"Another audience piece. Did Betty make it in today?"

"Yep." The snarky old woman was there every day, with her crinkled BIRTHDAY GIRL! balloon tied to her walker.

"Good. Grab her and one more. *Not* the giant baby this time. Please."

"Got it."

"I mean it, Evan. Not the baby."

"Don't worry," Evan told her. "I don't think that guy has washed his diaper in a month. Not going near him." But as he jogged out of the green room, he knew exactly where he was going. To the girl who'd cussed out the peacock on the front lawn. She was one of the only people in the audience not wearing a costume. And it was her birthday.

And she was hot.

He wound through the audience, stepping over outstretched legs and ignoring the smell of people who'd spent hours waiting— in hot costumes—in the late afternoon sun. Onstage, James threw the show to a commercial break. On a well-run, highly rated talk show, it would have been impossible to find the girl among the tightly packed house. But *So Late* was only 70 percent full, and half the audience looked like rejects from a furry convention.

The girl sat in the second row, eyes narrowed on the set. "They were coming to this show, yes? They must have been coming to this show," she said to the man beside her.

"Who?" Evan asked.

She jolted, sitting up tall with a light crease between her brows. "The ninjas. Are they next?"

"No. You are."

"What?"

"We need an audience member to play a game, and you're our lucky contestant. But we have to hurry. The show's going to start back up in a few minutes."

Her face fell into a frown.

She was going to say no. Maybe the guy beside her would do it. Or worst case scenario, one of those over-excited choir parents near the back. Their shirts would make for eye-gouging TV, but it had to be a better option than Ted the Man Baby.

"What do I need to do?" she asked.

"I don't know. It's, uh, kind of last-minute." Everything they did was last-minute. "But you'll get to go backstage. That's where the ninjas are."

She sprang from her seat as the lights dimmed. From across the room, he waved to Betty and the twins. By now, they knew their cue to shuffle their grandma backstage. The old woman had been a participant in every audience game the show had done in the last month. At first, she'd seemed reluctant and even a bit disgusted by James's onscreen persona. But with time and charm, the host wore her down. Now, Betty never missed a chance to flirt with James onstage.

Evan led the peacock fighter backstage and left her a few feet outside the green room. "I have to go help the other contestant. She's, uh, not exactly a spring chicken. Someone will be by to tell you what to do. Her name is Julia. She's about this tall." He held a hand to shoulder height. "Short brown hair. Kind of flops in her eyes all the time. Got it?"

No response.

He knew this must seem insane and confusing to anyone stepping onto their first television set, but it would take more time than he had to sort it all out. "So you're good?" he asked.

"*Gracias a dios*," she whispered.

Evan followed her gaze through the open door of the green room, where Tim and Tony were engaged in some sort of one-handed push-up competition. "Okay, good luck then."

Several minutes later, he found himself in a darkened hall, standing in front of one of the backstage monitors. There were a hundred things left to do before the taping was done, but he couldn't resist a quick peek at the screens. The girl stood on James's left side and Betty—with her birthday balloon—stood on the right. Both were dressed as Uncle Sam.

Uncle Sam from the early 1970s.

Onscreen, James put on his pipe-and-smoking-jacket accent. "Betty, I swear you're getting younger every day."

"It's my birthday, you know." She slowly lifted one hand from the walker and straightened her long white beard.

"You don't say." James looked directly at the camera, sharing the secret of Betty's daily birthdays with the home audience.

At this point, Evan suspected the home audience equaled the three people watching the show live and the other two recording it on their DVRs.

"And I understand we have another birthday girl in the studio. What's your name and how old are you today?" James asked.

The girl grinned and bounced on her toes. She was gorgeous, even in those ridiculous red and white striped bell-bottoms. "Marisol. I'm twenty-three."

"She's practically a baby," Betty said. The thin skin on her cheeks pinked and her blue eyes narrowed.

"Now, Betty. You're still my number one girl. Don't worry." James patted her arm. "Here's what we're going to do. Our guests tonight are from the not-quite-a-hit television show *Patriot Ninja Fighter.*"

Marisol squealed. The studio audience laughed.

Maybe for the first time all night. A burst of self-congratulatory hot air filled Evan's chest.

"I take it you're a fan?" James asked.

She nodded.

"Well, you're in luck." Even the host couldn't keep a straight face in the midst of her excitement. "Because they're going to help us play a game we call 'Uncle Sam'. That's it?" he asked to someone offscreen. "We couldn't come up with a better title? Fine then. Welcome Tim and Tony."

The muscle men strutted onstage, and the shorter of the two stood next to Marisol. She wasted no time in running her fingers up his arm. A ripple of laughter ran through the audience, growing louder and louder as she hammed it up. First, the petite Uncle Sam squeezed the guy's right bicep. Then the left, letting her mouth fall wide open.

"All right, all right," James said. "Any more of that and I'm going to have to charge you."

The audience rippled again. Their laughter echoed from the studio half a second before Evan heard it through the monitors.

"So what we're going to do is…" James's voice rolled on, explaining the rules.

Marisol and Betty would run to the other side of the stage, down a glass of "whiskey"—which was actually iced tea—run back, and concoct a replica of the Statue of Liberty out of all the grape-flavored bubblegum they could cram in their mouths. All in under three minutes. At the end, the wannabe ninjas would pick a winning sculpture.

Evan sighed. He'd seen this idea when he'd cleaned up the writers' room that morning. Someone—he suspected Julia—had crossed it off a list of ideas and scrawled a giant NO across the top.

On the monitor, Betty slammed her walker against the faux-hardwood, like a horse pawing at the ground before a race. But Marisol's smile slid from her face as she looked back and forth between James and the woman.

"I know what you're thinking," James said. "How unfair it is to put you up against someone like Betty, with all her age and experience and grit." He lowered his voice to a stage whisper. "She's got a liver like Fort Knox, and she won't hesitate to knock you down with her walker."

More laughter. Not the fake "ha-ha-has" the warm-up comedian forced out of the audience with threats and promises of candy. Real laughter.

Betty took off, not bothering to wait for a start.

"Well, go on." James pushed Marisol forward. "Someone in the audience has got a stopwatch, right?"

Evan chuckled as Marisol jogged toward the end of the stage. A muzak version of "American Pie" played over the PA system while she ran.

"Bet-ty. Bet-ty. Bet-ty." The woman slammed her walker against the stage as the crowd roared their usual chant. Not only did Betty appear in every conceivable audience game, but she won them all too. Who was going to take on an eighty-something woman who genuinely believed every day was her birthday?

"Mar-i-sol. Mar-i-sol. Mar-i-sol." A few voices rang out in the crowd.

That split-second decision to offer her tickets was paying off in spades. Super funny, really attractive spades.

"Evan?" A buzz of static followed the voice in his earpiece. "Someone puked in the holding area. Clean it up before we let the audience out."

• • •

The sugary, purple gum kept getting stuck in her beard, and eventually Marisol tugged the scratchy fake hair down around her neck like a tie. She wasn't quite sure what was happening, but this definitely qualified as her weirdest birthday to date.

"Time. Time," James January called out. "I don't know how long it's been, but I'm going to say long enough. When we get back, we'll see which one of these fine young women has created a true fucking masterpiece. Sorry, I mean, bleeping masterpiece. If I just say bleeping, will you still put the bleeps over the audio?" The host deadpanned into the camera, and the lights went dim.

"Stay here for a minute." James disappeared behind a scarlet curtain.

"Commercials," Betty added. "That's when he goes off and yells at everybody backstage."

"Good to know," Marisol said.

"Now I'm just going to warn you, I've got this thing in the bag. They bring me up on my birthday every year. And every year I win a prize. I think the birthday gods must be smiling on me."

Marisol bit her lip, trying—and mostly failing—to keep a straight face. "I appreciate the warning."

A girl dressed in head-to-toe black appeared behind Betty with a chair. On the other edge of the stage, the guy who'd given her the wristband took both of the purple, slobbery blobs to James's desk. A man with giant headphones ran toward a camera. Someone else rushed the stage to refill a mug of water on the desk.

This is what happens during commercial breaks?

James reappeared beside her, and the lights came up another degree. "Welcome back. Now let's bring out our celebrity judges. Tim and Tony from *Patriot Ninja Fighter*!"

They strode out on stage, more shiny and oily than before. For a brief moment, Marisol wondered what she'd have to do to get a job as an official ninja greaser. She knew she'd never leave nursing behind, but a second occupation wasn't out of the question.

"Tim and Tony, why don't you take a look at our replicas?" James asked. He pointed to the desk. Beside Marisol's sticky mess was a perfect replica of the Statute of Liberty. It stood nearly three feet high, and an embossed card below it said "Betty" in flowing script.

Clearly, someone had purchased a statue and spray-painted it purple. And it wasn't Betty.

This is why she always wins.

"Wait a minute." Betty clomped her walker against the floor. "What's the prize? You didn't tell us the prize."

"Hey, Betty. Let's not get greedy here," James said. "Who's to say you're going to win? Beauty is in the eye of the beholder, you know."

Marisol couldn't hold in her laughter any more. How was this happening? How was she standing on the stage of a show she'd never heard of, between an elderly woman and an Englishman, while they judged her ability to recreate the Statue of Liberty out of bubblegum? Suddenly, her face appeared on the overhead screen, and the entire audience laughed along with her.

"The winner gets dinner for two at a restaurant of her choice." James fell back into the stage whisper. "As long as it's Wonton Queen or the food court across the street at the farmer's market. And the loser has to grease down these two before the next segment." He jerked his head toward the celebrity judges.

"I forfeit. I forfeit." Betty hoisted herself up. "I want to grease those fellas. You got plenty of time to sow your Quaker Oats, honey." She hefted the walker toward Tim and Tony.

Thunk. Thunk. Thunk.

The audience stared in stunned silence. Across the stage, the ninjas wore identical expressions of mildly contained horror.

"Looks like we have a winner, folks." Even James was having a hard time keeping a straight face, and he lifted Marisol's arm in victory. "I think we could all use a commercial break."

The theme music played over the speakers, and the lights dimmed once again. The girl in black scurried onstage and carted away the sculptures. The twins wrestled their grandmother away from Tim and Tony. The wristband guy reappeared with a stack of papers for James.

"Do I go back to my seat now?" Marisol asked.

"Just a second," Wristband Guy said. "Good job, by the way."

"This'll work," James said. "Keep her backstage, okay?" He vanished behind the curtain.

"Me?" she asked. "Keep me backstage?"

Wristband Guy brushed a blond curl from his forehead. "Yeah." He pulled back the curtain and she followed. "James wants to bring you back on. Take off your clothes though. I mean, the costume. The costume. Shit." He pressed a button on his earpiece. "Nobody throw away the gum. We need the gum."

Then he was gone.

Marisol pretended not to be completely lost as the prop girl stripped off her costume. Onstage, James explained to the audience that he was about to tape a segment for tomorrow night's show. "I know, I know," he said. "You want to think the magic of late-night television happens in real time. Sorry, folks."

A few chuckles from the audience. The theme song played again, and James brought back his show voice. "You may remember tonight's first guest, well, from last night's show."

The prop girl gave her a nudge. "That's you."

Marisol stepped on stage. She caught a glimpse of herself in the monitor and saw the confusion written in her face. The audience laughed, and the sound wore away the last of the stress she'd been carrying. For the first time in weeks, Marisol felt like she could breathe.

Might as well end this birthday with a bang.

"Welcome back, Marisol." James sat at his desk and gestured toward the beige armchair beside him.

She sat and crossed her ankles. "Thank you."

"Now the seven of you who watched last night's show saw what happened. But for the rest of you, well, I'll let our guest tell you what happened."

"Me?"

He nodded.

"They made me dress up in this itchy beard and red, white, and blue hippie pants. And a big hat." She held her hand a foot above her head.

"Wait? Hippie pants?"

She knew there was a better English word, but here among the lights and laughter and adrenaline, it wasn't coming. "Like the hippies. You know, peace and love."

"Ah, of course. Hippie pants. I'm not always down with the American slang. I don't know if you noticed, but I'm not American." Stage whisper again.

"Me either," she whispered back.

"Really? Why are you here then? Vacation? Visiting family? Taking a chance on the American dream?"

"A conference."

"That's no fun. Next time say you're an international spy or something, yeah?" He winked at the camera. "Because nothing could go wrong with that plan, right?"

"Well, maybe—"

"So after you put on the outfit…"

She did her best to explain the gum building and the ninjas and Betty's eventual forfeit.

"And where did you go for dinner?" James asked.

"Dinner?"

"With your gift certificate." He gave her an exaggerated wink.

"Oh." She couldn't quite remember the name of the place he'd mentioned. "To the Wobbly Queen?"

It was clear he was trying not to laugh, and just watching him made Marisol lose it. "That's not the name, is it?" she asked.

"It is now. Who did you take with you to the Wobbly Queen?" He leaned in. Marisol could see the lines in his makeup, marked by sweat and laughter. Suddenly, she wanted to go along with everything he said. To see how far they could take this ridiculous bit. To see how many laughs they could get.

"I wanted to take the ninja fighters, but"—now she mimicked the host's stage whisper—"they were busy." She lowered her voice a half octave. "Betty."

James grinned, and the audience cheered. A few whistles in the back. Marisol sat up taller.

"If I'm not mistaken, you're wearing the same clothes today as yesterday. Must have been some date." He crossed his legs and leaned back in his chair.

"No. It was terrible."

"Terrible? How? Does this person have a name? Was it so bad you want to call him out on national television?"

For three infinite seconds, Marisol's brain blanked. She'd had plenty of terrible dates in her life, but she couldn't actually use those poor guys' names. Instead, she scrambled for a solution, clawing at anything—or anyone—close by. And just when she thought she'd have to roll over and give up the game, her eyes landed on a shadow along the far wall, the dim lights reflecting off one yellow curl.

"Him." She pointed.

The cameraman panned in the direction of her finger, stopping on the fat man in a baby diaper.

"No!" Marisol laughed. "Him."

This time the camera and lights found the right guy. "Evan? Our intern?" James asked. "Let's bring him out."

The audience clapped as cheesy porno music came in over the speakers and Evan lowered himself into the chair beside her. "You're ridiculous," he whispered.

She sat up taller. "Thank you."

"Evan, if we're being honest here, you look like the kind of guy who has no clue what he's doing with women," James said.

Marisol leaned in. Wristband Guy had practically forced her into the audience, and then he'd tossed her onstage. Certainly he could handle a little payback. "*Nada*. He needs lessons, James." She sat back in the lumpy armchair, grinning as the rumble of laughter echoed in her ears. "He needs an internship in dating."

DAY TWO

The note in Evan's mailbox felt like an initiation. Like he would open the studio door to find a candlelit secret passage. Someone would throw a robe over his shoulders, make him take an obscene pledge to the network, and induct him into the secret world of *real* television. Of *real* writers. But when he opened the door to room 214 Evan stumbled into the remnants of a fraternity party gone stale. Sandwich wrappers crinkled under his shoes. The smell of feet and mold grew stronger with every step, and a mysterious shit-colored stain covered the only free spot on the couch.

"Good. You're here. Welcome to the post mortem. We're about to get lunch." James pointed to the couch. "Sit."

Evan dodged the stain and perched awkwardly on the arm of the couch. James sat in a tattered recliner in the corner. Julia—looking well rested for the first time in weeks—sat in a wooden chair, one hand poised over her laptop and the other running over a broken nub on the chair's back. Writers and production assistants filled the other spots, faces Evan had grown to know but whose names remained a mystery.

"Has it come in yet?" one of the writers asked.

As if on cue, all of the other eyes in the room turned to the wall clock. 11:55.

"No," Julia said. "And it's not going to. Not after last night's show."

"One decent show isn't going to make up for a month of steaming shit," one of the writers said.

Everyone froze. Evan didn't even let himself breathe. This was not the welcome he'd expected.

"Who's responsible for that, huh Jerry? Not just me." James's voice held more defeat than disgust. More resignation than rage. "Just go. Go."

Before Evan could register what was happening, the door slammed shut behind the writer.

"Anyone else want to bail in the next"—Julia glanced at her laptop screen—"two minutes?"

Silence.

"Sorry, what's happening at noon?" Evan asked. Maybe they needed him to order lunch before then?

"Oh, right," James said. "Everybody, Evan the intern. Evan, everybody. Well, everybody but Jerry. He'll be back though. He always comes back."

Mumbled hellos and a few waves followed.

"Wednesdays at noon. The witching hour." James snarled. "Assholes, all of them."

Julia cleared her throat. "What he means is, the network lets us know if we're getting another week every Wednesday at noon. No word means we get to keep going. If they email us the closing notice, Friday's our last show."

"Oh. Wow. Okay. That's… interesting." He'd known the show had been universally panned by the critics. And the network was pissed at their fumbled chance to take this hour of late-night. But they couldn't even be bothered to come by in person? Or at least call? And none of that answered his biggest question: Why had he been summoned here in the first place?

The second hand moved in slow motion, and with every tick Evan tensed further. He forgot about the stained couch and the thick stench of rot and mold. He forgot about everything except the call he'd have to make. About how—if the email came—he'd have to swallow his pride, pick up the phone, and say, "You were right, Dad. I'm coming home."

From the recliner, James began to mutter, and before long the entire room was counting along with him. "Ten. Nine. Eight. Seven. Six." *The world's saddest rocket launch.* "Three. Two. One."

The voices dropped out and for two long beats, everyone stared at one another, their faces masks of disbelief. Then the eruption happened. Shoving, cheering, claps on the back. Someone pulled a six-pack out from behind the couch and cracked open a beer.

Evan's entire body drooped, and he closed his eyes. Another week without an execution. Another week he wouldn't have to make that call.

"You've got mail! You've got mail! You've got mail!" The robotic voice sliced through their excitement, and Evan watched as the sound drained the blood from their impromptu party.

"Seriously, Julia? 'You've got mail?'" someone asked.

"It's called irony." She didn't bother to look up, her focus consumed by the glowing laptop screen. "Dear James: We regret to inform you—"

"Son of a bitch." James smacked his hand against the recliner. "I'm sorry, guys."

But Julia ignored him. "We regret to inform you that your ratings last week did not meet the criteria agreed upon to merit continuation of the show for another week."

"Bunch of dumbasses wouldn't know good TV if it smacked them in the ass."

"James, shut up and listen," Julia said. She cleared her throat. "*However*, given the online interest in last night's show, we are willing to extend *So Late It's Early* for another week. Next Wednesday we will reassess, and…"

No one moved.

"And what?" James asked.

"They want us to up our ratings."

"How much?" James asked.

"A little. A 0.22 in the eighteen to forty-nine bracket. Last night was nearly that. We can do that, no problem."

No problem? That's a huge problem. A 0.22 hadn't happened even on the day the show premiered, when the network was throwing money at it instead of trying to sweep it under the rug.

Evan began planning the phone call to his dad. At least he'd have ten more days before he had to face the music. He finally stood, hoping the mystery brown stain hadn't somehow seeped into his jeans.

"So the lunch order?" he asked.

"It's on the way. We sent one of the other interns. The one with the blue streak in her hair? Looks like she killed a Smurf?" James shook his head.

"Penny," Julia said. "She's bringing pizza."

"So, uh…" He jammed his hands in his pockets. "You want me to…"

"Have you seen anything online about last night?" she asked.

"No." He'd stopped googling the show. Every swipe the critics took put him one step closer to ending up back in Peoria.

"Have a seat. We've got a lot of work to do."

An hour later, they'd watched last night's monologue, torn it apart, and put it back together again. Then the same with the celebrity interview spots. And Evan still had zero clue why he was in the room. He'd been tempted to pull out his phone and find out what people were saying about last night's show. But when one of the writers tried to check his email, the look Julia gave him could have slaughtered a dozen puppies.

"You've got to listen to what the guests are saying. It's obvious you don't give a shit. If *you* don't give a shit, how is the audience supposed to care?" Julia kept laying into James. And the writers. And the PAs. Like a tiny, crazy-haired Jack Russell, she dug in and wouldn't let go. And the bigger, slobbery dogs all stood back and licked their wounds when she was done.

Except James.

"You tell me how to give two shits about a couple of Eagle Ninja Fighters. Maybe if we weren't on week-to-week we could get a guest or two whose greatest accomplishment in life doesn't involve monkey bars."

"*Patriot* Ninja Fighters. It's *your job* to make them interesting," Julia said. "Besides, if we can get this intern dating segment off the ground, we can cut the interview time slots in half. At least until we can get some better guests."

Evan's face prickled with the stare of every person in the room. "Intern dating segment?"

"Somebody show the poor kid already," James said.

Within the minute, someone had shoved a tablet under his nose. Evan's own picture stared back at him from the front page of a celebrity gossip blog. In it, his eyelids drooped, and an I-just-ate-three-pot-brownies smile crossed his face. "*So Late It's Early* Finds Its Stride Among the Lovelorn and Lonely." As he read the headline, his eyes kept creeping across the screen to the other side of the picture. The side where the girl sat, mid-laugh, with dark hair reflecting the studio lights.

"This is maybe the worst screenshot of me ever taken. But I still don't get it."

"Worst? Seriously? Did you even watch the show?" Julia cued up the segment from last night. "The entire time you look like you're about to puke on her shoes. The. Entire. Time."

"I probably was. I'd just cleaned up someone's vomit in the holding area."

"Just watch." Julia hit play, and Evan's stupidity sucker punched him in the gut. Four years as a communications major meant he'd been forced to watch himself on-screen dozens of times. It always felt awkward and uneasy, but even after a hundred takes of the worst projects, he'd never in his life looked as ridiculous as he did on last night's show. That stupid pot-brownie smile? Not just a random screen grab. It appeared every time the girl glanced his way. At least there was no way for Julia to say he wasn't listening. He kept looking at Marisol like she was about to tell them all the meaning of life.

"Cut him some slack. That girl was way out of his league. Probably couldn't help it," James said. "Besides he's still green. Looks like he's fresh off the boat. Where are you from anyway?"

"Illinois. Peoria."

James let out a broad laugh, and the entire room—even Julia—

seemed to relax. "Well, if we put you on, this will definitely play in Peoria. Somebody give him the pitch."

One of the writers handed Evan a sheet of paper filled with scrawled handwriting and a few doodles in the corner. The only thing he could make out were the words across the top.

"Evan Becomes a Lady Killer (Figuratively. No Emails Please.)?" He took a deep breath and read it again. "Featuring Evan the Intern?"

"Think *Love Connection* meets *The Pickup Artist*," Julia said. "Like it or not, we're all hitching our wagon to your dumbass star."

• • •

Marisol would have preferred to wear her usual uniform, a pair of scrubs accessorized with a layer of bug spray and a pair of rubber boots. But anything—even the world's smallest bikini or formal ball gown—would have been preferable to this.

She tugged at the skirt one more time and straightened the sleeves of the jacket. Her mom was tall and built like a board. Trying to fit her own curves into the confines of her mother's scratchy wool suit was almost more than Marisol could handle. She was, quite literally, playing dress-up in her mother's clothes.

And the reflection in the full-length mirror of her hotel room proved it. She turned away, preferring to stare at the pinstriped wallpaper over that supremely awkward version of herself.

"*Sí*. Yes, it fits. Everything is fine, *madre*. I am not late. It starts at—" Marisol glanced at the alarm clock, and her throat went dry as the desert. "I have to go." She dropped the phone onto the bed. It bounced off the thick, maroon bedspread and clattered to the floor. But there was no time to search for it, not when she had exactly five minutes to scramble for her stuff, make her way from the seventeenth floor of the hotel to the ground level, and find her way to the biggest interview of her life.

Mistake. Mistake. Mistake. Sending me here was a big mistake. Marisol repeated the mantra as she waited three eternities for the elevator to arrive. She repeated it as she pried off her sensible black pumps and ran toward the hotel's conference center. And she was in the process of repeating it when the looming, gray-bearded man flung open the door to the interview room.

"I am very sorry." Marisol tugged on her left shoe and put on her best nonplussed smile. "The elevator was not working." Even to her, it sounded like a flimsy lie.

The man didn't say a word, and soon Marisol sat facing him across the table. She folded her hands neatly on the cool wood surface. Then on her lap. Then the table again. She stole a glance at the clock. For being only two minutes late, this was some kind of silent treatment.

"Melinda Gutierrez?" he finally asked.

"Marisol. Marisol Gutierrez. Melinda is my mother."

"It says here—"

"Yes, very sorry." She'd barely sat down and already she was two apologies deep. "My mother had a last minute medical emergency. I am here on her behalf. On *Ahora's* behalf."

"Oh, yes. I see here."

She expected a small smile. Or some acknowledgment that she was in the room.

"Well, let's get down to brass tacks," he said. "I've been looking at the information your mother submitted, and I've got to say I'm not convinced the Della Simmons grant is going to fix your financial trouble."

Marisol blinked twice. Hard. *Financial trouble.* Those were exactly the words her mother had used when she broke the news. Or rather, when Marisol pried the news from her.

"Twenty thousand dollars will go a very long way toward keeping our brigades strong." Already, her mother had cut the frequency of the brigades in half. Now, instead of packing her nursing gear and heading out into Nicaragua's North Atlantic region—the area where Marisol had been born, where much of her family still lived—every three months, she was going twice a year. "This money could be the difference between life and death for some people."

"Yes, but what is the long-term plan to get out of this crisis? Do you have a strategy for long-term change? Better ways to secure your government funds? We don't want to dump water on one fire only to see another blaze pop up in a year." The man scratched his beard as he looked at the papers in front of him.

For the hundredth time since she agreed to come on this trip, Marisol wished she could pick up the phone and call her older brother. This was his arena. Goals. Projections. He spouted long-term plans in his sleep. But he'd moved to the United States for two years to get a master's degree in public health. Now he called every Sunday to give her a recap of the things he was learning and tell her his plans to bring them back to *Ahora*. Marisol had never seen him so happy before. Neither had their mother. Which was exactly why she'd sworn Marisol to secrecy. She was afraid Felipe would hear about their financial woes, ditch his finals, and come running home. Only to find there was nothing left for him to save.

"Who really knows what will happen in a year?" The words were out before she could stop them. She'd spent hours practicing for these interviews. Hours stripping off her usual go-with-the-flow attitude and replacing it with the sheen of a type A businesswoman. "I mean, we have grants scheduled to come in with the Nicaraguan government. In one year, this will not be so much of a problem."

"Hmmm." He flipped a page. "On your expenses it says you intend to devote half of the grant to hiring a new physician. What happened to the old one? And why wasn't his or her salary included in those expenses?"

I am a responsible adult. I can make this work.

"Our usual doctor had to take some time away. He is working on a master's degree in public health. It makes the growing pains hard, but when he returns, *Ahora* will run better than before."

"Hmmm."

She fought the urge to offer more and more information. To fill the silence with her rambling.

"And your job with *Ahora* is what exactly, Ms. Guiterrez?"

"Nurse. I work in the Managua clinic—Managua is the capital—"

"I'm well aware of the capital of Guatemala."

Marisol held her breath a beat. She would *not* correct him. Her mother would die a thousand deaths if Marisol corrected him. "I work in the Managua—Nicaragua—clinic, but four times each year—two I guess, now—I travel with a medical brigade on the Atlantic coast. It takes four weeks each time. My job is to supervise the vaccinations and to guide the volunteers."

"Guide the volunteers how? It says here most of your volunteers are doctors and dentists."

"Sometimes the volunteers are not prepared for the conditions. Also, translation. English to Spanish. Spanish to Miskito. Miskito to English. And navigation. We travel by boat. Sometimes on horseback." She went on, steering the conversation right where she wanted it to go: the day-to-day of *Ahora* operations. She could talk for hours about the families she'd forged relationships with. The crying babies she'd watched grow into rambunctious toddlers. The people she'd treated for malaria, ensuring those toddlers wouldn't grow up without parents.

Like she nearly had.

Years and years had passed since Marisol and Felipe's biological mother died. Years and years since Melinda welcomed them into her home. But not a day passed that Marisol didn't miss her biological mother.

Marisol didn't mention that. Or the times she'd helped a few of the volunteers navigate more than just the rainforest. The brigades got lonely, and she was not someone who did lonely well.

"Very well." He flipped a few more pages. "And your presentation is scheduled for…" More flipping.

"Next Thursday." The thought of it still made her insides slosh. If only she'd had a little more time to prepare. If only her mother hadn't kept this secret for so long. If only Felipe hadn't left. If only she really *was* a responsible adult. "It is called Diabetes Self-Management in Central America: When Pumping It Up Is Not an Option."

"Pumping it up?"

"Yes. Insulin pumps. I am diabetic, and—"

"Is this going to be a humorous presentation?" The man's face puckered, as if she'd squeezed a lemon down his throat. As if sputtering out the word "humorous" made him nauseated.

"No. There are some funny parts. To try to keep it interesting, but—"

"And you won't be submitting a film to the festival?"

"No."

"That's too bad. The top prize is fifteen thousand dollars. We like to see our grant finalists taking advantage of every opportunity. I believe both of the other finalist organizations have submitted something."

Marisol fought to keep the pleasant smile on her face. She suspected she was failing. "Unfortunately, *Ahora* did not have the resources to make a film this year."

"Hmmm."

Three more vague "hmmms" and the interview was over. Until tomorrow, when she'd sit through another. And the day after, when there was another. Followed by an entire week of meetings and workshops and presentations. And if any of those things didn't go exactly as planned, they'd be followed by an entire life of searching for a job she loved as much as her work at *Ahora*.

An entire life of knowing she'd let her family down.

DAY THREE

With a month and a half as a Los Angeles resident under his belt, Evan couldn't imagine ever getting used to all this. The near constant sunshine. The tourists. The street performers. The traffic. Nothing about Peoria could have prepared him for the traffic. Especially since he'd spent most of the last summer driving his grandpa back and forth from the VFW to his apartment at the Senior Village.

And speaking of Gramps…

Evan turned down his radio and hit the speaker phone button. "Gramps, let me call you back."

"You little weasel. You said you weren't going to be on television." Gramps's voice rattled with years of cigar smoke and a lifetime of inhaling God-knows-what at the factory.

"Gramps, I've really got to go. I'm working right now *and* driving." He wove his decade old Ford Focus onto the highway, praying this would be the time he'd end up in the right place. He'd already dragged himself into three conferences today, and none had a bubbly brunette who loved ninjas.

"But that show isn't on until the middle of the night."

"We tape it in the late afternoon. I'm running some preshow errands. Can I call you back tomorrow?"

"When are you going to be on again? And don't tell me you don't know."

"Hopefully never," Evan muttered.

"Huh? This dang phone. So tiny you can't hear a word."

"It was a fluke. I'll call you back tomorrow. Okay, Gramps?"

"The van is taking us to the grocery store tomorrow."

"Saturday morning then?"

"I'll hold you to it, kid."

Evan knew he would. If he didn't call by noon on Saturday—Peoria time, no making excuses about West Coast time—Gramps would call in the cavalry at 12:01. "Stay out of trouble, Gramps."

Thirty minutes of too much honking and too much sun later, Evan wound his way up a narrow hillside to the slew of buildings surrounding Universal Studios. He'd hoped one of the hotels would hang a giant sign—"This is the Conference You're Looking For" or "Turn Right Here, Evan!" But they simply towered above him, gleaming and nondescript. An electric blue trolley full of tourists followed close behind him, and every time Evan glanced in his rearview mirror the driver looked more and more annoyed. He jerked the car into the nearest hotel parking lot and let them pass.

"This is bullshit." Evan threw the car into park and pulled out his phone. Certainly Julia had been joking when she told him not to come back without the girl. *So Late* was going to start taping in an hour. If he left right this second, he could make it to the studio in time to seat the audience. Assuming there was an audience—he hadn't been there to lure in unsuspecting game show hopefuls. Or distribute the scripts. Or put out snacks in the green room. Basically, there would be no show if he didn't turn around and head back this very second.

The phone chimed in his palm, announcing a text.

Julia: **Update?**

Evan shrank from the words on the screen. Maybe he could ignore it. Say he didn't want to text and drive. Especially on company time. She would have to appreciate that, right?

Ding.

Julia: **Pull over and call me. Now.**

So much for the head-in-the-sand approach. He still couldn't understand why this had become such a big deal. Yeah, a few random Internet forums and late-night celebrity "news" programs had gotten a whiff of his spot. One had said they wanted to see the "intern's orgasm face" again on an actual date with the girl. The headlines were almost as bad.

So Late It's Early *Finally Jumps into the Kiddie Pool: Intern Makes a Splash.*

James January: Saved by the Lovesick Intern's Bell.

Late-Night Waterboarding Continues: So Late It's Early *Grabs a One Week Reprieve.*

Every time, the tabloids bought into the idea that James and the writers planned the segment. But despite that, everyone seemed to believe Evan was actually as big of an idiot as he'd seemed. Or bigger. One forum even started meme-ing his stupid grin. Before long, an entire thread was dedicated to creating erectile dysfunction ads using his image.

By the third time he'd seen his face in connection with the words "if your erection lasts more than four hours," Evan was ready to hop in the car and head back to Illinois. Even if it meant admitting his father was right, that using part of the settlement money to come to Los Angeles was irresponsible and stupid.

"Julia? I'm not having any luck. I think—"

"We found her. She's at the Universal City Hilltop Hotel." Julia barked the words. "Penny, no. I said take these to Four B. God, why are the interns so incompetent this year?"

"Because instead of thirty you're down to three?"

"What? Did you hear what I said? Right next to Universal Studios."

Evan glanced out his window. Fifty yards away, the giant Hilltop *H* stared back at him. "How do you know?"

"Huh? No." Julia's voice muffled. "Black. James only takes his coffee black."

"Julia?"

"What?"

"It sounds like you really need me there. What if I—"

"We *need* you to make this work. I made a few phone calls. Pretended there was an emergency or something."

"Or something?"

"Look, I didn't say there was nuclear warfare going on or anything. Relax."

"You called every hotel in Los Angeles with a conference going on and pretended there was an emergency?" Evan stared out the window at the tourists. Parents with giant diaper bags in one hand and toddlers holding the other. Clumps of middle-schoolers, moving as a single unit while one or two exhausted adults trailed behind. A couple holding hands as they hiked toward the theme park. "Isn't that a bad idea?"

"Bad ideas don't work. Go there, find her, and get her to meet us at the studio tomorrow."

Click.

Evan shoved open the door and made his way into the hotel lobby. Stiff armchairs and leather couches littered the open space, and sun poured in through the massive floor-to-ceiling windows. To his left, a dozen or so business types sat at a bar, their sleeves rolled up, martinis in hand. To his right, the front desk, where a blonde woman clacked away at a computer.

"Hi. I uh…" He had no idea what to say. *Hi, I'm stalking one of your guests?* Could he pretend to be a pizza delivery guy? Even without the pizza? Was it too late to march out of this place? Would Julia really fire him? "I'm looking for Marisol. She's a guest here."

The clerk peered at him over her thick plastic glasses. "Last name?"

"Yeah, uh…" He could go with Julia's emergency bullshit, but then the poor girl would come tearing down the stairs thinking there was an actual emergency. There was no way she'd agree to come to the studio after that. "I'm not sure, actually."

"Sorry. Need a last name. Hotel policy." She turned back to the computer screen.

"You can't ignore the policy, just this once?"

"No."

"What if I told you it was important?"

Her head jerked, only a fraction of an inch. But it was enough to tell him she was listening.

"Well it is. Really important, I mean," he said.

"Really important how?"

He pulled out his phone and prayed this would work. Prayed the woman was one of those people new enough to Los Angeles that they were still impressed by the magic and thrill of Hollywood. "Look."

The clerk's eyes widened as she watched the clip. She laughed and groaned in all the right spots, and hope started to climb inside him. All he had to do was explain the show wanted to bring Marisol back. Maybe he could even promise the clerk free tickets in exchange for making the bit happen. "That's Marisol. The producer—"

"Boy, you have got it *bad*." She hit the repeat button and chuckled as the segment played again. "That *is* really you, right? You look taller in person. She's pretty though."

"Yeah, that's not—"

Her pleasant customer service smile turned to a wicked grin. "Is this your moment? Your grand gesture? Are there cameras?" She fluffed her hair and produced a tube of lip goo from the counter.

"It's not like that. I—"

A tall, thin man in a suit and tie squeezed into the tight space behind the front desk. The nametag on his chest read "Jim, Manager. Let me help you."

"Is there a problem, Linda?" he asked. "You seem to be having a lot of problems lately."

Her face went slack, and she shoved Evan's phone back across the counter. "None at all. Thank you for staying with us, Mr. Howard."

Evan glanced over his shoulder. No one except the crowd at the bar. "Oh. No, thank you. It was a lovely stay." Automatically, his voice deepened, making him sound like a grade A douche bag. Why did he always sound like an idiot lately? "I can't thank you enough for your assistance."

He waited for the man in the suit to slip away, but neither of the hotel staff moved.

"Linda?" Evan asked.

"Yes, Mr. Howard?"

Last shot, Evan. Make it work. "That drink special you told me about? The grand gesture?"

She bit back a smile and nodded.

"Is it being served at the bar this afternoon?"

Jim the Manager picked up a stack of paperwork but didn't leave. "I don't know if we have that on our menu, sir. Perhaps—"

"Oh, it's definitely on the specials today," Linda said. "You should visit the bar before you leave. See if you can make—I mean *drink*—one."

Evan kept his head down as he moved toward the bar, cutting through the maze of people in dark suits. They seemed to fill every corner, bringing with them the smell of faded perfume and fresh booze. Sandwich board signs popped up at odd intervals, all with arrows pointing down a dim hallway. DELLA SIMMONS GRANT FINALISTS, THIS WAY.

Evan snagged the last seat at the bar, ordered a beer, and said a prayer that Linda really believed in grand gestures.

• • •

The first time the hotel room phone rang, Marisol ignored it. The only person who knew she was in Los Angeles was her mother, and she wouldn't be calling on the room phone. Her mom saved her pep talks for the cell phone, which was why Marisol was also ignoring that. But after today's interview debacle—squirming in her chair while a woman with the thinnest eyebrows Marisol had ever seen stared her down—she was considering turning the phone off for the next week and a half. It couldn't be hard to pretend she'd run out of minutes.

The second time the room phone rang, Marisol's heart rate skyrocketed. What if it was someone from the conference? What if they needed her for something important? What if she'd missed a meeting? She grabbed for the receiver with her pulse thudding her in throat.

"Hello?"

What if things had gone so poorly the last two days that they wanted her to leave?

"Miss Gutierrez?"

"*Sí.* I mean yes." *Calm down.* The second Marisol had agreed to go to this conference, she'd pulled out all the English-speaking stops. For two weeks, she'd dusted off and polished her English until it shined like her uncle's bald head on Christmas morning. She didn't need any misspeaks clouding her chances of getting the grant.

She was doing that all on her own.

"This is Linda from the front desk. We have a—"the woman let out a giggle before clearing her throat"—package here for you."

"A package?"

"Yes. We need you to come down and get it immediately. It's waiting for you at the hotel bar."

Click.

Marisol stared at the phone for a full three seconds before heading toward the elevators. Who would send her a package? And why would they send it to the hotel bar?

By the time she stepped into the lobby, she'd decided it must be from the conference. Probably more paperwork. This week was nothing but grant interviews, and they'd already given her two binders full of information. They'd probably killed three forests' worth of trees to put together handouts for the actual conference.

"Hi." She smiled at the bartender, a sexy muscly type—her type—and wished she was here for fun, not work. The way he smiled back made her suspect they could have a lot of fun together. She leaned one elbow on the marble bar top. "There is a package here for me? Marisol Gutierrez?"

Hot Bartender kept polishing the glass in his hand, but his green eyes never left her face. Behind him, dozens of small mirrors reflected the room around them. And his backside. "That's quite the pickup line," he said.

"No. The woman at the front desk—"

"Hey. It's me. I'm the package."

Marisol turned away from Hot Bartender and toward the direction of the voice. Her brain scrambled to put a name to the face, but it kept coming up short. Then a curl flopped across his forehead and everything jolted into place. Wristband Guy.

"Okay, that sounded terrible. Sorry. Evan, from *So Late It's Early.*"

"Hi, Evan." She wasn't sure what to think. How had Wristband Guy found her all the way across Los Angeles? Was she about to become the victim of some international kidnapping scheme? Was he one of those weirdos who'd gather every piece of personal information about her? Mail her love notes and toenail clippings every month?

"You want a drink or something?" he asked.

"No."

The low rumble of happy hour barely filled the awkward silence between them.

"I guess you've seen the show? The one where you were on the other night."

Marisol shook her head. "I think this hotel does not have the right channel. I tried to watch, but it was playing a show about identical cousins?"

Evan shifted in his seat and took a big gulp of the beer in front of him. "The host, James January, he really liked you. He sent me to ask if you'd come on the show again."

"He sent the wristband guy?" Something felt off. This guy was definitely going to send her toenail clippings tomorrow.

"I'm an intern. He's taping the show right now, so they sent me. Also, they, uh, want us to be on the show together."

"No, thank you." Maybe if she sprinted out right now, he wouldn't have time to follow her back to her room. Maybe if she transferred to the hotel next door he wouldn't show up here again. She'd be on the hook for two really expensive hotel rooms, but a little more *financial trouble* seemed like a small price to pay in this scenario.

"Wait. Please? Let me explain. I can call the show and put our producer on if you want. I'll prove it." The sincerity underlying the desperation in his face stopped her in her tracks. He looked like the type of guy who changed tires for old ladies and volunteered at animal shelters.

And if he is going to send me his toenails, he has already found me.

Marisol sat on the stool beside him. "Explain."

Through a half dozen more swigs of beer, he explained the plan. On Monday, James would claim the show "found" footage of their horrible date. Evan would play the part of the bumbling, naïve intern—with a serious case of lovesickness. Marisol would act annoyed and exasperated. Essentially, the whole thing was a setup so they could turn him loose on a new unsuspecting woman every week.

"They'll probably find plants for the next one though," he said.

"You are going to date a plant?"

A grin broke his serious demeanor. "Audience plants. The show'll hire an actress to sit in the audience this time. Then I'll go on a fake date with her. Rinse and repeat."

"I cannot." Absolutely not. The conference—this grant—required her entire focus. Her job was on the line. Her mother's job was on the line. The health of hundreds of people without access to medical care was on the line.

"No? You won't even consider it?"

Marisol shook her head. "I have other things I must worry about right now."

"We can work around your conference stuff. When does it end?"

"It starts on Monday."

"Oh. Okay. Great, so you have a few days. We can tape some stuff tomorrow night. It'll only take an hour or two. Won't interfere with your work stuff at all. What do you do again?"

"I am a nurse."

Something in his expression changed. Softened at the edges. "Cool."

Over his shoulder, a small group of high-heeled women caught Marisol's eye. Two, with their hair in tight buns and their suit jackets slung over their chairs, and another with a close cropped style that set off her perfect pixie features. From afar the pixie looked sweet and approachable. But based on this morning's interview experience, Marisol knew she was a force of nature—a monsoon to be exact.

The woman—Hillary Huffington—had quizzed her for twenty minutes about things like planned giving strategies, supply costs, and community-driven action. Marisol wanted to sink further into her chair with every question. She'd read the *Ahora* mission statement and financials a dozen times on the plane. Her mother had conducted three mock interviews, and Marisol had aced them each time. By the time she'd landed in Los Angeles, Marisol had convinced herself she had a fighting chance at the money.

The interview with Hillary Huffington had nearly ended in a knockout.

Marisol had been the one to take all the blows.

"You okay?" Evan's face bobbed into her view before he glanced over his shoulder. "What's so interesting?"

"Nothing." She shook her head, trying push away the entire thing, but she couldn't get her gaze to budge. Who were those other women? Why did they look so familiar? And why did they seem to be having such a good time? To Marisol, Hillary seemed as pleasant as an angry scorpion. On steroids.

"Who are those people?" Evan asked.

"I don't know."

"You're staring at them like you know."

A stack of folders sat on the table in front of one of the women. A bright blue logo danced across the front and slashed purple letters wrapped around it. Marisol had seen that logo before. She leaned forward, straining to make out the writing.

"Um, hi?" Evan pulled back, forcing Marisol to realize how much of his personal space she'd invaded. She'd almost forgotten he was there. And she'd almost ended up in his lap.

"Sorry. Can you read that?" she asked. "On the table behind you—the one with the three women?"

He looked over his shoulder again, giving her an up close and personal view of his slightly overgrown sideburns and hard jawline. Somehow, she'd missed the fact that Wristband Guy was cute. Really cute. Definitely not her type—Tony and Tim the Ninjas were more her style—but Evan was not bad to look at. Not bad at all.

"I can't tell. Hold on." He extricated himself from the bar and headed toward the table of women, pausing a beat as he walked by. If Marisol hadn't been watching so closely, she wouldn't have noticed Evan's gaze shift to the folder.

He snickered all the way back to the bar. "People United for Body Euphoria."

The words dislodged the memory, and Marisol's stomach swallowed itself whole. People United for Body Euphoria. One of the three finalists for the Della Simmons grant. One of the three finalists who'd sat through an interview with the Scorpion Pixie. And, of the three finalists, they were the only ones sitting with her over a bottle of red wine. Marisol's chances of saving *Ahora* were being flushed further down the toilet every second.

Marisol flagged down the bartender. "Mojito, please."

"Are you having a drink with me because you can't stop thinking about how terrible their name is?" Evan asked. "Or because you've decided you want to go on a fake date with me?"

"Neither." She put her face on the bar top, ignoring the sticky substance hitting her cheek. "What is wrong with their name?"

"People United for Body Euphoria? P-U-B-E."

She shrugged. "So?"

"They've named themselves after pubic hair."

"Oh!" Marisol almost felt like smiling. At least *Ahora* would never be compared to pubic hair. Maybe that was why they were meeting with Scorpion Woman, so she could give them some pointers on avoiding embarrassing acronyms.

"So you know those Pube ladies?" Evan asked. His smile left a deep crease on both sides of his face. An easy smile that wasn't quite as dopey as the fake, pretending-to-be-in-love one he'd worn onscreen. This was his real smile, she could tell.

Marisol barely knew this guy, but at this point she'd spent more time with him than anyone in Los Angeles. And she had to tell someone. Anyone. As she sucked down her mojito, she spilled the whole story. Her job, the grant, the way she'd ended up taking her mother's place at the conference. How she felt like a puppy dog paddling in a pool filled with sharks.

A solid twenty minutes passed before she stopped for air.

"Wow."

"That is why I cannot do your show. I have to focus on the conference. I have to give a giant presentation next week, and I have not had time to prepare. I have to make them think I know what I am doing, but…"

Evan looked at his empty glass, then back at her. "You think you don't know what you're doing? You go out on these brigades all the time, right?"

"Every three months since I was eighteen—as a volunteer. And every three months since I graduated—as a nurse."

"Then I guarantee you know more about what you're doing than someone who would name their organization Pube."

She nodded toward the table of women, who were laughing and pouring themselves more wine. It wasn't just their shiny lip gloss and perfect manicures that made her feel inferior. "I do not know how to do that. How to never say stupid things. How to be so perfect all the time."

Evan shook his head. "You're being too hard on yourself. You need to have some fun, and you had fun on the show. I saw you think about knocking Betty's walker out from under her during the audience game."

"I did not!" She had.

He held up a hand. "Hear me out. Have some fun. Relax. When we're done taping, James will make every person in the studio help you with your presentation. If there's anyone who knows how to pretend like he knows what's he's doing, it's James January. This is Hollywood. We can make your presentation shine." He leaned in closer and lowered his voice. "And you'll be way ahead of the Pubes over there."

Marisol dragged in a deep breath. The weight of the interviews and the presentation, the financial troubles—all of it—threatened to crush her into a thousand, jagged Marisol-shaped pieces. Maybe Evan was right. If anyone could help her put a veneer of perfection on her presentation, it *had* to be Hollywood.

"James will help me with the presentation?"

"Yep. You want to practice in front of an audience? You got it. You want someone in our graphics department to make full color charts and graphs of your…"

"Pump It Up."

"Of your Pump It Up presentation? Done."

"What if people see me on the show? And then they think I am not a very serious nurse."

"You aren't a very serious nurse."

Marisol pressed her lips together. Just because she was young didn't mean she wasn't serious about her job. "I am."

"You're a nurse. And probably a very good one. But you aren't a *very serious* nurse. Very serious nurses have asses the size of China. They're always scowling, and they *enjoy* jabbing needles into people."

She laughed. She couldn't help it. She did sometimes enjoy sticking needles into people. "But maybe everyone expects me to be a *very serious* nurse?"

"Maybe," Evan said. "But maybe not. Maybe they want a cool nurse who knocks down old ladies for a chance to grease down ninjas. Besides, no one watches the show. It's on the chopping block. It airs after midnight, and you said this hotel doesn't even have the right channel. So the chances of anyone from your conference seeing it are slim to none."

With a start, she realized hope had taken root in her chest. And the more she thought about it, the wider its branches spread. She pictured herself onstage, commanding the attention of everyone in the audience. With the help of the show, she could make the presentation look like a million dollars. Make *Ahora* look like a million dollars. And then she could call her mother to say those two little words they all needed to hear. *We won.*

"I have one more condition," Marisol said.

"Done."

"I did not tell you what it is."

"Then tell me."

She grabbed a piece of paper from the bar—some flyer the conference had set out on every available surface—and scribbled down her phone number. "I want to be a contestant on *Who's Got the Coconut.*"

DAY FOUR

When Evan started at *So Late*, Friday afternoons had consisted of a few menial chores, a couple of coffee runs, and kicking off early for happy hour with the other interns. But by week three, Friday had become pure, unadulterated chaos.

Now, Friday was the day the skeleton crew scrambled to pick up all the balls they'd dropped during the week. Friday was the day he spent running from one task to the next, completing the dozens of tedious jobs left undone by the long gone interns. Friday was the day James January locked himself in his office and manically dissected the show's numbers while creating a frame-by-frame, joke-by-joke analysis of each episode.

Without fail, at one o'clock James would emerge with a piece of paper in hand, his fingertips smudged with ink. "We had a major drop off after the monologue," he'd say. "Somebody write me some decent hooks, damn it." Or "We got a big boost online this week, but our live numbers tanked after Thursday. Why the hell can't we do Thursdays?" Somehow the man knew exactly what each of his thirteen viewers were doing during every second of the show—when they peed, left for snacks, or passed out in a drunken stupor.

Last week, Evan managed to escape James's clockwork complaints by organizing the props. This week he planned to do the same, and he stood in front of the prop closet, surveying the damage. It was somehow worse, even though he'd spent hours last Friday tagging and sorting the contents. Musty junk brimmed from every corner, barely leaving him a place to walk. But if he was lucky, no one would find him for days.

Or at least hours.

Julia would turn the studio upside down, or maybe worse, if he didn't show at exactly four o'clock—the call time for his "date" with Marisol. The producer had almost flipped the entire place over last night when he'd told her about the promises he had to make.

"You promised *what?*"

"She has this presentation. It's—"

"Not that, Peoria. Tickets to *Who's Got the Coconut?*"

"Not tickets, exactly. She wants to be a contestant." Evan had assumed it wouldn't be a big deal. The show ran under the same network umbrella. And everyone knew *Coconut* didn't choose its contestants randomly. There were interviews and some top secret formula that seemed to weigh the decibel of the contestant's scream, the ridiculousness of their costume, and the likelihood they'd drop the f-bomb on television. Even on her own, Marisol was a shoo-in.

"James and Sammy Samuelson do *not* get along." Julia rubbed her temples—not like she was soothing a headache. More like she was gathering her fury.

"They don't?" he asked.

"Why don't you know this stuff? Don't you want to work in television?"

"You said to do whatever it takes. I did whatever it took."

"I meant to offer her oral or whatever. Not this. God, James is going to lose it if he has to grovel to Samuelson."

Which was why, this morning, Evan shunned his other duties in favor of organizing the prop closet. Again. He curled a four-foot rubber snake along the edge of the table, then built an entire pyramid of fake dog turds.

"This is why the show is failing." The voice startled him. Plastic shit clattered to the floor. "We spend all our money on poop and not enough on decent writers."

Evan cleared his throat. "Hi, Mr. January. I didn't realize you were in here."

The host sat on a footstool in the back corner of the room. His blue T-shirt blended in with the light blue walls, and when he ducked the right way he disappeared behind a tower of boxes. Boxes—Evan knew—that held the remains of a plastic skeleton, an urn Evan was too scared to open, and fifteen pairs of red high heels.

"This is my think tank. Being around this mess settles my mind. Unsettles my stomach, but, you know, everything's a trade-off."

"Sure." Evan fumbled with the snake. He was alone with the host of a late-night talk show. Had a captive audience with a man who could potentially launch his fledging writing career into orbit. He needed to say something. Pitch something. Make the man laugh. "You want me to go? I don't want to disturb you."

"Hand me that femur, would you?"

Evan racked his brain, trying to remember which bone was the femur. He grabbed the biggest piece of skeletal plastic he could find and handed it over. "This one?"

"That'll do." James waved the bone around like the conductor of an undead orchestra. "I heard you found the girl."

"Yeah. Kind of. Julia found her, but—"

James shook his head. "Look, Cletus. If you want to get ahead in this business, you've got to start taking credit for anything you can. You went to the conference and dragged her back to the studio, right?"

"Not exact—" Evan stuttered at James's raised eyebrow. "Yeah. I convinced her."

"Good. I know you're not as dumb as you look." He punctuated each syllable with a swing of the femur. "For whatever reason, people loved your dumb-as-a-box-of-press-on-nails shtick, so we're running with it. But we've got to make it big. We're going to launch a full-out social media war with this thing, so go big or go back home."

Evan laughed. His mind couldn't handle the sheer weight of the words. Like he couldn't comprehend what James was telling him. *Social media war?* "I think people liked the girl—Marisol. Don't know how much it had to do with me."

"What did I just tell you?"

"I look as dumb as a box of press on nails?"

"Well, yes. But come on, man. Take credit for something here. You're a bloody intern. You make this bit work and we get another week. Maybe two. The show gets picked up for twenty-six weeks. And then guess what?"

"What?"

"You'll have a job here. Probably a half dozen other job offers too. Maybe even a show that doesn't have thirty piles of dog shit on the ground. Now go find the rest of the writers and make sure they don't screw up your shot."

Interns weren't offered jobs out of the blue like that. It didn't happen, at least not before the end of their internships. But the words crept under his skin, buzzing until he couldn't ignore them anymore.

Five minutes later, Evan shoved open the door of the writers' room. He didn't knock, and he didn't ask for permission to join them. He'd always kindled a hope that this internship would lead to an offer. For a few weeks, that flicker had almost gone out. But now the host's words had sent it into wildfire territory. "James said to help."

The guy closest to the door nodded and pointed at an empty folding chair. "What time is she coming?"

"Around four. Depends on the bus schedule, I guess."

"You didn't send a car?"

"I can do that?" Evan blinked. Marisol said she'd taken the bus to the studio the first time, and they both assumed that was how she'd make it back tonight.

"Not now. It's too late," the guy said. "Go pick her up when we're done here. The buses are always late. Julia isn't going to want to be here all night."

"Yeah. Okay."

"I'm Andrew." He jabbed a pen at his chest, then introduced the rest of the writers in the room. "We were brainstorming desk pieces for next week. Let's run what we've got for the date instead, so lover boy here can go get the girl. Then we can pick this back up."

James's words buzzed louder. *Take credit for something here.* "Evan."

"Huh?"

"My name is Evan."

"Until we get a six-month pick up order, you're whatever we say you are. Let's go."

Evan listened as they spitballed, lobbing ideas back and forth across the table like a television show version of the world's slowest ping-pong tournament. A few ideas rang out as mildly funny, but none had that thing. The thing that made the studio audience erupt into laughter. The thing that pulled the home audience from the edge of sleep and made them turn up their televisions.

"What do you think?" Andrew asked. "Want to run through one of these? Let's do the first one: Accidental Dim Sum."

He didn't want to run through any of these. They were—as James would say—shite. Complete shite. *Go big or go back to Peoria.* "We need to use Marisol more."

"I'd use her six ways to Sunday," one of the writers chimed in.

Evan ignored him and focused his attention on Andrew. "There's too much of me in these. I mean, sure, I can look like a mooning idiot and people will laugh, but it'll get old fast. People liked the first one because she was so unpredictable."

"So what do you propose?" Andrew looked bored. And impatient.

"Keep it unpredictable. Go semi-scripted instead. Give her a few lines and ideas, then turn her loose."

"She's not a professional, man. I think that's a bad idea."

Maybe it was. Evan barely knew Marisol. She had no comedy training. She was being consumed by this grant stuff, and she wasn't exactly excited about being on the show. Giving her open stage to make or break his writing career—all of their careers—might be the worst idea he'd ever had.

Evan took a deep breath. "Do it semi-scripted."

• • •

Every time her mother called, Marisol let the phone go to voice mail. She replied with a variation of the same text again and again.

Sorry. Very busy. Will call soon. Everything is fine.

It wasn't fine.

She'd gone down to the hotel lobby for breakfast to find the Pube ladies sipping coffee with Mr. Morgan, the man who'd interviewed her the very first day. Emboldened by caffeine—or perhaps pure desperation—Marisol pulled up a chair.

"So nice to meet you. Are you looking forward to the conference?" she'd asked.

The women cocked their heads, like confused puppies. "Right. You're the girl from Nicaragua."

Marisol noticed the way she'd spit out the word "girl." Like Marisol was getting ready for her first day of kindergarten.

"Excuse me," Mr. Morgan said. "I'm going to get some more of those eggs."

The second he was out of earshot, Pube One morphed from pleasant business woman to sneering she-devil. "Feel free to leave now."

"Excuse me?"

"You can't just leech onto our networking efforts," Pube Two said. "It looks desperate."

Marisol stabbed her eggs and pretended she wasn't sitting at a table with demons in suits.

"The Hilltop always does the best breakfast. Top notch." Mr. Morgan slid into his seat.

"It was a very good choice for the conference," Marisol said. "Are you from Los Angeles, Mr. Morgan?"

"Please, call me Chadwick. And yes, born and bred Californian here."

It was working. She could tell by the depths of the hate pooling in the Pubes' eyes. Marisol went with it. She inserted herself into every piece of conversation, making small talk and feigning interest in Mr. Morgan's job, which seemed to involve shuffling paperwork all day long. By the time Marisol got up from the table to get ready for her last interview, the cranky old man was wishing her luck.

Take that.

But the feeling didn't last. First, the iron in her room went on the fritz—leaving her with a burn along the collar of her shirt and the world's deepest wrinkles in her skirt. Then the elevator clogged, leaving a bottleneck of people for her to wade through. When she finally made it to the interview room—on time for once—she found a note jammed into the crease of the door.

She plucked it from the slit and unfolded the paper. "Afternoon interview cancelled?"

No explanation. No promise to reschedule.

She flipped open her portfolio and rifled through the papers, searching for someone to call. There had to be someone who could explain. Or fix this. She was *not* going down without a fight.

"Hey," someone said. "They cancelled you, too?"

She turned and looked into the face of an angel. An angel in a suit, with dark brown eyes and a darker brown beard. Under normal circumstances, Marisol would have assumed he was a celebrity on a break from a movie. Or a model who'd just finished a shoot.

She glanced at his nametag. CLINT MCINTYRE, DELLA SIMMONS GRANT FINALIST.

These were not normal circumstances. He was the enemy.

"Yes. I am going to call them," she said. "They will reschedule."

"Good luck. I couldn't get through."

She narrowed her eyes. If this guy was as tricky as the Pubes, he'd probably put the sign up himself. All in some twisted attempt to tank her chance at the money.

"Clint. Clint McIntyre. Appalachia Together." He pointed at the name tag. "You're with *Ahora*, right? I did a little online research. Impressive. Do you—"

Very tricky indeed. He was going to try to woo her with flattery. And his high cheekbones. Get her off guard and then swoop in for the kill. Everyone here was in for the kill.

"Listen to me, Clint. I know what you are up to. I will find out where this interview is supposed to happen. I only need to call them." She flipped another page, and the portfolio tumbled from her hands. Papers and business cards scattered around his perfectly shined shoes.

"Huh? Seriously?" He tucked in his shirt—even though it was already perfectly tucked.

"Very seriously."

"They cancelled on me too. Actually they kicked me out." He sighed. "You know what? Never mind. Everyone here is a jerk. I get it." He picked up a handful of her belongings and handed them over with an eye roll. "Here. Good luck."

Marisol watched him take two steps before the weight of her outburst pressed on her shoulders. The stress of the interview process was crushing her soul. Two weeks ago, if she'd run into a guy this good looking she'd have had him wrapped around her pinky finger—no all her fingers—in ten minutes flat. Now *she* was the asshole. "Wait. Please. I am sorry. These interviews are making me crazy."

Clint turned to face her. "No kidding. I was just trying to help."

"I am blaming the Pubes."

His eyes widened. "Maybe we're having different interview experiences…"

"People United for—"

"Body Euphoria. Of course. The Pubes." His shoulders relaxed half an inch.

Marisol gathered the rest of her belongings. "Your interview was cancelled, too?"

He nodded. "Not that it matters any more. But you should call. Maybe they'll answer if you call."

A few swipes at her phone later, and Marisol knew he'd been telling the truth. Straight to voice mail. At least she could breathe again. She wasn't the only one being blown off. "Do you think they will reschedule?"

"I hope so." He tugged at the sleeves of his suit jacket. "Those first two interviews were brutal. Number three was supposed to be my big comeback."

Sounds familiar.

Her unease slipped away, replaced by the creeping in of

camaraderie. She wasn't the only one who'd flubbed a few things so far. "Mine, too."

"This morning, they sent my boss an email. Apparently, a bunch of our paperwork went missing. Said we're being disqualified unless it shows up."

Marisol's heart stopped. "Is he sending it?"

"My boss can't find it. Maybe he never had it to begin with. Things are sort of disorganized." Clint sighed. "I need at least a gallon of coffee to deal with this day."

So not only had she stooped to Pube level, but she'd kicked him while he was down. "Let me buy you some," she said. "Since I was such a jerk."

His forehead crinkled, as if he were deciding whether to trust a snake.

"I am really sorry," she said.

He grinned. "You're not trying to lure me to a second location are you? So you can murder me?"

"No promises."

"I saw a Starbucks at CityWalk."

The bright lights of Universal CityWalk—even at midday—obscured the sky. People lumbered along with giant shopping bags, tripping over the kids running from store to store. Across the open-air plaza, a band filled the afternoon with the thump of bongos, and Marisol couldn't stop her foot from tapping along.

"My mother was supposed to come to the conference. But she hurt her back a few weeks ago and could not travel." She stared at the overly sweetened, overly sugared coffee in front of her. "Hold on." She fished out the brand new orange and pink case from her bag. It had been more than a decade since she'd been diagnosed, but sometimes whipping out a lancet and canister of test strips still made her self-conscious. Especially in a new place filled with new people. But she did it out in the open every time, ignoring the sidelong glances and stares.

Because maybe somewhere there was a little girl watching who was too scared to test in front of her friends. And maybe that girl needed to see someone like her, smearing her blood on a thin strip of paper out in the open. Ten years ago, Marisol could have really used the company of a few more people like her.

And today, she really wanted the coffee monstrosity.

"Does that hurt?" Clint asked.

"Sometimes a little. Mostly no." Marisol mentally calculated the carbs in the drink while the meter worked its magic and then adjusted her pump accordingly. By the time she'd finished, her coffee was cool enough to drink.

"So your mom…"

"She hurt herself on one of the brigades." Marisol shook her head. "She decided to challenge our dentist to a *very* intense game of UNO."

"The card game?"

"Our dentist is very serious about UNO."

"Clearly."

"And we are having some financial troubles, so we could not say no to the grant. *Entonces*"—she waved her hand toward the breezeway—"I am here."

"Your mom must really trust you then."

She did. Too much. Her mother seemed to have complete faith that Marisol would return home with both the grant and a foolproof plan to fix *Ahora*'s troubles in hand. "And what do you do? Are you a doctor?"

He laughed. "Hardly. I build stuff. Wheelchair ramps mostly."

"You are a lumberjack then, yes?" Between the beard and the broad shoulders, he did seem like a sexy, magazine-version of Paul Bunyan.

"Something like that. I technically work for a rural medicine clinic, but most of my work is on private homes. Patients of the clinic who need help making their homes accessible or even just livable." He'd obviously given this blurb a dozen times in the past few days.

"So you show up at someone's house with a hammer and your truck, then start building?"

"No. We have a whole project with a summer camp for 'problem' kids. They come down for the summer and do most of the work. They learn to build things. It increases their self-esteem. They stay out of trouble and do some good. That kind of thing. I mostly supervise these days. A supervisory lumberjack. Maybe I'll change my résumé when we get back to the Hilltop."

Speaking of getting back—Marisol glanced at the clock on the wall. It was much later than she'd realized. "I am sorry. I have to go back to the hotel. I have a…" How exactly to explain this? "I am going to the making of a television show."

Not quite a lie.

"Really? Which one?" He stood and followed her through the crowd back toward the Hilltop.

"*So Late It's Early.*"

His face brightened, and his eyes crinkled at the edges. Back at the hotel, if he'd looked at her like that, she would have assumed he had one thing and one thing only on his mind.

"I love that show," he said. "Doesn't get nearly enough credit. The host is hysterical. A friend of my little brother works there. Well, he's an intern. Small world."

Marisol drained the last of her coffee. "I have never seen it."

"Seriously? How'd you score the tickets? Maybe I can grab one for next week. If they aren't sold out. Did you have to pay?" He looked like a toddler about to stick his hands in a birthday cake for the first time, and Marisol couldn't help but laugh. Clint was the first person she'd met in LA who didn't want something from her.

And she had exactly what he wanted.

Except—kind, attractive, wheelchair-building lumberjack or not—he was still her rival. Assuming his boss found the paper that had gone missing. She couldn't afford to let him in on her Hollywood coaching session. Not with *Ahora* on the line.

"I got the ticket months ago," she said. "I heard they go very fast."

"Bummer. Well, bring me back a full recap."

Marisol nodded. Now she'd have to find a way to watch

the show. And pray Clint wouldn't watch it online before the presentations next week. And—her feet stuttered as they descended the last rolling hill, bringing the hotel into view—hide the giant *So Late It's Early Show* van idling in the parking lot.

• • •

Evan ignored the fact that Marisol had dressed like she was going to a business meeting instead of a "date." He ignored the giant leather folder in her lap, even though papers shot out at every angle. But he couldn't ignore the paranoid, cops-are-on-my-tail look she kept throwing over her shoulder.

"Are you secretly on the lam?"

"Lamb? No, I do not eat lamb." She didn't take her eyes off of the side-view mirror. "We should go, yes?"

He pulled out of the parking lot, and with every mile that passed her harried glances slowed. By the time they'd fully immersed themselves in traffic, Marisol seemed perfectly normal. Except the wrinkled suit and the folder.

Julia was going to lose her mind.

"So, how was your interview?" he asked.

"Cancelled."

In his periphery, Evan saw her deflate. "Is it going to be rescheduled then, or…"

"I do not know."

Silence thickened the open space in the van. He should have let it go. Maybe she needed time to stew. Or a change of subject.

"So when you go on the medical brigades, you camp in the villages?" Evan hadn't been camping in years. Before his mom died, his family spent half the summers exploring hiking trails, roasting marshmallows, and rolling out sleeping bags in the field behind their house. But once she was gone, his dad packed up all their gear and shoved it to the farthest corner of the attic.

"Sometimes. If there is no one to let us stay in their house."

"So, when you get to the villages you don't even know if you'll have a place to sleep?"

"There is always a place to sleep." She shrugged as if it were nothing to uproot her life every few months for a wild adventure that was certain to involve saving lives.

"That's really cool."

Marisol didn't respond.

A guard waved as they turned into the studio parking lot, and Evan gritted his teeth as he navigated the van between the maze of sports cars and luxury SUVs. Above them, the studio towered like a worn warehouse. In Peoria, a building like this would be filled with tractors and piles of manure. Here it was filled with egos and Botox and—apparently—a lot of fake dog poop.

So either way, full of shit.

Inside, the *So Late* crew clomped and paced in circles. Julia stood guard over a camera and boom mic. Andrew paced beside her, muttering over the stack of pages in his hand.

"What took you so long, Cocktart?" Julia's short hair stood on end. Never a good sign.

"Traffic."

She narrowed her eyes. "Go find Jim. He has a shirt for you." She shoved a handful of papers at his chest. "And look this over. We made a couple of changes, but read it quick because we're late." Julia pushed, and he stumbled forward. By the time he pulled himself together again, Julia had Marisol by the arm and was oozing charm. "We had a pop star here a few weeks ago, and she left behind the cutest dress. Let's see…"

Two minutes later, Jim the wardrobe guy had shucked Evan's T-shirt, tossed it into a pile, and threaded his arms into a button-down. He tugged Evan's arm and shook his head. "Orangutan arms."

"What?"

"You're like Stretch Armstrong. We'll have to roll these sleeves."

One more thing to add to the list. Evan's nerves were already working overtime, knowing he was about to be on camera—again—when he was solidly a behind-the-camera type of guy. Plus, the piece of paper Julia handed him? Full of *his* ideas and jokes. They'd actually listened to him.

And now he wanted to puke. His jokes would probably land. Crash-land, taking down the show in a firestorm of flying pieces.

"Julia. Hey." He scrambled after her, rolling up his own sleeves. Someone should tell her this was a bad idea. Insist they do a sketch written by professionals. "Julia, I—"

Her eyes roved until they landed on him. "Great," she said. "Let's go. We're in a crunch. Someone bring Marisol when she's out of makeup. *Someone* should have told her to come date-night ready."

Evan dragged in a deep breath. How was he supposed to know what to tell her? No one on this show knew what they were doing. *He* was supposed to be learning from *them*.

Julia herded him outside and across the street to the hole-in-the-wall dim sum restaurant. The neon red lights on the front of the building screamed WONTON QUEEN, and even from twenty feet away the smell of dumplings and soy sauce permeated the air. Inside, the restaurant was as barren as ever. Of the fifteen or so tables in the narrow restaurant, only two had customers. The humidity clung to his skin and clothes, and within a minute, Evan felt like he was swimming in MSG.

He waved to the owner, a slight woman with hair she was always untying and then retying in her bun. Her entire face crinkled when she smiled, which was every time the *So Late* crew walked through the door. Evan was pretty sure their afternoon lunch runs and late-night brainstorming sessions kept the restaurant in business.

"Sit." Julia shoved him into one of the vinyl booths. Lately, she had two modes: barking orders or soothing celebrities. And today she sat at a full 90 percent barking orders.

"I…" The table wobbled under his drumming fingers. He didn't need to make sure they didn't screw up his shot. He'd done it himself with this stupid idea. "These D&D jokes are going to appeal to about five middle-aged guys in their moms' basements."

"Who do you think our primary audience is? Besides, that's the point. It's comedy. The best way to get people to laugh is to let them feel superior to you." She rolled her eyes. "I have to go talk to Edna. She needs to put up the closed sign. We can't have half of LA coming in here to watch you dry hump this poor girl."

"Dry hump?" Marisol's eyes widened as she slid into the booth opposite him. Someone had curled the front pieces of her hair so they brushed away from her face and the ends landed at her collarbones. Which were perfect, delicate lines on her chest. Someone from wardrobe had shoved her into a dress with a considerable amount of cleavage on display.

"Perfect, Evan. Don't lose that look," Julia said. She stormed toward the front door and flipped the lock.

Why did he keep looking at Marisol like that? She wasn't the first attractive person he'd ever come into contact with. Hell, he had entire conversations with the *Who's Got the Coconut* models at least once a week, but he never acted like he was on the verge of a stroke.

He sat up straight and forced his face into a relaxed state. "She's being sarcastic. No dry humping. Well, I won't dry hump you. I can't promise anything about Edna over there."

The owner waved to them from behind the counter. "Evan, you need to poop? You look like you need to poop," Edna said. "The bathroom was just cleaned."

He begged the earth to swallow him whole. "I'm good Edna, thanks."

A boom mic appeared over their heads and a camera over Marisol's shoulder.

"Alright. Let's do this," Julia said.

Marisol looked at the producer. "I do not know my lines."

"That's okay." Julia flipped through the script as she talked. "The basic idea is that this is the date you mentioned on the show. So remember you asked Redneck Romeo here to dinner with your gift certificate, and he's a complete idiot."

"Evan is an idiot, got it." Marisol smiled at him.

The effect was almost immediate.

"Perfect, Evan. Don't lose that expression," Julia said. "Marisol, order whatever you want off the cart. Other than that, you don't actually have to say anything. Action!"

Evan pushed his lingering self-doubt out of the way. Like it or not, he'd put his money on the table, and now he had to stick around to see where the ball landed. Hopefully it wouldn't land them all in the cancellation line.

Edna strode to their booth with the dim sum cart. She lifted the lid and steam sprang out, leaving behind dozens of tiny dome-covered plates. "Chinese broccoli? Sesame balls? Shrimp rolls? Noodle plate?"

"Noodle plate and shrimp roll," Evan said, doing his best to ignore Marisol.

That dress was not making it easy.

"Can I have the sesame balls?" Marisol asked.

Edna put two plates in front of Evan, one in front of Marisol, and began wheeling her cart away.

He tore into his food, stopping to glance at Marisol every few bites. "Do you have plans after this?"

"No."

"I'm the Dungeon Master tonight. You can come over if you want."

She froze, a sesame ball halfway to her lips. "You have a dungeon?"

"No. Dungeons and Dragons?"

She shook her head.

"It's a story game about fantasy adventures. Your basic exercise in collaborative storytelling, with an overlay of tabletop combat game." He crammed in another bite, talking with a mouth full of noodles. "Stop me if this gets too basic."

"Okay."

He droned on, expecting her eyes to glaze over.

"Do you make up new characters every time?"

"You develop them over time. It's a persistent game world. You gain experience points as you play. Then you use them to improve your character." He took a deep breath, pulling in every last bit of his D&D knowledge. "My game's been going on for years. When we last left our intrepid adventures, they'd just finished fighting their way through the temple of the evil Cult of the Ebon Hand."

"Ebon Hand?" Marisol stabbed his noodles and took a bite. "What is that?"

"Okay, hold on." Julia ground her jaw. "Marisol, do you play Magic the Gathering?"

"Dungeons and Dragons," Evan offered.

"Whatever."

"No, but I want to. Do you get costumes?"

"No," Evan said. "That would be weird."

"*That* would be weird?" Julia asked.

Marisol stole another bite from his plate. "These are very good."

"This is my new favorite customer!" Edna called out. "You want some more?" She appeared at the table and unloaded half the cart in front of Marisol.

Evan hid his laugh behind one hand.

"Let's take a five-minute break." Julia strode off without waiting for an answer.

Marisol came around to his side of the booth and grabbed the remaining shrimp roll. "Sorry, I think I messed it up."

"It's fine. Julia's kind of stressed right now. She's wearing a lot of hats. We just didn't expect you to be into the game. It's sort of weird."

"How long does this game take?"

"D&D?"

She nodded.

Evan leaned back in the booth. Finally, something he'd learned in college was useful in real life. "Usually lasts about seven hours. Three hours of actual play. One and a half hours of sundry delays, and two and a half hours of dick jokes."

"I know a lot of dick jokes."

Her words caught him mid-drink, and water spewed everywhere. The table. The food. Marisol.

She shrieked and jumped out of the booth, wiping madly at her dress while her shoulders shook with laughter.

"Sorry Edna," Evan called out.

"What are you two doing?" Julia marched back to the booth.

"It was an accident." He waited for her wrath to sharpen. Who knows where she'd gotten that dress, and he'd probably ruined it.

"Well, do it again for the camera, please. Somebody dry off her face."

"Do it again?" Marisol's eyes widened.

"Is that okay?" Evan asked. "I mean—"

"This time you should do it bigger," Marisol said. "Where is Edna? Wait until she is here and get her too."

"Perfect," Julia said. "Yes. Heighten it. That's perfect. Okay, let's go again."

By the time they finished taping, he'd recited every fact he knew about Dungeons and Dragons. Three times. And each of those three times, Marisol played a different part. The first take: interested. The second: confused and bored. And by the third take, she'd recited half the facts back to him, as if she were an expert on the game.

By the third take, she'd also been too drenched to carry on with filming.

"Great. We've got some good stuff." Julia handed her a stack of napkins the size of a small child. "It's about time the writers got something right around here. Anyway—"

Take credit. "I wrote it. I mean, with help from the other writers. And from Marisol because well…" Evan gestured toward her waterlogged dress.

Julia cocked an eyebrow. "What happened to five middle-aged guys in their moms' basements? Never mind. We'll talk about it later. Marisol, we need you to come back to the show tomorrow. Maybe Sunday too."

"You do?" she asked.

"We do?" Evan asked.

Julia nodded. "We want to shoot a few more of these. Take us through the rest of the week. If you say yes, I'll make Evan give you a private, backstage tour of *Who's Got the Coconut*."

"Julia, she's really busy with the conference—"

"And Evan I'll need you to write up some more ideas tonight and bring them with you tomorrow." The producer gave him a look that dared him to challenge her again.

Which he wouldn't, and she knew it. The thrill of seeing his ideas come to life had already hooked him, straight in the gut.

Marisol's face stayed unreadable. Her dark eyes locked on his.

"I know you're really busy," he said. "But I'd really appreciate it. We all would. And we can make sure we put a link up to your organization on our website. Right, Julia?"

"What is it?"

"A public health organization. It's really cool. She goes through the rainforest—"

"Down boy," Julia said. "Whatever. That's fine. As long as it's not some weird fetish website, it'll be fine."

Marisol bit her bottom lip then looked between them. "And I still get the private tour of *Who's Got the Coconut*?"

Julia nodded. "I'll have Evan talk to our guy over there."

"And I can keep the dress?"

"You can absolutely keep the dress."

Marisol took another bite of shrimp roll before she finally put him out of his misery. "Have someone pick me up at my hotel."

DAY FIVE

The second she stepped into the sound stage, Marisol knew she didn't belong. Around her, staff members in *So Late It's Early* T-shirts hastily threw together an art studio, and the set was wall-to-wall leggy blondes, paintbrushes, and easels. The last time she'd held a paintbrush was in primary school, and the last time she'd been a blonde—well, that was an ill-fated month at age seventeen.

All more signs she shouldn't have agreed to this.

"Perfect. You're here." Evan's voice came bounding out from between the blondes before his body did.

Perfect would have been doing the show last night, getting her tickets to *Who's Got the Coconut*, and spending the rest of the weekend locked in her hotel room prepping for the conference. But somehow, she'd been talked into it. Maybe it was Julia's promise of the backstage tour. Maybe it was the thrill of creating something. Maybe it was the way Evan made her laugh harder each time he spat water everywhere.

Maybe it was just Evan.

Long day. You were slap happy. That is all.

"When do I get my tickets for *Who's Got the Coconut*?" she asked. All night long she'd dreamed of winning the elusive grand prize—ten thousand dollars could eke a little more work out of *Ahora* even if she didn't come home with the grant—and all morning she'd been up researching and quizzing herself on the prices of household items. Laundry detergent: eleven dollars and ninety-nine cents for fifty ounces. A broom: eighteen dollars and ninety-five cents. Industrial-sized box of tampons: entirely too expensive.

"We need a little bit to work on that." He rubbed the back of his neck with one hand. "How about Friday?"

Friday was the day the grant winner would be announced. After that she'd be free to devote all of her time to scraping her way to the top of the *Coconut* pyramid. And maybe she'd get to see Evan before she went home. For purely platonic reasons, of course. "Friday will be good."

"And I was thinking we could do the backstage tour tomorrow," he said. "After we finish taping. Is that okay?"

"Will I be able to touch the Wheel of Terror?"

"Sure."

"How about the Trumpeting Turnips?"

"You can touch anything you want."

"Anything?"

He looked at her from the corner of his eye, and a smile fought its way across his face. "Are you flirting with me, Ms. Gutierrez?"

"Me? Never." She held out a flash drive. "Here is the information for my posters."

He slipped the drive into his pocket. "I can drop them by your hotel on Monday. That way you'll have them for meeting with James on Tuesday."

Now she had plans to see him four days in a row. And maybe once more a week from now. This was not what she was supposed to be doing in LA. She was supposed to be focused on networking and presentations and ironing her suits. Not on the way her stomach flip-flopped when he looked at her that way.

"Hotel bar?" she asked.

"Deal."

One of the blondes slid by with a paintbrush in hand. Someone had expertly applied a smudge of pink paint across her cheekbone. It gave her a breezy, confident, carefree look. Marisol had once been that girl. Full of confidence, riding the waves of *que sera, sera*. Until everything at home had gone straight down the toilet.

In the last couple of days, she'd gotten that back. At least in those hours when she was here and not at the hotel, feeling two sizes too small to fit in there.

"Evan?"

"Yep?"

"Thank you. For bringing me on the show, I mean."

He winked. "My pleasure."

Half an hour later, Marisol wore another starlet's cast-off dress and stood under the studio lights. The room smelled faintly antiseptic, like someone had coated the whole place in rubbing alcohol before they'd arrived.

"Why does it smell like that?" she asked.

"Porn," someone said.

"Porn?" She glanced around, half expecting to see the blondes had stripped off their smocks—and everything else.

"Sometimes they shoot adult films here. It was all we could get on short notice." Evan looked away sheepishly. "Anyway, don't worry. We made sure everything got cleaned this morning before you got here."

She cringed. "Do not touch anything, got it."

"Also, if weird porno music starts playing from the side speakers, just ignore it. Jerry found a CD, and he won't stop messing with it." Evan rolled his eyes.

"Do not touch anything. Ignore the porn music." Marisol raised a brow. "Anything else? What am I supposed to do for this part?"

"This is a good one." His explanation started off slowly, but with every breath his excitement seemed to build and build. By the end, Evan had gone into hyperspeed English, and Marisol could barely grab on to one word before the next flew by.

"This one is about you picking up women?"

"Right."

"And all I must do is stand there and hand you these lines?" She gestured to the fishbowl filled with strips of paper.

"Basically, yes. Think of it like you're coaching me. But you can always improvise if you want. Don't feel like you have to stick to what's on the paper. If you think of something better, go with it."

"Like if you need a pep talk because all of the ladies are turning you down?" she asked.

"Exactly. And I promise, with these lines, they will all turn me down."

"Let's get this show moving," Julia called out.

Someone rolled the camera closer, and someone else escorted Marisol and Evan to stools on the opposite end of the stage. The blondes took their places at their easels, and then the red light on the camera glowed.

James January walked out from backstage, complete with a beret and palette full of paint. "Welcome to Paint and Crank. A true artistic experience, guided by both *moi* and a baggie of crank." He handed out individual baggies of a powdery white substance before getting up close and personal with the camera. "Some places limit you to wine, maybe beer if you're lucky. But not us. Here, we nurture the inner artist."

Marisol tried to keep a straight face as the blondes tore into baggies and began rubbing what looked like powdered sugar all over their noses. The camera swung in her direction, and the red light on top shot straight through her shaky wall of decorum.

"What is going on? Are they supposed to be doing drugs?" She didn't know whether to laugh or chastise them all.

"Evan you were supposed to explain this to her." Julia put one hand on her hip and muttered something to the camera guy. The only words Marisol could make out were "intern" and "hopeless."

"I thought I did. Okay, you know those paint and wine things?"

"No." She ignored the fact that every face in the room was watching her every move. "I do not think we have this in Nicaragua."

"You know what, that's even better. Go with it." Evan leaned in closer. Close enough that Marisol could see the tiny scar a half centimeter above his lip. "Just be yourself. And if things get weird—well weirder—just keep it going. You'll be fine."

She nodded. Everything was so much more complicated than she'd expected. And every day seemed to add another layer to balance.

"This time when the camera turns back to us, I'll start talking to you. Pretend like it's just us. Maybe this time, pretend like you're a drill sergeant?"

She straightened herself on the stool. "Okay."

The camera pointed at them again. "Marisol, I don't know if these pickup lines will work," Evan said. His eyes widened, and he looked at her like she might be his fairy godmother.

Marisol shook the fishbowl in her hands and channeled her inner drill sergeant. "Are you questioning my tactics?" She jerked the bowl toward him. "I have tested every one of these lines. They will work."

Evan pulled a slip of paper from the bowl. She recognized the glint in his eye—the one that said he was fighting laughter of his own. She'd seen it at least a dozen times last night, and the familiarity let her relax a little.

Without another word, he crossed the stage to one of the blondes. The girl slashed a paintbrush against her canvas with her eyes closed. Her arm moved at a superhuman rate, but she stopped completely when Evan approached her.

"Hey," he said. "Do you like antiques?"

After an awkward pause, the girl rubbed her nose. "Yes."

"Good, because I've got some junk. And no one's laid a hand on it in years."

The girl smacked him with her paintbrush and turned away. Evan slunk back to his stool.

Marisol licked her lips, trying to keep her giggles under control, and put on her best no-nonsense, take-no-prisoners voice. "You can do better than that, Peanut."

Evan broke. "Peanut?" he sputtered. "Do you mean peon?"

She glanced offstage, expecting Julia to yell "cut" or for the red light on the camera to click off. But Julia stayed quiet, and the camera kept rolling.

"Are you correcting your superior, Peanut?" Marisol demanded, thrusting another paper into his hand. "Try again. Do not be so awful this time."

Evan trudged across the stage to a new girl. This one had apparently done so many fake drugs she'd gained laser focus. She bent over and kept her nose an inch from the canvas as she painted something so tiny no one could see it.

"Hey," Evan said. "It would be a lot easier for me to sweep you off your feet if—"

The girl was enraptured. By her painting.

Marisol couldn't resist jumping in. "Do not let her ignore you," she called across the set.

Evan nodded and started again, practically screaming this time. "I was saying it would be a lot easier for me to sweep you off your feet if you stood up."

Finally, the girl tore herself away from the canvas and straightened, revealing herself to be two heads taller than Evan. And probably thirty pounds heavier.

"Great," Julia called out over the laughter on set. "I think that will do it."

"Wait." Marisol waved her hands overhead. "He should really sweep her off her feet, no?"

For a minute, Julia and Evan and the exceptionally tall blonde looked at one another without saying a word. Marisol's throat went dry, and she wished she'd kept her mouth shut. This wasn't her project. She didn't know what she was doing.

"Nice," Evan said. "We should do it. If it's okay with you?"

The blonde shrugged. "Good luck, kid."

He grinned and gave Marisol a nod. If anyone had reminded her that thirty seconds ago she'd wished she hadn't spoken up, she would have called them a pathological liar.

"Let's roll," Julia said.

Evan started again. "I was just saying it would be a lot easier for me to sweep you off your feet if you stood up."

This time, when the Jolly Blonde Giant stood, Evan picked her up like a groom carrying his bride over the threshold.

"Ooof." He stumbled, knocking the girl's feet into her easel.

The easel crashed into the one beside it, taking out a canvas, a palette of paint, and the blonde holding it. And then she took out the girl beside her who took out the easel next to her, until the entire "Paint and Crank" studio went down like dominos. In the end, only Evan and the girl in his arms were left standing.

Marisol buried her face in her hands, only half succeeding in containing her laughter.

"Great job, guys." Julia helped set the girl back on her feet. "Let's get this cleaned up, and we can move on."

The set fell into chatter as everyone chipped in and began setting things upright. Someone ran out with a rag and a bucket of water and began scrubbing the paint from the floor. Marisol carried her stool offstage, half bouncing with excitement.

"Good job." Evan took the stool from her hands. "Great addition."

"It was good to begin with. You wrote all of this last night?"

"And this morning. Not just me either. A bunch of us had ideas and we bounced them around until we found something that would work."

He was trying hard, but his words couldn't mask the pride on his face.

"You missed one great idea," Marisol said.

"Really?"

The pieces were clicking into place, and all she wanted to do was stay in this moment. To keep laughing and making stuff up. Seeing how far they could go down this really weird rabbit hole. "I should do one. As an example for you."

"You're a genius." He started digging through the bowl. "Hold on."

A few minutes later, he'd handed her a slip of paper and made her promise not to read it until it was time to say the line. The light on the camera went red, and Marisol put on her best badass impersonation.

"Peanut, watch a master."

A snort came from somewhere out in the crew.

"Jerry, keep it down," Julia called out.

"Sorry."

Marisol marched over to James, who was working away on a paint-by-number drawing of a dinosaur. "Hey there," she purred.

James's eyes widened and one shoulder twitched upward. He was trying not to laugh. At her. This man—whose entire career rested on entertaining people—thought *she* was funny. It felt like being perched at the top of the world's tallest roller coaster, anticipating the glorious rush to come.

She unfolded the paper Evan had tucked into her palm and leaned forward.

I should kill him. But even as she had the thought, she knew his choice of line would hit the mark. She sucked in her cheeks, knowing she probably looked like a bug-eyed fish, but it was either that or burst at the seams.

"What's the difference between a trust fund and an erection?" she asked.

James rested a hand on his chin, like a less muscular, more world-worn version of *The Thinker*. "Well, I honestly don't know."

"I don't have a trust fund."

• • •

Evan's lunch break flew by in a blast of pats on the back, a barrage of script ideas—it seemed the writers were suddenly inspired to write—and a handful of sidelong glances at Marisol.

She'd killed it on the last sketch. Perfect delivery, perfect composure. And after they'd begun tearing down the set, she'd plopped down beside him with her biggest grin to date. "That was fun," she said.

"Yeah. It's been a while since anyone has had fun around here."

Even James had a hopeful look on his face when he'd left for the day. A look Evan hadn't seen since his first week on the show.

"Well, this is a pornography set," Marisol said. "I think some people have had fun."

"Good point. Also remind me to bathe in hand sanitizer before we leave here tonight."

"I think soap and water works best. That is my professional nurse opinion."

"Noted. Do you have a second to talk about the next sketch?" He and Andrew had turned it over and over again. The physical comedy was all there, but it was missing something. Something neither of them could quite put their finger on.

She nodded. "What is the next one?"

"This one is me on a date with one of these girls—"

"You have gotten over me so quickly?" She threw a hand up to her chest.

"Well, it was a tough road, but I'm working my way through the pain."

She gave him a smile that caused a different kind of pain. One he enjoyed more than he cared to admit, even to himself. *Get it together.* "So I'm on a date—"

"Is it the girl you knocked over? It should be her. We can say you knocked her out, and when she woke up you convinced her she had already said yes."

"Perfect." He scrawled her idea on his notebook. "So I'm on a date."

"Yes, and…"

"And it's supposed to be on the beach. But really it's only a sandbox and a fan. There are some cardboard cutouts of waves in the background."

"Okay?" The furrow of her brow said she wasn't following.

"You still haven't seen the show, have you?"

"I tried to watch on my laptop but the hotel Internet was too slow. It would not load the video."

The irony. Thousands and thousands of people, including him, made a pilgrimage to Los Angeles every year. They stuffed themselves full of Botox. They pulled late-night shifts at diners while flogging themselves with auditions—or, in his case, packets of written material. And still most of them would never make an actual appearance on television.

Marisol had never even seen the show, and she was already becoming a star.

Their star. The star the show needed more than ever.

"One of the bits James always does is that the show is broke. We kind of are, I guess, but James does it in a self-depreciating kind of way. He's always making fun of the sets, taking jabs at the network for not giving us any money."

"So you made a very cheap beach to fit his jokes?"

"Exactly. But it's missing something." He handed her the script. "You'll read these lines."

She chewed her bottom lip as her eyes moved across the page. A strand of hair crossed her cheek, and Evan found himself wanting to tuck it away.

You're screwed.

"What if I am the one moving the waves?" she asked. "While I am telling you the things to say? Picture it." She made a rowing motion with one hand and cupped the other on the side of her mouth. Her very pretty mouth. "Evan! Be a better date or you are going to die cold and alone."

The clomp of combat boots snapped him out of his daze.

"I thought I was doing the waves," Penny said. Her blue-streaked hair gleamed brighter than ever, and she'd tied her *So Late It's Early* T-shirt in a knot at the back. Like him, she'd stayed on board while all the other interns had scrambled for life rafts—begging for other network shows to take them on.

"Marisol, this is Penny. She's an intern, too."

"Too?" Penny scoffed. "More like the *only* intern. I'm having a great time filling the audience. And cleaning up the set. And organizing the props."

Guilt seeped into Evan's stomach. In his rush toward the writers' room, he hadn't given a second thought to who'd be stuck with his bloated daily to-do list. "Sorry, Penny. It'll be better after this week."

Assuming there was an "after this week."

"Whatever. Julia put me in charge of all the social media." She turned to Marisol. "We need to talk about your accounts."

Marisol looked back and forth between them. "My accounts?"

"You know, Facebook, Twitter, Insta." Penny waved a phone at them. "You're not that old. You have some of this stuff, right?"

"The show is pushing our stuff really hard online," Evan explained. "That's where the stuff with you and Betty really hit it big, so they're trying to drum up buzz about it that way."

"We don't want you to post anything about the show on your accounts," Penny said. "I'll put everything on the show's accounts. If you want to post something in a week or two that's fine. But nothing while your segments are airing, got it?"

"Got it," Marisol said. "Also I think it's better if you do not use my last name." She turned to Evan. "Because of the conference."

"Agreed."

Penny shrugged. "Whatever. I doubt anyone cares that much. I'll post some on-set photos after I'm done doing all of my job *and his*." She threw Evan a glare before she clomped away.

"She's a little bit prickly. Don't worry about it," he said. "And you're definitely doing the waves. Great idea."

"I will not give you any more great ideas if you make me say I have an erection again."

"You loved it, and that was the best take we had all day," he said. "Besides, you're the one who told everyone I didn't know how to act around women."

"You made me race an old lady in a walker!" Her wide smile betrayed her protest.

"And it was awesome."

She swatted his arm with his script. "So we agree you deserve it. Now let me see the rest of this."

By the time they started rolling on the second sketch, they'd bounced so many ideas back and forth his brain couldn't keep up. The crackle of creative chemistry between them kept sparking fires, and Evan struggled to write them all down before the next one started. And the smoke from those fires blurred the view of the quieter, smoldering one he was trying hard to ignore.

"Action." Julia's voice rang out over the sparse set. In final edits, the screen behind them would become an ocean, but for now it was a solid, stark green. Someone had dragged a plastic child's sandbox from the prop room and flopped it down in the center of the room. Beside it sat a bottle of wine and two glasses. A giant fan blew so hard bits of sand pelted Evan's face and mouth. Behind him Marisol pushed and pulled a thin stick attached to a row of wooden waves. It gave the segment a certain terrifying-circus-puppet-show vibe.

"Pour her a glass of wine," Marisol shouted over the roar of the fan.

The girl sitting beside him in the sandbox looked over her shoulder, sending a metric ton of blonde hair whipping across his face. "Who is that?" the girl asked. Her name was Monica, and she was a twenty-something actress who'd been on the show once or twice before. Not enough that anyone beyond a few hardcore fans would remember her face.

Assuming the show had any hardcore fans left.

"No one. It's no one." He pulled the cork out of the wine and picked up a glass. "Wine?"

"Sure."

He tilted the bottle at the exact moment the fan oscillated in their direction. Wine splashed all over his shirt, and sand coated the inside of the glasses.

Monica—like a pro—began drinking, straight from the bottle.

As the sandstorm slowed, Marisol called out more tips. "To develop intimacy, start with short bursts of physical contact. Lay a hand on her arm. Or help her brush her hair out of her face."

"Sorry," he whispered as he reached forward and wrapped a fist around the ends of Monica's hair. He yanked. Monica stifled a laugh as the chunk of blonde extension they'd slipped into her hair came loose in his hand.

"Ouch!"

"Like that?" he called.

Marisol kept moving the waves. "Not exactly. Try again."

Evan dragged in a breath. If they succeeded in bringing the show back to life, he'd have a career path already laid out. Clear of the thorns and hurdles he'd been fighting since he decided to come to LA. But there was a good chance he'd never have another date again.

Evan went for it, just like they'd discussed.

His hand darted forward, and the next thing he knew Monica's entire left boob was in his grasp.

She froze, mouth open in horror.

Behind the sandbox, Marisol's face darkened with pent-up laughter. And when she finally let it out, Evan couldn't stop himself from cackling along with her. Within seconds, everyone in the studio was in an uproar, and he knew right then that they had something special. Something that had been missing from the show's chemistry since the day it went live. And with the right marketing and the right editing and a good helping of luck, maybe they could turn this late-night ship around after all.

"You can let go of my boob now," Monica said.

"That'll do it," Julia called. "I think we've officially hit too tired to function. Marisol, Penny will call you a cab." She shook her head as she walked away, but Evan knew this crazy marathon day had begun to soften her shell. She was more like the old Julia.

They all were.

The camera switched off, and the lights dimmed. Slowly, people began putting the set away. Penny pulled out her cell phone, the same I'm-too-good-for-this expression on her face. "You want them to pick you up in the front or the back of the studio?"

Evan shifted his feet and jammed his hands into his pockets. He needed to pack his stuff and get out of here in time to beat the traffic. He had wine all over his shirt, more scenes to write for tomorrow, and a toxic-waste-level amount of dirty dishes in his apartment.

"I'll take her back," he said. "You want to get some dinner first?"

Stupid idea, Evan.

AMANDA HEGER

Penny sighed. "Are you taking care of this, or am I?"

Marisol cleared her throat. "Dinner would be good."

Best idea ever, Evan.

If a friend from home had come to visit, Evan would have brought them to one of LA's major establishments—In-N-Out Burger or Pink's Hot Dogs or Roscoe's Chicken. Someplace where they'd be surrounded by other tourists and a barrage of languages. A place where they could go back to Peoria and drop the name of the restaurant to their other friends.

He brought Marisol to Wilma's. The tiny diner at the edge of Hollywood had thick burgers, greasy bread, and all the crinkle-cut french fries you could eat. It smelled like salt and butter, and it was impossible to leave without a ketchup stain somewhere on his person.

It was his favorite place in all of Los Angeles.

It felt like home.

"This okay?" he asked. "They have the best cheeseburgers."

Marisol glanced around. "Perfect."

The diner had a steady crowd but no wait. A low-key, seat yourself kind of place, where the waitstaff always seemed more interested in refilling his drink than shoving him out the door. Even when he spent hours in here, drafting idea after ridiculous idea for his submission packets.

His legs ached with exhaustion, and he plopped down in a booth across from Marisol. "That was the most fun I've had since I started at the show."

Marisol smiled. A real smile. By now, he'd watched her enough to know her fake smile made her look a little too perfect, like those models in makeup commercials who'd just been "caught" faking their six-inch-long eyelashes. But when Marisol was really happy, her eyes went a little buggy and her mouth opened wide, revealing that single crooked tooth on the bottom left. When she was happy, she let her imperfections show.

"You ready?" A gum-snapping waitress interrupted, barely

looking up from her grease-stained notepad. "Or do you want to hear the specials?"

"Cheeseburger, please," Marisol said.

"Same."

The waitress didn't write a single thing on the notepad in her hand. "You're the kid that's always in here, right? And you're her. I knew it was you. They didn't believe me. Hold on."

The waitress disappeared behind the counter and returned with the cook in tow. Red and brown smudges stained his apron and a tuft of black hair stuck out from beneath his hairnet. "Hot damn. It is them." He pulled a five-dollar bill from his back pocket and slapped in the waitress's hand.

"No one here believed me that the Cheeseburger Guy with the notebook was the same one from all over the Internet. But then I saw her." She pointed at Marisol. "And I knew I was right on the nose."

Under the table, Marisol nudged him with her foot. "I thought you said no one watches the show?"

"Oh, honey. His lost puppy dog face made the rounds on every clip show this side of China." The cook looked at them both and shook his head. "This place'll spit you up and eat you alive. So when you find a boy who looks at you like that"—he jabbed his spatula toward Evan—"you take him and get the h-e-double-hockey sticks out of Dodge."

"I think we'll have two cheeseburgers. Medium." Evan put an edge on his words. He didn't want to explain it was all fake. And not just because the show needed people to believe it was real.

The cook and the waitress shuffled off, but they left behind the stares of half the diner. The other half were buckled to their phones, fingers swiping away.

"Do you feel like everyone here is looking at us?" Marisol asked.

He did. "I think we're being paranoid."

"Do you think anyone wants James's autograph? Maybe I could take orders and charge for them. One hundred dollars each. Then I would have enough money to spend all of my time at the show. I would not have to worry about the grant at all." Her voice said she was kidding, but the crinkles around her eyes were dead serious.

"I love that you have no idea how unpopular our show is."

"It is that bad?"

"You'd probably have to pay the people in here before you could give them his autograph."

Her shoulders slumped, and Evan found himself wanting to take it away, the pressure that sometimes looked like it was about to consume her. "Any news on the Pubes?" he asked.

Her frown deepened, and her gaze rolled over the old black and white photos on the wall before landing on him again. "Why do they call you the Cheeseburger Guy?"

"I'm a regular, I guess. This place reminds me of home. When I was a kid my grandparents owned a—shit. Hold on." He whipped out his phone and began trying to calculate the time difference between Los Angeles and Peoria. Noon had come and gone, and he hadn't bothered to call Gramps. If he was lucky, he could maybe catch him before bed. His fingers dialed home before he'd finished the math.

His grandfather picked up after one ring. "Lies, kid. They'll eat you up inside."

"Hi, Gramps. It wasn't a lie. I just had a really busy day." He glanced over at Marisol. "Sorry," he mouthed.

Here he was, at his favorite diner in the entire city, with a gorgeous girl across the table—and he'd picked up the phone to call an old man more than a thousand miles away. Apparently, he was almost as horrible with women as his character on the show.

"Lies and pies will make you fat with shame. Don't get fat, kid."

"I'm really sorry. I know I said I'd call—"

"Do I gotta spell it out for you? You said you weren't going to be on the show anymore. But it says right here you'll be appearing with that parrot guy next week."

Maybe Evan would have to cave and call his father. Check to be sure Gramps was taking his medications as prescribed. He'd always been prone to pontification, but usually his ramblings made some semblance of sense. "Parrot guy? Says right where?"

"You know. The one with all the stupid hats. Always looked like a real asshole to me."

Paul the Parrot Man was Monday's scheduled guest. And he did look particularly smarmy. Maybe the meds were working okay. "Gramps, please. Focus. Where did you see that?"

"On my computer. Somebody from the senior center put it on there."

"Put it on where?"

"On my computer!"

"Okay, Gramps." This was going nowhere. Fast. He'd have to google it when he got home, see what the website guy was promising for next week. Evan tried to pry himself out of the conversation with a solemn promise to call tomorrow with more details, an oath to tell the whole truth about the show, and a pledge to not let the "Hollywood weirdos" talk him into getting calf implants.

"I've got to go now. Can I call you tomorrow?"

"I know you've always had them chicken legs, but the risk ain't worth it."

"I promise. Talk to you later."

Evan hung up before his grandpa could slide in another offhand remark. Once the old man had hit seventy-five, he'd decided everything was on the table for discussion—no matter how random or offensive.

"Sorry, I was supposed to call him this morning. He gets really weird if I don't call."

Marisol cocked her head to one side. "Does he live close to here?"

"No. He lives back home. Illinois. That's in the middle—"

"I know where it is. I lived in St. Louis for a little while."

"Oh, well. That's where he lives. Near my dad." He ignored the pang in his chest. The one that still came every time he said "my dad" without "my mom."

"And he collects parrots?"

"No. He's just a little crazy. Can't quite do it on his own anymore."

"And you talk to him every day?"

"When I can. He saw me through some hard stuff when I was younger. I try to pay back the favor."

The waitress pushed her way through the crowd, holding a tray of food overhead. "Look out. Look out. We've got a couple of lovebirds over here, and they need their fuel." She slid the plates onto the table, leaving behind a burst of steam and a chocolate shake. Tons of whipped cream. Two straws.

"That one's on the house," she said with a wink.

Marisol fumbled with something under the table, twisting and turning in all sorts of odd directions.

"You okay?"

"Yes. I have to check something." She flopped a small pink and gray box on the table. It was the size of a small cell phone, and a tube ran from one end and disappeared somewhere under the table. She pulled an orange case from her bag and began unzipping.

"You're diabetic. I mean, I recognize the supplies. My grandpa has the same meter." *Your grandpa?* Had he really just shoved his foot so far down his throat that he'd compared her to his grandpa? "But you're a lot prettier than he is. I mean, here." He shoved the shake across the table. "I'm going to stop talking now."

Evan pulled a fry through the ketchup and tried one final time to focus on the dozens of red flags flying in his face. Coworker. Potential Internet celebrity. Leaving the country in two weeks.

"I can share." She handed him a spoon, and all those flags faded into the distance. "But only because you are cute when you talk to your grandpa."

DAY SIX

Even if porno music hadn't been blaring throughout the studio, Marisol would have known something was wrong. Everyone stood in a tight circle, looking at their feet while Julia's nostrils flared.

"How many times did I tell you to leave that shit alone, Jerry?" She spoke between gritted teeth, and her voice hovered a centimeter below a scream—still barely able to be heard over the constant *bow chicka wow wow* coming over the speakers.

A bearded man in a *So Late It's Early* T-shirt flinched at her words. "It's Sunday. I thought we could all use a little fun."

"I'm going outside and coming back in ten minutes. This better be fixed by then." Julia stormed off the set, and everyone followed. Everyone except the bearded man, who scrambled in the other direction.

Marisol tiptoed into the hall, holding her coffee in one hand and her notes in the other. After dinner last night, she'd gone back to the hotel with every intention of practicing her presentation. Instead, she'd found herself scribbling idea after idea for sketches. It started with an idea that spun off of something Evan said over dinner. Then it moved to a few new ideas. And the next thing she knew, three hours had gone by and she had over a dozen ideas. Ideas of other "Lady Killer" skits.

But now, in the light of day, it seemed stupid and silly. These were professional writers. Showing them her handwritten, scrawled ideas would be akin to asking a lawyer to let her question a witness. Nope, she'd simply stuff this notebook into her bag and be done with it.

"There you are." Evan rounded the corner and stopped a foot ahead of her.

"What is going on in there?"

"Jerry put the CD on again, but this time he got it stuck in the player. Can't get it to turn off. Julia's pissed—as usual—and the camera guy keeps saying he needs a raise if he's going to have to shoot anyone in assless chaps. I tried to tell him all chaps are assless, but…"

Marisol pushed back a laugh. "Wow."

"Just a regular day here on the set of *So Late It's Early*." Something different glinted in his smile today. Something like mischief. "Let's go." He nodded toward the side door.

Ten minutes. The memory of Julia's words inched their way into the space between notes of the cheesy music. Marisol knew she definitely *should not* follow this funny, cute guy into the dim hallway. She definitely *should* go back and wait with the others, finish this last taping, and then return to hotel and work on her presentation.

But when he kept looking at her like that—like the two of them shared all the inside jokes the world had to offer—all the *shoulds* and *should nots* faded into the background. "Go where?" she asked.

"I was thinking we could take that *Coconut* backstage tour?"

"Now?"

"Come on." He grabbed her hand and tugged her down a maze of nondescript hallways, straight to a Plexiglass booth tucked away in one corner of the building. Rows of *Who's Got the Coconut* memorabilia hung along the walls—glittery shirts and mugs and giant buttons shaped like dollar signs filled every space. A cash register stood in the corner, darkened and dead. A sign on top stared back at them. CLOSED.

Marisol tried to focus on the wall-to-wall glitter in the booth instead of the way her hand fit inside Evan's. Or how disappointed she felt when he let go.

"Hold on." He glanced over his shoulder before jamming a key into the brass lock. Two clicks later, he tugged Marisol into the booth behind him. "Okay, what size? Small? Medium?"

She jerked her head back. Was he really going to steal from

this souvenir stand? Not even she wanted an *I Lost My Coconuts in California* button that much. "Evan, I—"

"Try this one." He handed her a red polo shirt before grabbing a second one from a cabinet beneath the cash register.

"I am not going to steal anything." Had she misjudged him? She was all in favor of harmless mischief, but petty crime was something else altogether.

Footsteps echoed from the other end of the hall, and they dove behind the cash register. Evan put one finger to his lips, eyes wide. Marisol tried to hold still, but her legs kept shaking. All she could imagine was the booth flinging open to reveal a muscular security guard with a mustache and a stun gun.

Maybe if she stood slowly and put her hands up—

"Why the hell are you on the ground, Evan?"

She looked up into the face of a burly man with a mustache. But he didn't look like any security guard she'd ever seen. He wore one of the glitter coated T-shirts from the wall, and with every breath more gold flecks showered the ground around them. He stepped past them and flipped the CLOSED sign to OPEN.

Evan stood and pulled her up beside him. "Hey man. Sorry, I thought you were Julia. Marisol this is Bourbon. Bourbon, Marisol."

"Hi." She lifted a hand then turned to Evan. "What is going on?"

"Put on the shirt and find out," he said.

She plucked the red polo from the ground and held it up at eye level. A miniature version of the game show's logo clung to the left breast, and just above it the word STAFF had been embroidered with black thread. "This is okay?" she asked Bourbon.

"As long as you bring it back and don't get anything too disgusting on it." He powered up the cash register.

Evan rolled his eyes and gave her a nudge with his elbow. "Trust me."

She tugged the shirt over her dress, not caring that she looked like a lumpy, mismatched version of herself. For the last month, her sense of adventure had been shut away from the light. Left to die a slow death. But something about this place and these people had started to unlock it. Something about Evan—and the way he always laughed a little too loudly at her jokes—had started to unlock it. And if that meant she had to wear a polo that smelled vaguely like a fish tank to feel alive, so be it.

Bourbon pulled a bottle of bourbon out from the bottom drawer of the cash register. "To young love." He tipped it in their direction before taking a big swallow. "You've got twenty minutes."

Marisol glanced at the floor, wondering if she should correct his young love comment or ask what was due to happen in twenty minutes.

Evan didn't give her the chance to do either. "Let's go. You're going to want all twenty."

A handful of steps later, they stood in the middle of a gray hallway, in front of a slightly darker gray door. Spray-painted block letters ran across the surface, announcing STAFF ONLY. But a tiny sign beside the door matched the logo on her borrowed polo shirt.

Evan undid the lock and held open the door. "This way."

She barely had both feet in the door when the lights flickered on. Followed by the sound of a thousand angels filling the space with their praise—or maybe that part was in her imagination. It didn't matter. At that moment she was standing on the stage of *Who's Got the Coconut.*

In one corner, Sammy Samuelson's pulpit loomed, giving him a bird's eye view of the contestants. It also kept him from being splattered with paint or water or goo or whatever other messy substance the contestants would be forced to endure. On the other end of the stage, the champion's throne glistened with the same shade of glitter that covered the knickknacks in the souvenir stand.

What she wouldn't give to sit in that throne with the winner's crown pressing down on her head. Maybe a smattering of prizes at her feet. A giant check with her name scrawled across the front. For now, she'd have to settle for just the throne.

"I see you're practicing for your big day." Evan walked closer, his hands jammed into his pockets, as she settled into the seat.

She couldn't stop smiling. Or running her hands along the arms of the chair, even if it meant glitter flakes clinging to her palms. "That man, Bourbon? He's in charge of the tours?"

"Yeah, not exactly. I guess James is in some kind of feud with Samuelson. I don't really know. This is more of a workaround."

"Thank you."

She wanted to say something else. Something about how this strange American game show had helped distract her as a young girl, when she sat in the doctor's office or the emergency room. Even in her own living room, watching people in costumes makes fools of themselves for random prizes let her forget—for an hour at a time—that she would have to deal with her diabetes forever.

Marisol had years to adjust to pricking her fingers, tracking every morsel she ate, and being hooked to a small machine nearly twenty-four seven. She was no longer that scared girl watching television, but sitting on this stage, in this throne, she remembered her all too well.

"You okay?" Evan asked.

"Better than okay."

"Want to see backstage?"

She stood and followed him to the edge of the stage. "Do they keep the tank full of fish back there?"

"I don't think they do the fish thing anymore. PETA did a whole protest." Evan held open the velvet curtain and flipped on the backstage lights, revealing a tomb of game show props.

A barrel marked PURPLE SLUDGE sat next to another barrel marked BLUE SLUDGE, which sat next to another, marked CHARTREUSE SLUDGE. Marisol pressed her fingers to the glass of a dunk tank, imagining icy water sloshing against the sides. Across the room, Evan climbed a step stool and peered down a double set of giant orange tubes—a piece from the classic Gopher Dash game.

"I never really understood the logic of this show," he said. "Sludge? Thrones? Guessing the prices of toasters?"

She balked. "It makes perfect sense."

"Explain it then." He crossed his arms.

Marisol opened her mouth to explain, then snapped it shut. "Either you understand or you do not."

"Fair enough. This one has been around since the nineties, right?" Evan's voice echoed through the tube, and when he pulled his head out something in his expression had changed.

"I think yes," she said. "I used to watch the show and plan how I would attack the gopher tube."

"You have to dive through—" Evan started.

"On your stomach," they both finished.

"My mom was obsessed with this show." He shook his head. "She hated television. Was always threatening to throw it out if I didn't go 'experience the greatness of nature.' But she never got rid of it, probably because she wanted to watch *Who's Got the Coconut.*"

"And now you work on a television show." Marisol grinned as she wandered to the next game, a balance beam of sorts. Every six inches or so, a bucket popped up on the beam and clear spikes rimmed each hole. *This one must be new.* "What does she think of that? Or maybe she does not mind because you are working next-door to her favorite show?"

"She died. When I was sixteen."

She started to tell Evan she was sorry, then bit the words back. Those words had never brought her much comfort, and half the time she'd end up comforting the person who uttered them. "You know what we must do, yes?"

His brow furrowed. "No?"

She stepped toward the orange tubes and forced her way next to him on the step stool. There was barely enough room for one person, but they wouldn't be on their feet for long. "We must dive through the gopher tubes in her honor."

His eyes narrowed. "We must?"

"Ready, steady, Freddy!" She called out the show's catchphrase and leapt in headfirst. The red polo shirt kept at least some of her dress plastered to her body, but the too big sleeves made wiggling her way through more difficult than she'd imagined. Heat made the inside of the tube sticky, and everything glowed orange. The twin tube beside her stayed silent, and there was no shadow to suggest a twenty-something guy crawling beside her.

Maybe I should have just said I was sorry.

She kept scooting on her stomach. Ahead, light and fresh air beckoned from the first hole in the pipe. For a half second, Marisol considered ignoring it. She could climb straight through, end this embarrassment, and apologize. Then they could make their way back to the set, face Julia's wrath, and finish out this very weird situation.

"When you're a contestant, you have to go faster than this." Evan's voice rolled through the tubes, and soon his shadow passed her—clearly the hare to her tortoise.

"What? How?" She tore forward until she could poke her head through the first hole.

Evan was already there, his head bobbing back and forth as he yawned. "Geez. Are you sure you want to be on this show? I don't want you to make a fool out of yourself on national television."

"Says the man who is taping whole sketches that make him look like a fool on television."

"Well played."

Marisol laughed. How strange this would look if anyone walked through the doors. Two heads protruding from orange tubes on an empty game show set, taunting each other. Smiling.

Flirting.

"I do not have to take this kind of abuse." She ducked low and took off, moving through the tunnel at lightning speed—if lightning wore a dress and tried to squeeze its way through a tight space while thinking about what it would be like to kiss the guy beside her.

She couldn't pinpoint the exact moment she'd moved from not-my-type to let's-lock-lips, but now it seemed there was no going back.

She pushed through faster and faster, until she emerged from the tunnel. "I win!" She threw her hands in the air before collapsing to the ground

Two seconds later, Evan squirmed out beside her, panting and ruffled. "You cheated."

"I did not."

He ran one hand over the top of his head then looked her straight in the eye. "Thank you."

"For kicking your butt?"

"For that too."

She pushed her hair back from her face. "My mother died too, when I was small. It is…" There was no single word to describe it. Suffocating? Lonely? Aching? "Hard."

"I thought your mom was back in Nicaragua?" He blinked a few times. "Sorry, that didn't come out right."

"She is. I was adopted."

"Do we need to do another round of the Gopher Dash in her honor?"

"No, I think one round was enough for today." Her mental clock kept ticking. Julia's ten minutes had to be up by now, but Marisol couldn't bring herself to move from this spot.

"My mom was the one who got me into television. Even if she didn't realize it." Evan stood and dusted off his pants. "Gave me an old video camera when I was six. By twelve I'd made a half dozen short documentaries."

"What were they about?" She peeled herself from the floor.

"Let's see. There was one about the neighbor's dog. Hard hitting. Another about the best way to care for baseball cards. That one started quite the controversy. But my seventh-grade masterpiece was all about the girls' locker room. What goes on there? Were there communal showers? Pillow fights?"

"Are you serious?" Marisol found herself climbing the windy stairs to Sammy Samuelson's podium, with Evan's footfalls—and warmth—on her heels.

"Mostly it was me interviewing my friends about what we'd heard. I think there was one girl who agreed to be interviewed, but she kept talking about the tampon machine, so her part got cut."

When she reached the top, Marisol turned to look out over the set. Stadium seating filled the back of the room, and from here the host would have a full view of every costumed game show hopeful in the building. Of every messy movement occurring on the stage below. And when she turned, Marisol had a perfect view of the hopeful, messy guy looking back at her.

Looking at her like *that*.

She inched forward, feeling more like the old Marisol. The one who kissed who she wanted, when she wanted. The one who was always ready for an adventure. Or three.

Evan's gaze flicked from her face to something beyond her shoulder and back again. "I think we…"

Maybe it was the rush of standing on the stage of her childhood dreams. Maybe it was nothing but proximity and the loneliness of travel. But Marisol wanted to kiss him mid-sentence. She wanted to break off all his words and most of her common sense. She wanted to kiss this guy who probably tasted like mint and California sun.

"Can you guys scoot a little to the left?" Penny's bored voice sliced through the air. "I can stick this one through a filter but that's not going to help the weird shadows on your faces."

• • •

Stupid, Evan. Stupid, Evan.

The words in his head matched the pace of Julia's footsteps as she paced back and forth across the set. "Ten minutes. Ten. Not twenty. Not thirty."

"It wouldn't have mattered." He gestured toward the overhead speakers, which kept playing the porno music—although someone had managed to get the volume down from ear-hemorrhaging to migraine-inducing. He did regret something about those stolen minutes on the game show set, but it wasn't that he'd been away too long.

Should have kissed her. Instead, like a chump, he'd acted like the whole thing was a setup, posed for one of Penny's Instagram photos, and then high-tailed it down the steps and back to the rented set.

"Fine. We have to be out of here in an hour anyway." Julia said. "We'll go with what we have. I don't know why we even bother."

She growled and stomped her feet. "We are a professional TV crew. *Why* can't someone figure out how to unplug a freaking CD player?"

Obviously, the sheen of yesterday's hope had rubbed off after one night's sleep and a quick shower. There had to be something else they could do. Incorporate the music? Scrub it out in editing? That would probably cost a fortune. Go somewhere else?

"Maybe we can shoot on location somewhere? Marisol?" he asked.

She appeared beside Julia, her features closed off. "Yes?"

"Are there any places in LA you really wanted to visit? Landmarks? Tourist traps?" he asked.

She tapped a finger against her chin. "The Hollywood sign. The place where all the handprints are in the ground. One of those buses that take you to all the celebrities' houses." Her eyes were starting to light up, to give off the flicker he kept searching for.

"We can't do any of that stuff on a weekend, Newbie." Julia kept her wrath aimed at Evan. "It's a madhouse of bad khaki shorts and snotty children on the weekends. Hollywood Boulevard will be wall-to-wall weirdos."

She was right. It would be nearly impossible to film anything in the crush of tourists. And Marisol had been perfectly clear that this weekend was all she could offer. *Stupid, Evan.*

"Tuesday afternoon I am supposed to come back to the studio to give my presentation to James. If you want…"

He definitely wanted.

"That gives us two more days to hammer out the details. See, Julia? It's going to work out." He punched the producer lightly on the shoulder and was met with a death glare. But Evan couldn't bring himself to care. He didn't know when he'd become so stupidly optimistic, but he suspected it had something to do with spending nearly every waking minute about to fall off a creative cliff with Marisol close by.

"Fine. I'm sending everybody home." Julia threw up her hands. She stormed off and before long most of the crew followed, leaving

Jerry to carry the last pieces of equipment from one end of the stage to the other.

"Hey, I, uh need to give Bourbon back his shirts. Want to come?"

"Sure."

A second chance. There was no way he was going to be so stupid this time.

When they got to the *Who's Got the Coconut* set, Evan ignored the booth of overpriced, over-glittered junk and popped open the door to the set. "I think I left my notebook in here." Somehow, the lie came out convincingly.

"Which one? The one with all of our notes?" Marisol's eyes widened.

"Yeah. Can you check the podium?"

Her response was a beeline up the spiral stairs. He waited a beat before following, watching her hips shift as she moved. Watching everything about the way she moved.

"I do not see it."

He reached for her waist, praying his heart would stop pounding so damn hard. No dice. It only beat faster as she turned and met his gaze. And it nearly exploded when he laid his fingers on her neck, letting her dark hair flow over his hand.

"I found it," he said.

"Found what?" But her smile said she'd found it too.

"This." He pressed his mouth to hers, so gently at first—too gently. As if he might break her, or break them both, with how much he wanted this. Wanted her. Marisol's mouth melted into his. Her arms wrapped around his neck, and then they were crashing into one another. Tasting. Breathing one another.

She pulled back, two fingers covering her lips. "Wow."

"Good wow?"

Then they were kissing again, and Evan forgot everything. Where he was. Who he was. When he was. He shattered into a hundred thousand pieces with each brush of her tongue against his.

The lights flicked on and off.

They broke apart, but his body put up the mother of all protests. If it was Penny again, with her damn social media—

"Ahem." The nasal voice came from below, and Evan peered into the audience seating. A tall, beanstalk-like guy in a red polo shirt adjusted his glasses, while a group of fifteen or so tourists with glittery name tags stared up at them. "Do you have permission to be here?"

"Oh. Uh, yeah." Evan pointed to the red polo shirts. "Doing some last minute clean up."

"It *is* them. The ones from the *So Late* clips." A girl in the back elbowed the girl beside her. "We totally ship you guys. Everybody on my JV volleyball team watched it on the bus to one of our games. Do you—"

The cold sting of panic shot through his veins. He didn't have permission to be here. And this girl was going to put them on the spot, ask them questions he didn't want to answer. Not yet. "Watch out for Studio Seventeen C. I heard they were having some technical difficulties." He grabbed Marisol's hand, and they darted down the stairs.

Away from the stares of the crowd.

Away from the bright lights of the studio.

Toward—he hoped—another real moment together.

DAY SEVEN

Nothing could kill the butterflies—all three dozen of them—floating around in her stomach. Not the lack of coffee in her hotel room. Not the six a.m. wake-up call. Not even the bonus check-in call from her mother.

"*Sí.* All of the interviews were cancelled that day. I am sure they will reschedule. I will find out today." She pulled a sea green button-down from a hanger. Not even having to stuff herself into a suit seemed bad today. Not after a day like yesterday.

"Have you met anyone interesting there?" her mother asked. "Conferences are always a great way to network. Make connections. You never know when all those business cards will come in handy."

Okay. Maybe lying to her mother murdered one of the butterflies.

"I am working on it."

"I know you are, honey. Thank you." Her mother's sniffle traveled all the way from Puerto Cabezas and wormed its way into the cracks in Marisol's heart. Her mom—the always level-headed, always prepared, always everything—had built *Ahora* from the ground up. She'd fought for government grants, recruited volunteers, and somehow raised two children who wanted to be exactly like her.

And now everything she'd worked for balanced perilously on Marisol's shoulders.

A dozen more butterflies: dead and gone.

"How is your back?" Marisol asked, trying to paddle her way out of the panic sloshing at her sides. "Have you heard anything from Felipe?"

"Back is about the same."

"You need to have the injections," Marisol said.

"We'll see."

Her mother's code for "done talking about this."

"Felipe?" Marisol prodded.

"Called yesterday. Said he'd been trying to get ahold of you."

"What did you say?"

"Told him you'd been having phone trouble."

Marisol sighed. She hated keeping things from her big brother—even if she knew keeping this secret was in his best interest. "I will email him." She'd ignored her inbox—and every other electronic device—all weekend. It was easier to live in her bubble of funny people and funny things—and not so funny kisses—without the distraction of the computer or the television. But now it was time to head back to the real world.

Starting right now, with her brightest, most businesslike smile, a pair of sensible pumps, and a promise to her mother that she'd network the hell out of this place. And first things first, she'd march down to the registration desk and get her interview rescheduled.

One sardine-packed elevator later, she stood on the ground floor. She followed the DELLA SIMMONS PUBLIC HEATH INITIATIVE THIS WAY signs through a labyrinth of mostly vacant conference rooms, until she finally stumbled upon a line of people at least a hundred deep, all waiting to get in.

So much for marching in and demanding the interview.

"Well, hello. Mary Anne, right?" The woman smirked and shifted an expensive purse from one forearm to the other. Exactly what Marisol didn't want to face this early in the day—or ever. Pube One, front and center on the first full day of the conference.

"Marisol."

"Right, right. They've got quite the line here. Hope you don't miss the first session."

"Me too." Marisol couldn't quite tell if the woman was being genuinely nice or a genuine asshole. She put on a warm smile, just in case. "Did you have a nice weekend?"

"Oh, you know. The usual. Dinner with a few of the conference sponsors. Oh, we did a private screening of our documentary." Her eyes widened. "Went really well. Here. You should come see it. The public screening is Wednesday night." She pulled a sheet of paper from her handbag. "A little tip: get there early. It's a fan favorite to win, and you don't want another replay of this situation, do you?" She gestured toward the marathon-length line before she gave Marisol a little wave and strutted away.

Marisol crammed the paper into her folder without reading it. Her stomach twisted tighter with every step she took toward the registration desk. Why did she constantly feel like the only person who had no clue how to maneuver this whole conference schmoozing thing?

"There you are."

Every head turned in the direction of the voice. Clint stood a head taller than everyone in the vicinity, and his suit was even more impeccably tailored than the one he'd worn the other day.

It should be a crime to look that hot this early in the morning. "Me?"

"Yeah. I think I found the guy to talk to about the interviews."

"Not here?" She nodded toward the chaos ahead.

"Nope. Already waited in this line for twenty minutes just to be told they didn't know. Come on."

She glanced over her shoulder. Everyone stared. Every. One. The logical part of her brain knew they were looking at him. The Pube-induced paranoia part of her brain said they all knew about her appearance on the show—just like the girl the day before.

They strode past the line and down a hallway scattered with people in business suits. Wafts of hairspray and cologne hit as they marched by, and Marisol began to wonder if they were headed for a secret passage. Or maybe a wardrobe that would lead them to a magical land full of grants and kind interviewers.

"How was the taping?" he asked.

Marisol's feet stuttered. "The taping?"

"Yeah, *So Late It's Early.* You were going to see it the other day, right?" He laid a hand on the doorknob in front of them.

"Oh. Yes. It was... strange."

His face broke into a grin. "That's why it's so awesome. I called my brother. He's going to call his friend and see about getting me tickets. Ready?"

No. Definitely not ready. "Yes."

Inside the room, the horrible Scorpion Pixie Lady sipped coffee while the man who'd raked her over the coals in the first interview scrolled through his phone. Other important-looking people filled the rest of the space, and suddenly Marisol felt like a wildebeest who'd wandered into a pack of lounging lions.

"Clint—"

"Ah, Mr. McIntyre." Scorpion Lady sauntered over and draped a hand on his arm. She was old enough to be his mother, but the vibe she gave off was anything but maternal. "Did you finally come across your paperwork? It will be such a shame if we can't consider Appalachia Together for the grant. You have such strong qualifications."

He cleared his throat. "We're working on it. In the meantime, I'd still like to reschedule my last interview."

"Me too." Marisol stuck her hand out. "Nice to see you again."

The woman clasped her outstretched hand before leading them both to a table at the far end of the room. Marisol stared at her feet while Scorpion Lady flipped through a leather-bound planner. Clint had not only figured out the mystery of rescheduling, he'd gone out of his way to bring her along. He might have been her competition, but he fought fair. More than fair. And she kept spinning lies about the show. If she were a good person, she'd tell him the truth. See if he needed help with his presentation the way she did. Maybe James would let him sit in on her lessons.

"How about Thursday afternoon for you, Mary Anne? Say three o'clock?"

"Marisol."

"Oh, yes. Sorry. I'll put you down for three. See you then."

Marisol started to protest. Her presentation was scheduled for two on Thursday. Getting from one to the other would be a flaming hot mess. But Scorpion Lady was already halfway across the room by the time Marisol found the words.

RIP: every last butterfly.

• • •

It should have been harder, running back and forth from the writers' room to the coffee kiosk across the street. Making sure Penny didn't get stuck sweeping off the stage *and* counting wristbands *and* running scripts between departments. But it wasn't. Not when his mind could wander back to the set of *Who's Got the Coconut*. To Marisol pressed against him with her face in his hands.

With those memories front and center, Evan walked to the parking lot with his stack of wristbands. He had hoped the weekend would give the show time to catch fire, so he wouldn't be left begging for an audience.

Wishful thinking.

Maybe the stack weighed a little less than usual, but he'd still be hitting up the game show line for leftover superheroes and soccer moms who'd missed out on their chance at fame and housewares. And tomorrow he might have to pawn off an even thicker stack of wristbands if his sketches bombed.

"Figured you'd be inside gettin' all done up." Ted the Man Baby pulled a pack of cigarettes from his diaper before he swiped a wristband right out of Evan's hand.

"Done up?"

"For the show. My girlfriend saw you on one of those celebrity gossip websites." He jutted a thumb toward the woman behind him. Evan wasn't sure what her costume was supposed to be. Cutoff shorts. Pink-streaked hair. A lightning bolt painted above her left eye.

"It's pretaped." Evan held out a wristband to the girlfriend. Earlier in the day he'd watched as the crew edited together Friday night's dinner "date." Watching himself yammer on about D&D was embarrassing. Seeing himself watch Marisol's every move was something more akin to showing up to gym class naked—with a giant boner.

He tried to ignore the beating late-afternoon sun as he handed out the rest of the wristbands. A few more game show rejects. A few random passersby. A handful of people who showed up and actually asked to watch the taping. By the time the seats were full, it was time to do the one intern job he'd been looking forward to all day.

Evan checked his pocket for the flash drive, grabbed the giant, floppy portfolio full of posters, and made his way out the door. When he arrived at the Hilltop, he expected his legs to propel him out of his car. Propel him straight to Marisol, who he definitely intended to kiss again. Maybe right there in the hotel lobby.

Except.

Long gone were the adults in fanny packs and their sugar-crazed children. The place buzzed with the drone of businesslike chatter. The laid-back, overpriced vacation vibe had been replaced by the haughty laughter of old men and the occasional buzz of someone's cell phone.

This was not the kind of place where you could just grab a girl and throw her back into a kiss. Especially if that girl stood at the bar in a group of other well-dressed folks, commanding the attention of every person in a ten-foot radius.

Suddenly, Evan was all too aware of his sweaty T-shirt and jeans.

"Hey." He waved her down and hung back a few feet. "I, uh, have your stuff."

Marisol smiled, and Evan could see the relief in her features—something he wouldn't have picked up on a few days ago.

"Excuse me." She tugged his elbow, and he followed the clack-clack-clack of her heels to a table in the farthest, darkest corner of the hotel bar.

"Sorry. I didn't realize you'd still be… conferencing?" When he'd dropped her off the night before, he thought there'd been a little more to his promise of bringing the posters by than either of them had said aloud. Maybe in the light of day, away from the artificial glow of Television City, she'd decided they'd been a fluke.

"A long day, my brain hurts." She lowered her head into her hands then smiled up at him. "I am glad to see you."

He tucked a strand of hair behind her ear, finally able to breathe. "You want to get out of here for a little while? There's a—"

"Evan? No way. Hey, man." A guy with a beard and a vaguely familiar face slapped him on the back.

It took him a few squinting seconds to put the face with the name floating in his head, but when he did Evan burst into a grin. "Clint. Hey! What are you doing here?" In high school his best friend's older brother had been untouchable. The girls fell all over themselves to get his attention. The guys fell all over themselves to score invites to his parties. Evan and Matt watched from afar, as if they could learn how to be exactly like him with the right amount of time and sacrifice.

"I'm here for this public health conference." He gestured to the signs dotting the hotel landscape. In the next breath, Clint launched into a spiel about West Virginia and wheelchair ramps and camps for kids who were getting into trouble.

"Wow. So you guys are competing for the same grant?" Evan asked.

Clint nodded. Behind him, Marisol's face contorted into horror.

"But we're cool," Clint said. "Plus, there's a problem with our application. It's a whole thing. My boss is a nutjob. How do you guys know each other?" Clint asked.

"I, uh…" Evan tried not to look at Marisol, who was making a throat-slitting motion behind Clint's back. "I mean, we don't."

Shit.

"I forgot some things at the show," Marisol said. "This man was bringing them back to me. Thank you again." She picked up the giant portfolio, as if anyone would believe she'd left a two-foot by three-foot folder behind.

"Wow." Clint raised an eyebrow. "That's some service."

"Yes, *muchas gracias*." And then she was gone, fading into a crush of people who'd stumbled into the lobby.

He hadn't been able to show her the sketch. Or hand her the flash drive. He hadn't told her about his ideas for practicing her presentation. Or that Penny had made the *Ahora* links live on the show's website.

He hadn't kissed her again.

"Sorry man, didn't mean to block your game," Clint said. "Want to go after her? I mean, that look on your face is one thing. But driving all the way out here to hand-deliver whatever she forgot? Damn."

Evan shook his head. Marisol clearly didn't want Clint to know about the show. Maybe this had to do with her "serious nurse" hang-up. Which was stupid, especially where Clint was concerned. Evan had once seen him do six shots of Jack and then do backflips out of the bed of a truck.

The outskirts of Peoria were a weird place.

"Hey, how do you like working on the show? Matt made it sound pretty cool."

"It's okay. Ups and downs. We're kind of struggling—"

"Any way you could hook me up with a ticket? That show kills me."

"Yeah, no problem. What night do you want to come?" As soon as he said the words, Evan knew Marisol's secret would be out. *Shit.*

"How about tomorrow?"

He scrambled for an excuse. Any excuse. "It's a long way from here. At least an hour on the bus. Might not be worth it."

Clint shrugged. "I'm already in LA. What's another hour?"

"And there's a lot of waiting around beforehand. It's actually super boring. And hot."

"A price I'm willing to pay."

Evan gulped in a breath of chilly hotel air. *It'll be fine. Clint's cool.* "You sure?" he asked.

"Yeah. I'm sure."

Not much he could do at this point, not without giving away

Marisol's emerging starlet status. "Come by the studio around four o'clock. I'll make sure we have a ticket for you." Only fifty more tickets and maybe he could keep the giant baby from getting a seat.

Once Clint slipped away to mingle, Evan wandered into the main area of the lobby. He'd hoped Marisol would still be there, waiting to see if the coast was clear. But the armchairs were empty and only a handful of guests stood in the center, looking sweaty and worn. He pulled out his phone and jotted off a text.

I'm in the lobby. Clint's gone.

If the hotel had crickets, they would have chirped. Instead, ringing phones filled the space. None of them his. He wandered to the nearest sandwich-board style sign announcing the location of the conference. Tacked to the back, a single sheet of pink paper fluttered each time the lobby doors slid open or closed.

DELLA SIMMONS DOCUMENTARY FILM FESTIVAL

Evan glanced at his phone. More metaphorical crickets. For a brief moment, he considered leaving the flash drive at the front desk. At least then she'd get the chance to see her hard work pay off. But it had outtakes from the show and the sketch wouldn't air for hours. If one of the clerks decided to nose around before calling her room, Evan would be fired in ten seconds flat.

He checked his phone one last time then stepped out into the cooling night, leaving the conference—and Marisol—behind him.

DAY EIGHT

Moving halfway across the country for this internship made some things easier. Evan suspected he could order delivery every day of his semester in Los Angeles and never make it through half his options. In Peoria, he'd been limited to a half dozen pizza places and one subpar Indian restaurant. In LA, a trip to the grocery store meant the possibility of running into a famous director. In Peoria, a trip to the grocery store meant the possibility of running into his high school English teacher. In LA, it was easier not to care so much about fitting in. The entire place was overrun with people who didn't belong anywhere else—crazy creative types chasing their dreams were a dime a dozen here. In Peoria, he'd felt like the only one who cared more about watching Saturday Night Live than playing fantasy football.

But one thing was definitely harder in Los Angeles: extracting himself from a phone call with Gramps.

"They're called headshots, Gramps. And I don't have any. They're for actors."

"Looks like you're an actor now to me."

Despite all the miles between them, Evan knew exactly the pose his grandfather was striking. Sitting straight-backed in his recliner, tapping his left index finger on the arm of the chair. His interrogation pose.

"I'm not. It's just a thing. Short-term. I'm the intern—I have to pretty much do what they say."

"You aren't having to give any handy work are you? California is a weird place. Tilda at the senior center said her granddaughter moved out there and this director—"

"No, Gramps. No." Evan wasn't sure what was worse: that his grandfather was asking him about giving hand jobs or that he was seriously considering explaining the term was hand job, not handy work.

"Good. So if you send me about five of the pictures, that should be plenty."

"I told you I don't have any headshots to autograph. And, even if I did, I don't think anyone from the Peoria Senior Center will be interested in buying them from you."

"Kid, everywhere I go in this town someone asks me about you. On the CityLink bus. The grocery store. At Freddy's Tavern—"

"Why are you going to Freddy's?" The dingy bar was a favorite of the underage college crowd. The bouncers didn't care if you looked five or fifteen—as long as you had some kind of ID that said you were twenty-one.

The tone in Gramps's voice went from all-nonsense to no-nonsense. "Had to check on something."

Dad.

"He's drinking again, isn't he?" Evan asked.

"Maybe if you'd call him once in a while, you'd know."

Evan puffed out a deep breath. Digging up his resentments from their shallow grave was the last thing he wanted to do right now. "I better go. I've got a bunch of stuff to do before the taping starts."

"I don't got much time left here, kid. I don't want the two of you still fighting when I'm worm food."

Here we go. Again. "Don't play the old man card. We've been through this. I've really got to go."

"Send me the autographs."

"Okay." Anything to get off the phone. Anything to get out of this conversation. Maybe he'd grab a handful of napkins from the green room, sign those, and drop them in the mail.

His dad had checked out after Evan's mom died. Left with a teenage son, a sixty-hour a week job, and a wrongful death settlement several hundred thousand dollars deep, his dad went from casual beer at a cookout to a six-pack every night. Then more. Evan stopped counting. Eventually Gramps stepped in. He gave Evan's dad one of his famous come-to-Jesus talks, and for a time it seemed to work. But now—

"You need to get to wardrobe. They finally found a shirt long enough for your arms." Andrew shoved a few pages in his hand, snapping his head back into the present. "This is the sketch. Or the bones of it. You were right about doing these semi-scripted, Blue Balls."

"Blue Balls? Your nickname game is lacking today."

"Don't get too big for your britches there, Fuck Face. You still might screw this up and get us all fired. I've got kids that have to eat you know."

Evan's head nearly imploded. *No pressure.* "You have kids?"

"I've never met them, but I'm sure they're out there. And probably hungry too."

"You're an asshole."

"Yep. But I'm *our* asshole." Andrew clapped him on the back. "Seriously, good job."

Evan let himself gloat—just a little. He flipped through the pages, recognizing his ideas there, interspersed with Marisol's quips.

"Don't get too giddy there. Julia's got a massive case of the Tuesdays."

Tuesdays. The day before the network email would or would not come. The day before he'd know if all this public humiliation had been for nothing.

That gave him one more day to hope. One more day to pretend like this would go on forever. By some miracle, he'd save the show, have his pick of job offers, Marisol would never leave, and they could spend all their free time making out on game show sets. Denial would be his very best friend today.

"Any idea how it's looking?" he asked.

Andrew shrugged. "The Internet is bonkers. Did you know you're like the unofficial spokesman for erectile dysfunction meds now?"

He rolled his eyes. "What about the numbers?"

"Don't know yet. But it's sticking around. Some of the celebrity news shows ran a clip this morning. And I think one of the morning shows. The ones that call themselves news but are really just alcoholics sitting on a couch for four hours. You should ask Penny. She's been handling it all."

The last time he'd seen Penny, she'd practically been a fire-breathing dragon. *No thanks.*

But two steps out of wardrobe, Evan had to face another dragon. Julia.

"Why are we always running so late? We needed to start shooting five minutes ago. Where's Marisol?"

Evan glanced at his watch. He'd have to go back to regular intern duties in a couple of hours. Which meant James would start warming up for the show soon. "She's probably doing her presentation stuff with James."

Julia shook her head. "I cancelled it. Well, I never really set it up. Let's go."

"Julia, wait." He trailed behind her, praying he hadn't heard what he thought he'd just heard. "We told Marisol she'd meet with James today—"

She stopped, closed her eyes, and let out a ragged breath. "Evan. It's Tuesday."

"I know."

"You know what that means?"

"I know. But Marisol said she would do this if James could listen to her presentation and give her tips. Put the Hollywood shine on it." He felt stupid even saying those words aloud. He couldn't imagine how Julia felt hearing them.

"I know. I'm not an idiot. But we need the time for the shoot instead."

"We don't need that much time. We only need a couple minutes of—"

"We made some adjustments. It's going to need a little more time."

He'd seen the script. It shouldn't take more than a half an hour to get what they needed. Especially now that they all had a handle on what they were doing. "Julia—"

"Tape it," she said.

"Tape it?"

"Tape her presentation. Tell her James will watch it. Then you or Penny or whatever hobo you can find can write up some tips. Done."

"So lie?"

"I didn't say that. You did. Now go outside. Please." Her attempt at politeness was anything but. She stalked off before he could protest any further.

After he'd peeled off his *So Late* T-shirt and slipped his arms into the still-too-short sleeves, he made his way outside. The line of game show contestants snaked along the sidewalk. The usual suspects were present and accounted for. Unicorn. Giant Baby. Gorilla. But lots of fresh blood as well. A light breeze fluttered the wings of two women dressed as scantily clad butterflies. At the front of the line, three people huddled together dressed like they'd just stepped out of a maudlin production of *Cats*. At the back, a man with a black handlebar mustache, mullet, and green trucker hat goosed a blonde wearing entirely too much eye shadow. Evan wasn't sure exactly what constituted too much eye shadow, but like porn, he was certain he'd know it when he saw it. And this was it.

"Hi."

Evan jolted. Marisol's voice had reached his ear before he noticed she stood beside him. But once he'd noticed, he couldn't stop noticing. The way her collarbone peaked out of the neck of her shirt. The way she pulled her bottom lip between her teeth when he met her eye. The way she kept tucking her hair behind one ear.

She was nervous.

And so was he.

"Sorry about yesterday," she said. "I was a little freaked out."

He'd been freaked out, too. But her reasons had to do with things like saving lives and letting down her family. His reasons had more to do with whether he should have brushed his teeth a third time before heading over to the hotel. "You've got a lot on the line here."

"So do you."

"How about this: when the taping's over, we hit up Wonton Queen for some take out?" he asked. "Just us."

"Perfect."

He turned her toward the crowd, letting his hands rest on her shoulders. "Which one?"

"The pink butterfly."

"You think? I was thinking the woman with all the purple stuff on her face. Back there." He jerked an elbow toward the line and narrowed his eyes. He couldn't quite tell if Mullet Man and Eye Shadow Lady were in costume, but he suspected not. Either way, they'd make for great TV.

"No, no. Her man friend looks…"

"Unstable?" Evan watched as the man adjusted his trucker cap and winked at the woman beside him. Then at the woman behind him. Then at the unicorn.

She shuddered. "I was going to say like a perverted one. So, the butterfly, yes?"

Something in her voice made Evan turn. "What's wrong?"

"Nothing."

She was lying. He could hear it. Evan leaned in closer, leaving less space than proper between them. "What's the matter?"

"I feel like all of these people are watching us."

A million responses ran through his head. Things that—if this were a Hollywood rom-com full of beautiful people with beautiful cars and exquisite taste in clothing—would be the perfect script material to precede a long, lingering kiss.

"I guess that means I shouldn't kiss you right now?" he asked.

She glanced at her feet, then back at him. "Not if we want to keep pretending I am your wing girl."

"Hey! It's Marivan!" Like a sword, the shrill voice cut through every bit of traffic and chatter in the air.

Evan turned, trying not to flinch at the sound. "What's a marivan?" he whispered.

Marisol shrugged.

"MARIVAN! Over here!" Now every head in a half-mile radius stared either at Evan and Marisol or the source of the voice. And the source of the voice was jumping up and down while staring directly at them.

While his mustache flapped in the breeze. Mullet Man.

Marisol blinked several times. "Is that—"

"The love child of Fran Drescher and Ozzie Ozbourne?"

"Who?"

"Never mind. He's talking to us, right?"

"I think yes."

"Marivan! We came all the way from Oklahoma on my rig to see you. Can we get a picture?"

"Me?" Evan asked.

"The both of y'all. Get in here." The man held out his arms like he was ready to wrap them in a big hug. Or in Saran wrap, so he could take them back to his "rig" and murder them both on the spot.

Evan crept over to the line with Marisol at his heels. "You, uh, a fan of *Who's Got the Coconut*, sir?"

"What's that?" the man asked.

"You know, honey." Eye Shadow Lady smacked Mullet Man on the forearm. "The one with the tank full of those ugly sucker fish."

"I don't care about no game show," Mullet said. "I just want this here picture. Me, you, and our ladies."

"I am only his wing person," Marisol said.

"Sure, sure," Eye Shadow Lady said. "I think this one's gonna change your mind, sweetheart. Like ol' Tommy did here with me."

Mullet Man smirked and handed his phone off to the person in front of him—a man dressed as an exceptionally large caterpillar. Evan and Marisol ducked in beside the couple, and the caterpillar snapped the photo with one of his many arms.

"What time you start letting us into the studio? Anything we've gotta do to get a front-row seat?"

"You know this is the line for *Who's Got the Coconut*, right?" Evan asked.

"No shit? Where do we get in line for your show?"

My show. The words almost erased the weirdness of the situation. Almost.

How did these people not realize they were standing in a line filled with the world's worst Halloween costumes? Then he remembered every time the giant baby had slipped to the front row of *So Late* and ended up on camera, despite the fact that Evan always sat him in the back.

"We usually start handing out tickets around three o'clock," he said.

Julia arrived, barking like a general readying her troops for battle. "Are we ready yet?"

Behind her a cameraman scanned over the crowd, and Penny handed out release forms like candy.

"Y'all are shooting here. Well spank my momma's monkey." Eye Shadow pointed at the camera and nudged Tommy's elbow.

Evan glanced at Marisol, expecting her eyes to be lit with laughter. These people would be perfect for television. But instead, she watched the butterfly girls with keen interest. They kept typing on their phones, then staring at Marisol, then typing some more.

"Are all the right people here, Penny?" Julia asked.

Penny scanned the crowd, then nodded.

Right people? The line seemed like it was filled with all the wrong people—which, to be fair, made them the right people for television.

"Let's roll, guys." Julia gave Evan a nudge and pointed at the texting butterflies. "Those girls are way out of your league. Start there."

"But—"

The producer's eyebrows went so high they disappeared into her messy crop of hair.

Evan took a deep breath and let resignation fill his lungs. "Okay, fine."

The cameraman strolled over to them and the crowd went suddenly silent. When Evan and Marisol had come up with this idea that night at the diner, they'd imagined a group of people so enthralled with the idea of being on *Who's Got the Coconut* they'd barely notice him working the line and begging for girls' numbers. He'd never imagined they'd become an actual attraction.

"Now is your final test, young mealworm." Marisol stared straight into the camera as she said the words, dead serious.

No one watching at home would know how hard she'd laughed coming up with that stupidly funny line. How proud she'd seemed. How insanely beautiful she looked as she'd jotted it down on the notebook they'd passed back and forth over their plates of greasy burgers and fries.

And she looked just as beautiful now, watching as the camera followed him up and down the length of the line—following so close that turning around would mean a close-up of his nostrils. He wanted to shrug it off, tell the guy to give him room to breathe. But doing so would taunt Hurricane Julia.

"Hey." He leaned on—and stumbled against—the velvet rope separating him from the line. *Great.* Apparently he could still be awkward without trying.

"Hi." The butterfly batted her pink eyelashes and tossed her pink-streaked hair over one leotard-covered shoulder. Maybe leotard was too generous a description. A big slice of the stretchy fabric was missing, revealing the girl's flat stomach—which she'd covered with about a billion pink jewels.

"Hold on." Julia yanked him away. "You're supposed to look dopey. Not like someone killed your cat."

This girl probably modeled for off-brand lingerie companies on the weekend, while waiting for her big break. Which would probably come, because she was objectively gorgeous. But nothing about her held his interest. "Sorry, right. Dopey. No dead cats."

He approached again. But this time, he kept his eyes on

her face. No roaming. Not even to the horrible, garish wings on her back that would certainly block the view of anyone seated behind her—assuming she got into *Who's Got the Coconut*. Which she wouldn't. Not with her stomach showing. Everyone knew the network hated midriffs.

"Hey." He cleared his throat. *I can't believe I'm going to say this.* "I was wondering, do you know what's hung like a horse and winks?" Evan's upper body went stiff, bracing him for the smack that was sure to come.

Pink Butterfly giggled. "No."

Oh God.

The cameraman moved to get them both in the shot.

Evan's face burned as he pushed away his last morsels of self-respect. And then winked at the girl.

More giggling.

He laid it on thicker. "Can I get your digits?"

The butterfly fished a marker from between her breasts and grabbed his forearm. As the camera watched, she jotted down a series of numbers. Followed by her name. Followed by a heart. Followed by the outline of a butterfly. "So you won't forget me."

This was the opposite of what was supposed to happen. He was supposed to get rejected again and again. The Lady Killer was supposed to be so inept at picking up women he couldn't even get the weirdest people in the world to agree to date him.

"Cut," Julia said.

"What the Sam Hill is this?" Eye Shadow Lady shoved her way through the line. Butterfly's pink-rimmed eyes widened.

"Never mind. Keep rolling," Julia said.

"Listen here. You want to be happy like me and Tommy, you need to go after the right girl. This ain't the right girl for you, son."

"It's not?" Evan stepped back, half expecting her to pull a switchblade out of her cutoffs.

"Marivan. That's where it's at."

"Marivan?" He looked at Marisol, who shrugged.

"Your celebrity couple name. Come on now, you can't be as dumb as you pretend to be on the TV."

"What's going on?" Butterfly asked. She ran a finger along the numbers on his arm, then leaned in close. So close he felt her breath on his ear. "Is this part of the show? Will I be able to get a clip for my reel?" she whispered.

"Hole-y shit." Eye Shadow Lady wedged her way between them and gave Butterfly the smallest shove. "Girl, don't you respect true love?"

The cameraman kept rolling. And so did the rest of the people in line. In two seconds, a dozen phones pointed in the direction of the chaos. Followed by a rush of men in jeans and T-shirts—paparazzi—shouting and capturing their reactions with the click of heavyweight cameras. "Evan! Marisol! Come on, Evan. Lay one on her for the camera!"

"Marisol, any truth to the rumors about your porn star past?" another yelled.

"Evan, what's going on?" Marisol whispered.

"You were spotted leaving a set that has been long-rumored as an adult film hub. Certainly you have some explanation for that." The pap kept talking as he snapped photo after photo of Marisol's mortified expression.

"Where do you see your career going after this, Evan? What about you, Marisol? Will your patients still take you seriously?"

Evan grabbed her hand. "Let's go."

They took off, ducking through the side door and into the quiet air-conditioned studio. "You okay?" he asked.

Her hands shook, and she jammed them into her pockets. "Yes. I think."

"Are you sure?" He rested a hand on her lower back, trying to somehow quiet the unease between them.

"I thought you said no one watches this show."

"It's complicated. We—"

The doors swung open and Penny stepped in, holding her phone toward them. "You guys always pick the worst light."

"What the hell, Penny?" Evan asked.

"Whatever. Don't be so clueless." Penny snapped another photo. "Smile. It's time to give out the wristbands."

"When am I doing my presentation?" Marisol's voice quaked, and she kept her eyes trained on the floor.

"Are you sure you're okay?" He definitely did not want to drop the news about the presentation right now. Not when she looked like this, like she'd already been betrayed twice over. "It's kind of—"

She finally looked up at him. "When am I doing the presentation?"

Shit.

"I, uh... I'm not sure. Stay here. I'll find out."

• • •

Marisol paced the hallway, unsure of what to do next. Leaving seemed out of the question. Who knew when James would call her back to practice her presentation? But the idea of staying here while all those photographers swarmed outside made her stomach churn. The thrill of being recognized was being worn thin. Especially after those crazy people from Oklahoma and last night's near miss with—

"Marisol?"

"Clint?" She had to look twice. In a T-shirt and jeans he looked more human and less like a Calvin Klein model.

"Hey! So it worked, huh?"

Her face froze in horror. "What worked?"

"That whole delivery boy thing. Evan got you to come back to the show. I could tell he had a thing for you. Written all over the poor schmuck's face."

"What are you doing here?"

"Going to watch the taping. Same as you. Evan got me a ticket. Said if I waited here he'd give me a backstage tour."

The flickers of fear that started with the fight outside lit to roaring blaze. It took a solid three seconds for her mind to spiral to the worst case scenario: a world where no one from the conference took her seriously. Where her last interview got cancelled, again. Where no one showed up to her presentation. Where she'd be forced to go home and tell her mother she'd screwed everything up. Proving once and for all she wasn't responsible enough for anything.

Julia's head poked through the maze of doors. "Marisol, we need you."

Marisol forced her lungs to keep breathing as she contemplated her choices. One: go with Julia and hide from Clint for the rest of her life. Two: word vomit everything right there and hope he'd keep her secret. Or three: run.

She was out the door and halfway across the parking lot before she'd accepted her choice. So what if James didn't give her presentation pointers? So what if the show took the *Ahora* website links down? She couldn't breathe with the pressure and the accusations and the secrets bearing down on her like this.

Outside, she fell into a crush of people. They moved in one slow line, sweating in the sun and staring at their phones. To her right, two BIRTHDAY GIRL! balloons fluttered in the wind. Their bright red strings ended at the front of a walker and one all-too-familiar face.

"Betty," she whispered.

This was the line for the show. She'd tried to run away and ran straight toward it.

Keeping her head down, she jutted through a small gap. "*Con permiso.*" The bus stop was only a half block away. If she could just—

"Marisol? Wait! Are you okay?" The tone of Clint's voice said he was more confused than ever.

She walked faster.

"Hey, wait up. Please."

The prickle of two dozen eyes watching her every move was becoming entirely too familiar. She froze.

"What's going on? Are you okay?" Clint asked.

"I am—" the lie caught on her throat and she struggled to force it out. "I am fine."

"Marisol! Marisol. Over here. Just one more picture?" A man shoved a camera lens into her face.

"Who's this?" another asked. "Where's Evan?"

The paparazzi kept coming, and the roar of their questions grew so loud she couldn't hear herself think. How in the span of a few days had it reached this level of crazy?

"Come on." She grabbed Clint's arm and dragged him across the street to the relative safety of Wonton Queen.

Inside the restaurant, the smell of deep fried food and salty sauces billowed in the air. The tables sat empty except for one, where a middle-aged man with his back to the door lorded over a table brimming with small plates.

"You! Welcome. Sit." The kind voice came from the owner, and Marisol felt guilty she couldn't remember the woman's name. Something with an *E* sound. Eunice? Ella? Edna?

"Hi. Thank you." She dragged Clint to a table as far from the other patron as humanly possible. The chances a forty-something man eating dim sum at three o'clock in the afternoon would recognize her were slim to none. But then again Evan had also told her the chances of anyone from the conference knowing she was on the show were slim to none.

"What's going on?" Clint asked. "Why are we over here when we could be over *there* getting a tour? And why did all those people know you? And why does the woman working behind the counter know you?"

Marisol waved a menu at the owner. Maybe if they took one of every item off the cart, he'd eat enough to get sleepy and pass out. Then she could make a break for it. Tomorrow she'd convince him the entire thing had been a soy-sauce-laced hallucination.

Clint put a hand on her arm. "Marisol?"

Her phone vibrated. Evan.

Where are you?

In hiding, that was where. And she wasn't about to come out any time soon. She slipped the hunk of plastic into her purse.

"Earth to Marisol." Clint tapped a finger on the table, and then the crinkles in this forehead smoothed. "Is your blood sugar off or something? We can order—"

For one shameful second, she considered faking it. "No. I feel fine."

"Then what's going on?"

The older woman pushed the cart toward them, one wheel rattling against the metal and announcing her approach. "He says all plates are on him." She nodded toward the gentleman in the back.

"What?" Marisol asked.

At that moment, the man turned and gave a little wave. James January.

"Holy shit. Is that really him?" Immediately Clint began smoothing and tucking everything. His T-shirt. His hair. His T-shirt again.

"It *is* me." James made it to their table in three gangly legged strides. "Grabbing a bite before the big show?"

Marisol grabbed a plate of egg rolls from the cart and stuffed one in her mouth.

"James." The television show host stuck out his hand.

Clint's face blanked for an uncomfortable amount of time before he returned from whatever fanboy planet he'd visited. "Clint. Clint McIntyre. I'm a big fan."

"So *you're* him." James slid into one of the empty chairs.

"Him?" Clint tucked his shirt in again.

"My fan."

"Oh, ha. Right. I get it."

Clint had seemed perfectly comfortable at the conference, surrounded by CEOs, CFOs, COOs. Every kind of C-something-O title Americans loved foisting upon themselves. But here in front of a failing television show host, he'd become a hot mess.

Marisol took another bite of egg roll. At least these were as good as she'd remembered.

"It's usually not funny if you have to explain it." James turned his gaze on Marisol. "You need to get laid, my friend."

She nearly choked, spitting and sputtering until she caught her breath. "What?"

"You're practically making love to that egg roll over there."

"Wait." Clint pried his stare away from James. "You know *him*, too?"

Marisol closed her eyes and nodded.

"Not as well as she knows Evan," James said.

She sank into her chair.

"You and Evan are a thing?" Clint seemed to have lost all of his nervousness and replaced it with incredulity.

"No," Marisol said.

"That's not what the intertubes are saying." James pulled out his phone and slid it across the table. "Just click the little hashtag right there. Hashtag Marivan. Our interns are pretty smart, even if you could drive a train through the holes in their common sense."

Marisol tried not to stare at the photo currently on the screen, but it was impossible. In it, she was running through the crowd, grimacing as she pulled Clint along behind her. It had to have been taken only a few minutes ago.

"Has the Marivan crashed?" she read the words aloud.

"Well, has it?" James asked. "Inquiring minds want to know."

"I did not know anything about this. I did not know there was a Marivan." She clicked the hashtag and photo after photo loaded on the screen. Nearly every moment—even some she'd thought had been private—of the last few days stared back at her on that tiny screen.

Clint cleared his throat. "Speaking of inquiring minds—can someone tell me what's going on?"

James explained it all while she scrolled through more of the photos. The first handful were from today. The ones of her sprinting across the street with Clint brought out comments so nasty her stomach threatened to toss the eggrolls.

Slutting it up.

Didn't take her long to find a new dope. Must have run out of them wherever she came from.

Poor Evan. He can do better.

Follow me back, PLEASE. I love you Marisol!

Hot photos all day all night. XXX

She swallowed the bile climbing her throat and scrolled further. A few photos of the earlier snafu, followed by a hundred comments speculating on the cause. How had so many people already found the photos? And why did most everyone believe she was the one to blame, even though she wasn't in a majority of those photos?

She scrolled further.

A photo of her and Evan chatting. Standing a little too close. Looking a little too happy. She couldn't stand to read the comments on that one.

She scrolled and scrolled and scrolled. The photos kept appearing. How many people had grabbed her photo in the last few days without her knowledge? She scrolled to the very first one. She and Evan on the set of the "paint and crank" sketch. Posted on Monday by *So Late It's Early.*

She clicked through to the show's account, stopping to glance at its thousands of followers—followers like *PhillipFarmer* and *LacyinChicago* and *HotRamenDTF*—before taking in the hundreds of photos posted in the last few days. All with captions that painted her as a not-so-bright-love guru who was not-so-secretly in love with her protégé.

"Take this down." She shoved the phone toward James.

"I can't."

"Why?"

"I don't know how it works. I'm old. Besides, Penny told you she was going to handle the social media, right?"

"She didn't say it would be like this. She didn't say she would make people hate me."

"Oh, darling. You're famous now. People will hate you." James shrugged. "It's going quite well I think. I need to head over. I think I've stayed away long enough to make Julia batty by now."

"Wait." Marisol grabbed his arm. "When are we going to discuss my presentation?"

"Your presentation?"

"You know, for the conference? You are supposed to help me today? Help me with the Hollywood polish?"

James clearly did *not* know. He cleared his throat and took a step toward the door. "Maybe talk to Julia? She's usually in charge of things like that. Besides, you don't need any help in the polish department. Just be yourself."

No. No. No. Evan wouldn't have lied to her about this, right? Maybe James got into weird preshow hazes where he forgot everything except the show.

"What about my tickets?" she asked.

"Tickets?"

"To *Who's Got the Coconut?*"

"Why would you want tickets to that horrible housewife shite?" He waved to the woman behind the counter before he disappeared into the late afternoon sun.

The wet cement sloshing in Marisol's stomach solidified. They'd all lied to her. Used her. Julia. James.

Evan.

"Damn." Clint had his own phone out now. "I can't believe you didn't mention this."

"Sorry." She put her hand on his phone screen. "Please do not tell anyone."

"Why? It's awesome."

"No. It was an accident. Being on the show, I mean. And no one from the conference will take me seriously if they find out. Especially with all the things people are saying now."

"Like what?"

She couldn't find the energy to repeat them. "Stupid things."

"Can I ask a question? If you were so worried about people finding out, why'd you do it in the first place?"

Because they'd promised to help with her presentation. Because of the *Who's Got the Coconut* ticket. Because she didn't understand what she'd gotten into. Because it made her feel alive. More alive than sitting in a stuffy hotel trying to convince people she—and by proxy her work and her family and her patients—were worthy of their grant money.

A million reasons.

"I don't know," she said.

"Well, I think I do." Clint pulled a few dollars from his wallet and tossed them on the table. "You're human? It sounds fun. Plus, the show is funny. And hello? Look at James. Gorgeous."

"He is not really my type."

"Well, he's definitely mine. Come on. On the way over I'll tell you a few stories about Evan as a kid."

She didn't want to hear anything about Evan right now. Or maybe ever. It would be smarter to go back to the hotel and pretend he'd never stumbled into her life with his wristbands and his ideas and his weird grandpa. His kisses.

"How do you know him exactly?" she asked as they exited the Wonton Queen.

"Friends with my kid brother since they were tiny. In fifth grade, they called this sex line number from my parents' basement and ran up a three hundred dollar phone bill."

Her mouth fell open.

"Yeah, 1-800-Spank-Me or something like that," Clint said, tugging her back toward the studio. "Evan had to mow my parents' lawn for a year to pay back his half. And you should absolutely feel free to tell him I told you this story."

They stood near the gates of the giant warehouse-like studio now, and Marisol looked between Clint and the bus stop a few meters away. *Nope*, she decided. She would never mention it. Never tease Evan about it, because she wasn't going to speak with him again. She was going to get on the bus and hide in her hotel room until daybreak.

"You ready to go in?" Clint asked.

She looked at the building, willing her mouth to open. Willing her brain to force the words "I am leaving" out.

"Clint?"

"Yeah."

What if she'd misunderstood James? What if he had so much on his mind that he couldn't keep track of his schedule? What if she really never saw Evan again? "Do you think Evan is a good person?"

"One of the best."

"Are you sure?"

"Absolutely. Now come on, we can't miss the monologue."

She let him pull her inside, and they made their way to the set with just enough time to grab the wristbands Evan had left with one of the security guys. Unlike the first night she'd stumbled into the taping, the audience seats were full. Only two remained in the back corner, with a tiny sign marked "Reserved."

Evan appeared behind them. "Those are for you," he whispered.

"Thanks, man." Clint slapped him on the back and sat down.

Marisol couldn't find any of the right words. Everything kept swirling inside her—frustration, confusion, attraction. Why hadn't he told her how big this had become? Did he know about those rumors? What about the things he'd promised her? Were any of them real?

Those feelings between them? Real? Or was he only doing what he needed to do to keep her coming back to the show?

"You okay?" he asked.

Please be real. "When should I meet James for my presentation?"

"Yeah. About that."

"What about that?" she asked. Her heart sank further with each beat.

The lights flickered on and off. On the sidelines, Julia spoke into a headset. A plump man in a flannel shirt sauntered onto the set. The same warm-up comedian as last time.

"James is busy tonight. So we're going to tape it. And then, uh, he's going to watch it and give you some pointers." Evan looked at his shoes as the lights flickered one last time.

"Hello everyone, and welcome to *So Late It's Early*. Glad to have a full house tonight." The warm-up comedian clapped his hands together.

Finally, Evan looked her in the eye. "I have to go. I'm sorry."

She sank into her chair, feeling every bit a stupid, stupid girl. He'd lied. About all of it. Lied about how many people would see the show. Lied about James helping her with her presentation. Lied about them.

Ten long minutes later, the audience roared to life as James stepped onstage. Beside her, Clint became a freaking ray of celebrity-crush sunshine, beaming at the Englishman onstage. And Marisol slipped out of the studio, determined not be the show's pawn for one second longer.

DAY NINE

It had to be some kind of sorcery.

That was the only plausible explanation for how room 214 had become *more* disgusting in the week since Evan had last been there. It still smelled like moldy feet and had more stains than a hooker's bedspread. But the amount of garbage on the floor had increased threefold. Fast-food wrappers. Empty soda cans. A wine bottle. Pages and pages of scripts. The only clear surface in the room— besides the giant brown stain on the couch—was the rickety table where the playback equipment sat. And even that was covered in some sort of sticky film.

"What happens in here the rest of the week?" he whispered to Andrew.

The head writer shrugged. "Hell if I know. We used to think it was the interns. But now there's only, what, two or three of you?"

Evan nodded and cleared a spot for himself on the non-stained end of the couch. Soon the others filtered in, including Penny, each with their shoulders hiked closer to their ears than the last. This was it. In less than half an hour, they'd know if they'd get another week.

Whatever the verdict was, whatever twists or turns the executives decided to make, it would be on him. The stupid intern with the stupid ideas who stupidly convinced everyone to go along with them. The more he thought about it, the angrier he became. So much for a learning experience. The cancellation email hadn't even come yet and already he was picturing the headlines. The rude comments. The flight home.

Not to mention the bullshit with Julia not giving Marisol what they'd promised. He'd pay the price for that too.

"Hello? What do you think?" Julia stared at him like she'd been talking for ten minutes without a response.

"About what?"

"For crying out loud. I don't know why we bother with interns anymore." She rolled her eyes.

"Lay off him," Andrew said. "Bonerhead Bob's done a lot the last few days."

More than most of you. Evan bit back the retort. "I didn't hear the question. That's all."

"What do you think we should do about the Lady Killer segment? Every time we try to shoot the last one something goes wrong."

"I don't know," he said. "Maybe we should end it as is. Maybe Penny can be the new Lady Killer." He'd happily do all the intern duties alone if it meant he'd never have to appear on television again.

"Might not be a bad idea." Julia scribbled something on a notepad. "Penny will need to give you all of the passwords to the social media, her contact list, all that jazz. What do you think?" she looked at Penny.

"Uh, sure." Penny looked anything but sure. "But what about Marisol?"

"The public hates Marisol, especially after yesterday. I think we need fresh blood." Julia kept scribbling.

Evan wanted to protest, to stand up for Marisol. But it was true.

Last night, after the show wrapped, he'd headed straight to the back row. Everyone knew James disappeared into the bowels of the studio for an hour or so after the tapings—giving himself a mental critique of his performance—but not everyone knew he did it in the prop closet surrounded by fake dog turds and plastic skeletons. Evan would grab Marisol and march her straight to the prop room. Get her an audience with James.

But she was gone.

Clint said she'd slipped out before the show started. That she'd gotten freaked out by all the photos and the comments online. So when Evan got back to his apartment that night, he pulled up his old, inactive Instagram account.

The last time he'd looked, he had ten followers. All of them friends from college. Now? Fourteen hundred. On an account with a single picture—Evan at age six, sitting on Santa's lap while his parents smiled in the background.

He dug a little further, found the *So Late* account. And from there, he found the hashtag with the hundreds of photos. Photos of Marisol walking down the street with a cup of coffee. Photos of Marisol and Evan at the diner. Photos of him getting in and out of his car in the studio parking lot. A single photo of them kissing from atop Sammy Samuelson's game show podium.

He'd been tempted to stop there. Then he read the comments.

The stupid fucking comments.

Yeah, there were people who posted seventeen times in a row about things like true love and "Marivan" and how they wanted to smoosh Evan's cheeks. There were people who posted comments praising the show and the sketches. But no matter how many positive comments glowed on his screen, all Evan could see were the negatives.

When it came to him, the trolls fell into two camps: the why-are-his-arms-so-long camp and the let's-keep-the-erectile-dysfunction-memes-going camp.

But the comments about Marisol knew no bounds.

Her clothes. Her hair. Her smile. Her accent. Her skin color. It seemed the Internet brought out all kinds of crazy, but especially the chickenshit, racist, sexist kind. And once someone posted a photo of Marisol walking away from the show with Clint beside her, the comments only fell further down the rabbit hole of disgustingness.

That someone who posted the photo of Marisol and Clint: the show.

A fact he intended to interrogate Penny about as soon as they left this hellhole.

"You've got mail! You've got mail!"

Everyone jolted upright, gazes darting between Julia's laptop and the clock on the wall. Too early. The clock said they still had fifteen minutes of hell to wade through before they had to lay their necks on the chopping block.

"You've got mail! You've got mail!"

"Julia?" Andrew asked.

"You've got mail! You've got mail!"

"I'm trying." The producer's hands moved over the keys as the robotic voice kept announcing mail. "The computer's freaking out or something."

"You've got mail!"

She turned it around. Email after email popped up on the screen. From this distance Evan couldn't make out anything but the constant scroll of names and subject lines rolling by.

The door swung open and James sauntered in. He held a giant coffee in one hand and the plastic femur in the other. "Well, we meet again. Ten minutes before our fate is announced, and I have a few things I want to say."

"You've got mail! You've got mail!"

"Already?" James asked.

"I think something's wrong." Julia banged at the keys. "It's only supposed to do the 'You've got mail' thing when it comes from the network."

"You've got mail!"

"Shut the thing up already." Jerry crossed the room and unplugged the laptop's external speakers, but the email notification kept playing—just minus the surround sound.

"Back away from my laptop, Jerry," Julia said. "Right now."

But Jerry ignored her and pulled the screen closer to his face. "Holy shit."

One by one, everyone left their seats to huddle around the laptop, their murmurs cutting through the constant drone of "You've got mail!"

Evan couldn't take it. "What?"

He shoved his way to the front of the crowd, close enough to see the screen over Jerry's shoulders. The emails kept coming, but it didn't take long to see they were all from the same network address.

All with the same subject line: MARIVAN FOREVER. And the little preview box showed they all had the same attachment: the photo of Marisol and Evan kissing on the set.

At last the emails stopped. But there were still more than a hundred of them clogging Julia's inbox.

"What is this?" James squinted at the screen. "Why are the execs emailing you with this fanboy bullshit?"

"You've got mail! You've got mail!"

"Here we go again," Julia said.

Evan squinted at the computer screen. Who at the network had lost their mind and forwarded Julia the same email again and again? Someone was getting fired—and not just James January and the rest of the crew.

Except, Evan realized as the screen finally stopped moving, it wasn't the same email. Same subject line, same photo, but each had a slight variation on the length of the text.

"Is it a virus?" James asked.

Evan almost snickered. Marivan did sound a lot like a virus.

"Shut up and listen." Julia pulled the computer and onto her lap. Like a group of overgrown preschoolers settling in for story time, the rest of the room fell in around her. "Dear James and Julia," she read. "As you can see, you have a vocal group of fans—a group that clearly includes some hackers, as they were able to obtain my personal email address to use in their electronic letter writing campaign."

"What kind of asshole says 'electronic letter'?" James made a hoity-toity face as he said the words, but the bounce in his knee said he was desperate to hear more.

Julia cleared her throat. "One of my interns has set up a filter that will bounce the incoming emails to you. I don't know how this works, nor do I care. However, if I have to deal with this misery every day, so do you. It is quite obvious someone from your show began circulating the rumors about cancellation—"

"Don't think it counts as a rumor if it's true," Evan said.

"Do you want to hear the rest of this or do you want to keep interrupting?" Julia asked. She didn't wait for a response. "While we do not endorse such tactics, we do appreciate the fervor of your fan base. Therefore, while you have not met the requirements to extend the show, we have decided to reassess on Friday"—she took a deep breath, and the smile that had started to creep up her face disappeared—"when the executive in charge of finalizing these decisions returns from vacation."

The drumbeat of silence filled the room.

Evan reached for the computer. "Can I?" He ignored the return of the raging "You've got mail!" notices as he read the executive's email again. At the bottom, in a mess of numbers and information Julia hadn't read aloud, their ratings glared from the screen. They needed a 0.22, and they hadn't made it. But the 0.20 they had accomplished was higher than any week the show had aired. Ever.

"We almost made it," he said.

James grabbed the computer from his hands. "Let me see."

"You've got mail! You've got mail!"

"Find a way to shut that damn thing off," James said, but he didn't move. His eyes roamed over the screen, and Evan knew the exact moment the host caught that number along the bottom. "We really did. A 0.20. I didn't think our little bastard engine that could would ever see more than a 0.15."

A congratulatory murmur went through the crowd, a low-key sort of happiness tempered by the task ahead. And by the constant yammering of the computer announcing more mail. James slammed the laptop shut mid-notification.

"Okay, first things first. Who set up the 'electronic letter writing campaign?' I'm probably supposed to punish you for giving out that asshole's email address, but first I want to congratulate you on being a genius."

Everyone stared, letting the tension pull tighter and tighter.

Until one person raised their hand.

Penny.

"Okay, fine," James said. "Congratulations. If anyone asks, you got into a lot of hot water. Now on to business."

James's smug grin was back. The one that had earned him a cult fan base as a stand-up comedian but seemed to fade further with every week they awaited the network's email of doom. "What's the plan for tonight's sketch? The stuff with the weirdos outside? Did they edit it yet?" His questions kept coming, and it was a full thirty seconds before he paused long enough for anyone to answer.

And when he did, everyone turned to Evan.

"We, uh, well…" Suddenly the room was ten degrees warmer. "Things didn't go so well yesterday. I think you probably heard?" How could James not have heard? In less than 24 hours Evan had heard at least five different rumors about why Marisol had run away—and none of them came close to being weird enough to be the truth.

"That's why she was so keyed up at Wonton Queen?" James pulled his chin back, like Evan had dropped the truth about the tooth fairy in his lap.

"It was a small thing," he lied. "Some of the *Who's Got the Coconut* people—"

"That fucking show. You know how many prizes Sammy Samuelson takes home with him every week? One time—"

"James." Julia put a hand on the host's arm. "Focus."

"I hate that son of a bitch. And what's this I hear about giving Marisol tickets? Why would you torture anyone with that stupid show?"

"James. James." Julia set her jaw. "Back to business remember?"

"Fine."

"We only taped a few minutes yesterday before she left," Julia said. "The paparazzi came on a bit stronger than we thought. Scared her off."

Stronger than they'd thought? "What does that mean?" Evan demanded.

Julia ignored him. "We were thinking of scrapping the segment, James. It's not working anymore. It's getting too complicated." The look she threw Evan's way could have bent nails.

"Did you or did you not just read the email from the executive idiots?" James looked at her like she'd just suggested they set the entire show on fire and run away. "They want the Lady Killer. The Lady Killer fans are the reason we've got a two-day reprieve."

Julia cleared her throat. "James, it's only two days. I don't think... Maybe it's time—"

"Nope. It's not time until the fat lady yodels." James shoved the computer into Julia's hands. "Writers' room, now. Someone bring me every bit of footage we haven't used from the Lady Killer stuff." Somehow, the network's email had reenergized him. Like that little, simultaneous bit of taunt and encouragement had been exactly what he needed to care again.

"Evan? Where's Evan?" James asked.

Evan raised his hand, even though he stood only a few feet away from James's towering form.

"Get ready to grovel. You're going on the show tonight."

* * *

Another full day of workshops in the books. Another day of suits and heels and fake smiles. Finally, without the constant pull of the show, Marisol could focus every last drop of her energy on the conference. Put every brain cell to work on the mammoth job of getting this grant. Of making connections. Of making her mother proud.

And she did.

Mostly.

A handful of times her mind took off on its own, catching wind of something mildly funny. Something that could be spun into a funny skit or become the seed of an idea. And before she could stop, her brain ran with it—mentally pitching the idea to Evan.

Each time her brain went down that bumpy route, Marisol fought it back. She imagined the pain of telling her mother she'd lost the grant instead. She imagined how angry her brother would be when he found out what they'd been keeping from him. She imagined never going on the brigades again, losing touch with that last remnant of her family's history.

The love of her job, her family, the importance of her work—all were more important than a television show, no matter how much she loved that feeling of creation. Of molding something from the ground up and putting it on display.

"And that is why we must find new ways of engaging children with diabetes *and* their communities." She allowed herself a small smile in the mirror as she gestured toward the sign on her left—a giant poster board with statistics about the number of children diagnosed with diabetes who also lacked access to refrigeration for their insulin.

Her stomach rumbled, a reminder that she needed to check her own blood sugar levels and grab something to eat. After an hour and a half of rehearsing, her brain was beginning to leak from her ears. She stuffed her notes for tomorrow in a bag, slipped on a pair of shoes, and made her way downstairs. As the elevator dinged from floor to floor, she decided to take advantage of the perfect California evening and make her way to the CityWalk. Getting out of the hotel, and away from her fellow conference goers, even for a little while, would give her brain a chance to recharge.

"Excuse me." A woman dressed from head to toe in Hilltop Hotel gear called out from the reception desk.

"Me?"

"Hi." The woman adjusted the red scarf around her neck so all the gold Hs stood in perfect alignment. "I'm not really supposed to do this, but" —she leaned in conspiratorially— "do you think you could follow me? Just for thirty seconds."

Marisol's skin felt two sizes too small for the rest of her body. Suffocating. *Calm down.*

Certainly the hotel staff wouldn't be more gawkers. They probably had people who were *actually* famous in all the time. Maybe they just needed her to confirm her checkout time or something. "Can I come by later? I have an appointment." She didn't mention the appointment was with a margarita the size of her head.

"Not really."

Marisol ignored all the warning sirens sounding in her mind and followed the woman. The clerk's shoes had tiny *H*s on the backs of the heels, and Marisol stared at them as they snaked around the reception desk, past a giant fish tank, and into a small room off the main lobby.

"It's only a few questions," the clerk said. "Will only take a minute."

But once Marisol saw what was in store, she knew it would take less than a minute. Because no way was she staying to watch this debacle unfold. It had been weird and horrible enough in person; watching it replayed on television was like dumping an entire canister of salt into the wound. Yet, her feet refused to move, and her eyes refused to turn away from the giant TV in the center of the room.

"Sources say the stress of Hollywood was simply too much for the couple to withstand." A reporter with perfect hair and perfect teeth and perfect skin stared right into the camera. "What a shame."

The reporter saluted the camera before the shot faded. And then Marisol was staring at herself on the screen. And then Evan. And then at herself smiling at Evan. And then it was a whole montage of their skits, edited together to make them look completely, utterly, one hundred percent smitten with one another.

No wonder everyone is so confused.

No wonder I am so confused.

"Here she is!" The hotel clerk pointed to Marisol, and every person gathered around the big screen TV turned in their direction. "Now, I think we all know things aren't always as they appear on television. So let's be kind in our questions, yeah? And when they hand you that little card upon checkout, keep in mind this unique Hilltop Hotel experience."

Before Marisol could fully comprehend what was happening, hands and questions shot into the air.

"Who's the other guy?"

"Did you intend to make Evan fall in love with you?"

"Are you here illegally?"

It was the jolt her feet needed to move. She did an about face and marched through the lobby, ignoring the voices following her. Ignoring their questions as they replayed in her mind. Ignoring the memory of Evan's grin as they huddled together onscreen.

That last shot. The one where they looked like they might implode if they didn't kiss. That wasn't taken from their sketches. That was yesterday, before the cameras had started rolling.

Or so she'd thought.

She took off, not caring that she probably looked like a lunatic—arms swinging madly as she propelled herself as far away from the television as she could. Until that moment, she hadn't realized she'd been holding out hope. A feather light hope that what she and Evan had was real.

Marisol stopped in a dim hallway, where she was the only person in sight. The smell of food wafted by. Cheese. Fresh bread. Strawberries. She ignored her growling stomach and pulled out her phone.

She scrolled until she found Evan's number and pressed call. Time to settle this once and for all. She'd demand he tell people the truth about what happened. She'd demand the show leave her alone. She'd demand—

"We're sorry. The person you have called is no longer accepting calls or their mailbox is full. Please try again at another time."

Fine. She'd send him a text and *demand* he return her call.

Mid-demand, the phone vibrated in her palm.

Incoming call. Madre.

Her fingers hit ignore so fast Marisol barely had time to comprehend what she'd done. She'd call her back later, after she was done demanding—

Incoming call.

This time a phone number flashed across the screen. A phone number Marisol recognized, but one that belonged to someone who didn't know this throwaway American phone existed.

Felipe.

Her phone clattered to the floor, and spiderweb cracks crawled across the tiny screen. The battery fell from the back and slid along the floor, finally disappearing beneath a nearby cabinet.

"Damn, that sucks." A waiter carrying a tray of wine glasses and food paused beside her as she picked up the phone. "I know a guy who fixes—"

She waved him off. "It is fine. Better than fine."

"Ah, a Luddite, perhaps." He brought the tray down to her reach. "Here. Cheers."

Marisol took the wine. And then two of the cream cheese and salmon appetizers. "Cheers."

"You better hurry. I think they're about to start the first movie."

That's when she saw the sandwich board sign, taking up half the hallway. DELLA SIMMONS DOCUMENTARY FILM FESTIVAL THIS WAY. The conference must have spent half their budget on those oversized monstrosities.

Marisol glanced over her shoulder. She could chance going back through the lobby, say a prayer that the nosy hotel clerk and the legion of nosy gossipmongers wouldn't notice her. Or, she could sit in the dark for an hour with free food and drinks, while she pretended none of this had happened.

She hit a few buttons on her insulin pump and drained the last of her wine. Courage gathered, she tossed the remnants of her cell phone into the nearest garbage can and flagged down the waiter. "Another, please. You know what? I will do it." She took the two remaining glasses from his tray and poured one into the other. "*Gracias.*"

The lights had already gone down by the time Marisol slipped into the makeshift theatre. People filled almost every seat, and she shuffled her way toward an opening in the far corner of the room. "Excuse me. Sorry. Excuse me." She juggled her glass of wine and tiny plate stacked with appetizers until she could safely flop into her seat.

"Welcome to the third night of the First Annual Della Simmons Film Festival." The lights rose on the stage to reveal a man in a stiff tuxedo and shiny shoes. His hair had that Elvis Presley look. He pranced across the stage with his skinny microphone. "Tonight's feature film is from one of our three Della Simmons Grant finalists. And I have to say, the ladies behind this organization have made quite a splash this week. I'm proud to show you People United for Body Euphoria's documentary, *Capoeira's Children*."

Marisol shoved a cracker into her mouth and chased it with a swallow of wine. Maybe she could pretend like the whole *So Late It's Early* thing hadn't happened, but apparently the universe wasn't about to let her forget about the grant. Or that she was likely losing it to the Pubes. "Great."

"Shhh."

The heavy curtain parted, and the screen burst with color. A hundred houses appeared on a steep hillside, boxy and sitting one on top of the other. A dog barked somewhere offscreen, and a narrow path wound its way between the houses. A favela.

"Three years ago, People United for Body Euphoria's founder, Gloria Chambers, found herself in Brazil, staring up at the slums." The voiceover coming from the speakers reminded Marisol of a used car salesman. "And though she felt helpless against the crushing poverty, this American knew she had more in common with the Brazilian people than met the eye."

Marisol took another swig of wine as the movie cut to a shot of one of the Pubes in a silent dance studio. The woman had donned spandex from head to toe and rolled across the screen in some sort of slow motion breakdance.

"Capoeira!" Drumbeats rang out from every speaker, and Marisol jumped in her seat, sloshing wine onto her lap.

At first Marisol thought she'd had too much to drink. Or maybe time really was slowing. But the drums kept pounding, louder and louder. The woman onscreen kept dancing. And fighting. Or dance fighting? Whatever it was, the woman kept doing it. For at least five minutes, Marisol watched this display in both confusion and—not that she would ever admit it—admiration.

As suddenly as it started, the dancing ended, and the favela filled the screen once again.

"We're here today to find our first group of Capoeira warriors!" Pube One spoke right into the camera as she adjusted her giant safari-style hat. "Together, I know we can make a difference in these kid's lives. Oh! Look."

The camera followed her as she chased after a chubby kid in a red T-shirt. And then another, similarly overweight little girl with pigtails, and another boy—this one with cheeks so pinchable Marisol wanted to reach straight through the screen and hug him. In the span of a minute, the documentary showed her chasing a dozen children—all of who looked horrified when this crazy white lady, dressed like she was headed to the Serengeti, grabbed them by the arm and began yelling in stilted Portuguese.

Marisol hated the Pubes, but she had to hand it to them: submitting a mockumentary like this had been a bold move. The way people often stomped into—and over—foreign customs and lands, was something she'd seen hundreds of times. Even good people sometimes ended up hurting more than they helped.

"Childhood obesity," the announcer said. "It doesn't know skin color or religion or socioeconomic status. But it does fear one thing: Capoeria!" Onscreen the chubby children began learning to dance fight, and Marisol didn't bother to stifle her laugh as they toppled over like dominoes.

She laughed even harder when the time-lapse videography showed the children losing weight, their faces morphing into as they lost their last layers of baby fat. And she was still giggling when the lights came up.

Everyone around her stared in complete silence.

The tight-lipped woman beside her sneered. "I don't see the humor."

Apparently, neither did anyone else. The room burst into applause, and two rows up someone wiped a tear from her cheek.

"No way." Marisol's whisper floated into the brimming cheers. This was her competition? The grant money would be used to kidnap poor children—children who likely didn't have access to electricity or indoor plumbing or regular meals—and make them lose weight through dance fighting?

"What is wrong with you?" The woman next to her adjusted her salt and pepper bun. "Obesity is no laughing matter."

"I know. It is a very serious problem, I am sure." Marisol was at a loss.

"Well then you shouldn't be laughing." The woman straightened a little taller just so—Marisol suspected—she could look down her nose. "Obesity is very big right now."

• • •

On his first day, Evan had stumbled upon a wall of signatures and doodles in the green room. Classic television giants had scribbled their names across entire blocks. Rock stars had written expletives Evan had never before—and never since—seen. One child star had stuck an old lump of bubblegum to the wall, which set off a chain reaction of disgusting bubblegum lumps in every artificial color of the rainbow.

Evan was still in awe of the sheer amount of history contained in that single swath of cement. The studio's history, long before it housed this failing experimental talk show.

Evan waited to go on and watched the overhead monitors as James played to his strengths—making fun of himself and the network and the show. From this angle, no one could see the weaknesses—the constant state of backstage chaos, the disgruntled writers, the prop room overflowing with plastic dog poop. James kept it well hidden. Just as he kept hidden his apparent disdain for the guest currently sitting across from him onstage. Instead, James listened intently as Sam Samuelson talked about his new memoir, *This Gopher Dash Called Life: The Sammy Samuelson Story*.

"You good, Intern?" Andrew popped his head into the green room, and immediately his gaze went to the monitors. "This is some weird shit. They hate each other. I don't know why James bumped the parrot guy again."

"That guy's gross," Evan said. "Also I told him I wouldn't go on the show tonight unless he got Marisol on *Who's Got the Coconut*. So…" He nodded toward the monitor. "Sammy traded the tickets for a chance to plug his book."

Andrew shook his head. "You got some balls, Evan. Now let's go."

Evan stood and James's voice sounded over the speakers. "Let's bring him out, yeah? Please welcome our next reluctant guest: Lady Killer—figuratively, no emails please—Evan the Intern!"

The lights beat down on Evan's forehead, obscuring the faces in the darkened crowd. From this angle, no one would ever know the seats were filled by the ghosts of Halloween past.

He waved to the crowd as he made his way to the couch and squeezed in between the two men. Ever since James announced his half-cocked plan this afternoon, Evan's nerves had been suspiciously quiet. At first he'd chalked it up to being more comfortable in the limelight. After all, he and Marisol had been on television every day for the last week. Sometimes on multiple stations. But now…

A whole new ballgame.

He forced his knees not to bounce as he shook hands with the game show host on his left, then the talk show host on his right—never forgetting, not for one millisecond, that he was a random twenty-four-year-old from the middle of nowhere. And somehow, this had become his very weird life.

"So, Evan." James leaned back at his desk. "Anything new going on in your world?"

The audience cackled.

"More or less everything," Evan said.

"Why don't you tell us old men what it's like to play the field? To go out there and get your heart stomped on by pretty brunettes with sexy accents."

More laughter.

"It's hard."

"I'll say." James nodded to one of the Internet memes that

filled the overhead monitors. *If your erection lasts more than four hours, seek medical treatment immediately.*

Evan shook his head.

"Now, I'm a little confused, Evan." James leaned forward with his chin in his hands. "I thought Marisol was supposed to help you catch the ladies."

Evan pretended this was no different than the rehearsal they'd run through an hour before. "That was the plan."

"But?"

"But things changed."

The monitors flashed to one of the pictures of them kissing on Sammy's podium. The one Penny had posted to one social media outlet or another before it took off like wildfire.

"Yeah. We need to talk about this, kid." Samuelson crossed his arms tight across his chest. From his perch a few feet away, Evan could tell the game show host's blond hair was thinner in person than it appeared on television. The creases around his eyes deeper. The slack along his jaw looser. Apparently, the magic of television made this man look ten years younger.

"We do?" Evan asked. But he knew what was coming.

"Something about this photo looks familiar."

The crowd chortled.

"It does?" Evan cleared his throat. "I mean, it does."

"How did you get in to that super secure set, Evan?" James widened his eyes, sharing the secret mockery with everyone in the studio and onscreen.

"I bribed a guy."

"You bribed someone?" James's contorted his face into mock anger. "This girl must really have you by the 'nads, man."

"You better not have put your 'nads on my set," Samuelson added.

"No, no. Nothing like that." Evan wedged himself into the opening. "Marisol's a really big fan of your show. I don't know if you know this, Sammy, but I actually met her for the first time in line for *Who's Got the Coconut*."

"Ooooh." James tented his fingers. "The plot thickens."

"She really wanted to go on." Evan took a deep breath and forced out the words James had all but put in his mouth. "It was her birthday. But she didn't make the cut. So I decided to take her on a tour."

"Well, it looks like she got *something* on the show, if you know what I mean," Samuelson said.

"Well, why don't we given her a call then, eh?" James asked. "I want to hear from her what went down outside the studio the other day."

He pointed to the monitors, which had been split in half. On one side of the screen Marisol looked at Evan like he knew the answers to life. On the other, she held hands with Clint as they jogged across the street.

Evan hated looking at that picture. Not because she held hands with Clint—not that he loved that, necessarily—but because he could see the fear in her face. The slight look of panic that set in around her mouth, turning her usual brilliant smile into a scowl.

Penny wheeled an old pay phone onto the set—one of the few props they used on a regular basis. What people couldn't see, from home or from the audience, was the tech crew had patched Evan's phone into the studio's soundboard.

James handed him a quarter, and Evan stood to dial. *Please answer. Please answer.* He'd already left her two voice mails. The first one simply said he wanted to talk and James wanted her to appear by phone on the show. The second was a longer, rambling message telling her when he would call and why, what he would say, and how it wasn't true. He'd all but begged her to pick up the phone.

But she'd never called him back.

One ring came over the speakers.

The audience quieted.

Two.

The tension in that tiny phone booth pinned Evan's arms to his sides.

By the third ring, he knew she wouldn't answer. The voice mail clicked over, an automated message from a robotic voice—as far from Marisol's musical tone as he could imagine.

Just say it and hang up. Say it and hang up. "Hi, Marisol. This is, uh, Evan. Your, uh, protégé. I think I might be in love with you." He hung up as fast as humanly possible. Maybe faster.

James leaned back and crossed his ankles. "Well if that won't ruin a good relationship, I don't know what will, Sammy."

Brrrrring. Brrrrring.

Evan jolted.

"Is it her? Is it her? If it's her, I have a few things to say," James said. "As do a lot of people in this audience."

Evan had no idea if it was her. The old prop payphone might have been patched to his cellphone, but it didn't have caller ID.

Please be her.

Please don't be her.

He lifted the receiver. "Hello?"

"Evan? It's your dad. Grandpa's in the hospital."

DAY TEN

As long as Marisol didn't look closely, her reflection appeared confident and competent. But when she leaned in to the mirror, she saw the circles under her eyes and the days of stress worn into her skin. And it had all been for nothing. No game show tickets. No help with her presentation. Nothing.

"A little more lipstick, and no one will notice. It will be fine." She reached for her makeup bag and in the process dropped a tray of eye shadow on her laptop. The laptop she needed to take downstairs for her presentation. The same laptop that was now covered in pink and purple powder. "It will be fine. It will be fine." She grabbed a hand towel and swiped across the keyboard, rubbing as much of the sparkle as she could off of the keys.

With the motion, her PowerPoint presentation disappeared from the screen, hidden beneath a new window opening up. One that held all the things she'd been avoiding for the last week.

Her email.

"No. No. No."

For the last ten days, the Hilltop's basic Internet had trudged along at sloth speed, and the upgraded access cost an additional fee. A nonstarter with the constant drumbeat of "financial trouble" in the back of her mind. Plus, stomping all the way down to the lobby with her laptop had been too much trouble—especially now that the hotel clerks knew about *So Late It's Early*. Of course, now that Marisol was systematically avoiding everything—other than this presentation and interview—the Internet started to move. And move. And move.

She should close the window. Click the little *X* in the corner as fast as possible. Nothing good could come of sitting here, feeling homesick and helpless as she read messages from home. But still.

One email from her mother. Subject: **Everything Okay?**

Three from Felipe: **What is Going On?**

Followed by **Call Me, Please.**

Followed by **Call Me NOW!**

All too conveniently, Marisol had no way to call him, so she scrolled past all three of his messages without opening any of them. But he'd pulled a page from Marisol's own playbook and enlisted his girlfriend's assistance. The same girlfriend who happened to be one of Marisol's oldest friends. Annie.

No. Close the inbox. Close it. Her fingers hovered over the keyboard, sparkling with spilled eye shadow. It didn't matter how much she missed Annie. It didn't matter that her friend gave great pep talks and could organize anything—including a wayward presentation—within an inch of its life; Marisol needed to focus. Today, the cost of explaining anything was too high.

She double-clicked the first message from Annie.

> **Mari! I just saw your face on Extra! Are you really in LA? What's going on? I spent an hour falling down the rabbit hole of celebrity gossip about you and this guy. (He's cute!) Call me!**

Sent two hours later:

> **Hey Mari, Felipe is getting worried. I guess he talked to your mom about why you're in LA. I didn't know. I'm sorry. Can you call, please?**

And five hours after that:

> **Mari, I'm getting worried now too. Some of these websites are saying things. Well, I'm sure you know what they're saying. I love you. I'm here if you need anything. Let me know you're okay.**

"Saying things?" Marisol minimized her email and took a deep breath. She was absolutely, 110 percent *not* going to put her own name in the little search engine box on the screen. With less than an hour before her presentation, she needed to get her head in the game. Except...

Marivan Derailed by Love? Or by Sex Tape Scandal?

Ten clicks later she'd read a half dozen theories about her disappearance from the show. She'd been looking for a green card, and when Evan wouldn't propose she'd moved on. She'd wormed her way onto the show by sleeping with James January and extorting him with a sex tape—which was apparently extra-extortion-y because James was widely known in the US as the first openly gay late-night host. She had coke habit that cost more than what the show paid her.

"Everything costs more than what they paid me," she muttered.

She'd given the show hours of her time. Her ideas. And, up there on that podium with Evan, a little snaggle-toothed piece of her heart. James January and crew hadn't given her anything in return—except a few posters. Marisol tried to suppress her anger, but with each stray thought it inched higher inside her.

She pulled up a blank email and inserted the names. Her mother. Felipe. Annie.

Everyone,

Everything is fine. Those things online are not true, I promise. I will explain when I am home in a few days, but for now I have to go win *Ahora* some money. If they give it to me on one of those giant checks, I will send you a photo.

Mari

P.S. My phone isn't working. If you have an emergency, call the hotel. I am in room 1708.

She read it over again. Once, twice, three times. She needed it to be firm but lighthearted, and she needed to hide any trace of how horrible everything felt.

P.P.S. If they give me a giant check, I will need to buy a

**second plane ticket, because I am bringing it home to hang
on my wall.**

"Good enough." She hit send, closed her inbox before her fingers could do any more damage, and packed her belongings. She'd head down now, make sure she had time to hook up her computer, and check her teeth for leftover signs of lunch one last time. She would be early for once, and there would be no stopping her. Maybe stuffy interviews weren't her thing, but she could rock the hell out of a presentation. She'd been doing it for years back home—both on the brigades and off—and no one at the conference knew more about training community advisors than she did, especially when it came to diabetes training.

At least, that's what she told herself as she marched toward the elevator.

By the time she made it to the lobby, Marisol felt almost like herself. A little nervous? Sure. But also a little excited. When her presentation ended, she'd have fifty more people excited about training their own community health workers. And hopefully twenty thousand more dollars in her pocket.

"Marisol? Hey, I was hoping to find you." Clint caught up to her in a few lanky strides. He looked different than usual. His tie hung crooked, and his shirt had a certain rumple to it, like he'd picked it up off the floor an hour ago.

She looked past him toward the registration desk. No sign of the clerk who'd tricked her yesterday. "I have to set up for my presentation." She didn't want to be rude, but there was no more room at her crazy train inn. Any more questions Clint had about the show would have to wait.

His face flatlined.

"Is everything okay?" she asked.

"Yeah, about the presentation—"

"Marisol. Marisol! Just a few questions for you. Chuck Taylor, *Sizzling Celebrity Scandals.* How long are you planning to give Evan the silent treatment? Did you hear his message last night?" The man shoved his cell phone in her face, and it took her too long to realize he was snapping photos.

A woman with frizzy blonde hair poking out from under a baseball cap edged the man out of the way. "How long ago did you make the sex tape? Do you have any insider thoughts on James January's sexuality?"

A third cell phone appeared. "Do you think *So Late It's Early* deserves a renewal?"

The click of the electronic shutter was all it took. "Leave me alone." She tried to shove by, but they surrounded her like hounds at a hunt. Where were the hotel staff? Why weren't they rushing to free her from this mess? How did these paparazzi know where she'd been staying?

"Come on." Clint grabbed her around the shoulders and threw his body weight into the crowd. More cameras went off as the buzz grew louder. Formerly disinterested guests stood to see what all the fuss was about, and—at last—a man dressed in head-to-toe *H* gear began telling the paparazzi to leave.

When she and Clint had thrown enough elbows to scuttle past the chaos, Marisol ducked into the first open door she could find. So much for feeling like her old self.

"What was that?" she asked.

"Paparazzi."

"I know that. But why are they here?"

Clint ran a hand over his once perfect beard. "Maybe we should—" He nodded toward the door.

"No. I am not going back out there." She crossed her arms. "Not until they are gone."

At that moment, a man with a potbelly and a straw hat stepped into the room. His footsteps echoed off the tile, and his eyes widened when they landed on Marisol.

Great. Here we go. "No photos, please," she said.

"I'm sorry. Am I... Is this?" He glanced over his shoulder.

"It is. Minor emergency," Clint said. "This one's out of service. There's another men's room on the other side of the lobby. Go past the big television and hang a left." He escorted the man the three steps out to the hallway.

Marisol finally found the wherewithal to take in her surroundings. Sinks. Stalls. The smell of bleach. Urinals. In front of all those paparazzi, she'd grabbed her supposed lover and ducked into the men's room.

"I think someone from the hotel staff tipped them off," Clint said. "I caught one of the clerks giving me the side-eye while she was talking on the phone. At first I didn't think anything of it, but now..."

"Now everything is a mess." She reached for her phone before she remembered last night's debacle. "What time is it? I have to set up for my presentation. Do you think—"

"So you haven't been in there yet?" Clint's frown deepened.

"No. Why?"

He sighed. "Something happened to the circuit breaker or something. No electricity in Hall C. It went out right at the end of my presentation."

"No electricity?"

"None."

"Well, they will get it fixed, yes? Or move it to a new room? This hotel is full of empty spaces."

Clint shrugged. "They said everything is booked. Some new conference started today. A science fair. It's called Lab Rats or something like that."

"Science fair?" She needed to come up with a plan. Her presentation was the only thing that mattered right now. "I need to go. Can you look out there and see if it is safe?" she asked.

Clint pulled open the men's room door and poked his head out. "Looks like the security guards finally got them out. I'll go first. If no one notices, you follow." He pointed to her laptop bag. "Is that all you have? I thought—"

"*Mierda.*" Her posters. She must have dropped them in the chaos. "Brown folder. This big." She held her hands an arm's length apart. It was so bulky—how did she miss it flopping to the ground?

He stuck his head into the hall again. "I don't see them. Let's get you to Hall C and then I'll go back and look. Someone from the front desk probably grabbed them and put them in the lost and found."

He was a terrible liar. "Clint?" she asked.

"Yeah?"

"Thank you."

He nodded. "Ready?"

"Ready."

Clint slipped out of the bathroom. Marisol watched from her perch around the corner, holding her breath as she waited for another ambush. When none came, she followed.

Hall C was a tomb. Dim, cold, quiet. Filled with ancient old men. The only light crept through from the shaded floor-to-ceiling windows on either side of the room, and a hundred empty chairs lined up in perfect rows in front of the stage.

Her stage.

"Shut the door!" A voice boomed out from the front of the room, and Marisol jerked the door closed behind her.

"Hi." She approached with caution. "I am supposed to do the two o'clock presentation."

"Not anymore." The man hiked up his worn blue jeans and jerked his head toward the stage, where two other men huddled together near the podium. A patch on the front of his shirt said ROY, MAINTENANCE HEAD.

"Oh, I am sure you will fix the problem, no?" She did her best impression of a dazzling smile. Wide eyes.

It all felt flat.

"Not unless you know a good exterminator," Roy said.

Exterminator? She looked at Clint, who shrugged. Maybe somewhere in the constant surges of adrenaline her English had gotten waterlogged. "Did you say electrician?" she asked.

"Nope. See, you got one right there." He shined a flashlight across the room. Marisol only caught a flash of movement before whatever it was it disappeared. "And last I saw you had a whole mess of them under the stage. Probably making babies under there right now."

"Babies?"

"Look, I like God's creatures as much as anybody, but somebody's got to do something about this, and it ain't gonna be pretty. And there certainly isn't gonna be any presentation in here."

"Creatures?" Marisol asked. "I thought the electricity was out."

"It is. Because one of the damn rats chewed through every wire on stage. Son of a bitch fried himself three times before he finally gave up the ghost. They said the damn things are on steroids, but I think it's more like Hulk juice."

Hulk juice? Fried rats?

The man jumped onto the nearest chair. "There. There's another. Suckers are huge. They've gotta be multiplying."

Rats were no big deal. Marisol spent four months out of every year on a glorified camping trip. She could deal with rats. No problem. She followed the beam of his flashlight to a twitching nose and took a small step forward. But then the light illuminated the rest of the beast, and Marisol couldn't scramble away fast enough. Hulk juice be damned. That rat had apparently eaten the Hulk and all of his brothers.

"Maybe we should find one of the organizers?" she asked Clint.

"I'm afraid to move. Maybe we should play dead?" He said the words from the corner of his mouth, every other muscle mannequin-like.

"No. It will be fine." She took a step backward. The rat took one forward. One backward. One forward.

"Not fine. Definitely not fine," Clint said.

"I told ya," Roy said.

Only a rat. More scared of you than you are of it. Only a rat. Marisol reached into her bag and pulled out a piece of candy. One of the butterscotch discs she kept handy in case of a blood sugar emergency. If she could distract it for a few seconds—

"Here." She chucked the candy toward the rat, realizing a second too late that she hadn't unwrapped it. No matter—the animal's gargantuan paws tore through the plastic at hyperspeed. "Go." She took off toward the door with Clint at her heels. They slammed the door shut behind them, leaving poor Roy and his cronies alone with the beasts.

Marisol leaned against the wall and tried to calm her breathing. Fifteen minutes until she was supposed to go onstage, and she was ready to pack it all in, admit defeat, and hop on the next plane back to Managua. Between the sex tape rumors and the paparazzi in the lobby, she'd screwed up her own chances at the grant. And now giant rats had taken over her presentation room. Clearly the universe was trying to tell her something.

And she was finally ready to listen.

"I heard there was a problem with your presentation. That's so terrible." Pube Two appeared with a hand to her chest. "Bless your heart. It must be awful trying to juggle the stress of being an Internet celebrity with real work. I guess something had to give, right? It's probably for the best."

Marisol pulled upright, like the woman's bitchy tone was a marionette string attached to her spine. "What do you mean?"

"Oh, I just…" She shrugged, the picture of innocence. "What's the saying? If you chase two rats you'll lose them both?"

Marisol squeezed her fists tight against her side. "You."

"You're welcome. After your little meltdown during our movie last night, I knew you needed a break. This seemed like the best way for everyone. Well, maybe except the rats. But I think they'll survive. Tough little things. I also went ahead and explained everything to Mr. Peabody. That's who you're meeting with this afternoon, right?"

"Your movie was horrible," Marisol spat. "Capoeira is Brazilian. I don't think those people need *you* to come in and teach it to them."

"Tell that to all those little kids with BMIs in the overweight range. No more obese range for them."

Clint's voice cut through her rage. "Marisol? I think you should see this."

Clint. She'd forgotten he was there. She wasn't sure what was more important than giving this crazy lady a piece—or three—of her mind, but Marisol craned her neck to see what he was pointing at.

Down the hall, past the thick rope someone had put up and the DO NOT ENTER sign, a crowd waited. At least forty people milling around, shuffling their folders and tugging at their suits. People waiting to see her. People waiting to hear what she had to say about diabetes education. People who could take her words and ideas and make an actual difference in their communities.

"I guess you have some fans after all," Pube Two said. "Don't worry. I'll go ahead and tell them you had to cancel."

"Do *not* tell them anything."

"Ta-ta!" Pube Two waved as she flounced away.

Marisol looked at Clint. It was like the Pube's deceit had brought everything into perfect focus. "Can you help me?" she asked.

"As long as it doesn't involve going back in there with those rats."

"Tell those people the presentation is going to be on the patio."

"Where are you going?" he asked.

I'm going to talk to the bartender."

"The bartender?"

"Yes, please hurry."

"You're going to buy everyone drinks?" he asked.

"Not exactly. I think he's going to give them to us. After all, I do not think the hotel will want me to call Chuck Taylor from *Sizzling Celebrity Scandals* and tell him about their rat problem."

"Blackmail. Got it." He pushed forward at a full sprint, easily passing Pube Two and her dainty, designer-shoed walk.

Marisol shook out her fists and steadied herself for battle. *Okay, Universe. Time to shut the hell up.*

. . .

The smell of hospital invaded his nostrils before Evan made it through the first set of double doors. In the eight years since he'd been here last, he'd managed to forget how much death smelled like fake pine and latex.

"I'm looking for my grandfather, John Abramson."

The woman at the desk took a drink from her giant Styrofoam cup. "Room 413. That's the ICU, so visiting hours end in"— she twisted her neck to look at the clock behind the desk— "twenty minutes."

"Thanks." He jogged the few steps toward the elevator and pressed the up button at least three times.

Twenty minutes. Los Angeles traffic plus a flight delay and a resulting missed connection meant he only got twenty minutes to spend with Gramps. What if these were the last twenty minutes? Last Evan had heard, Gramps was still unconscious from the fall. They weren't sure when he'd wake up again—if ever.

"You like Los Angeles?" the reception desk woman asked. "I've been thinking of heading out there myself. Just got a divorce, always wanted to go, so I figured why not."

"Excuse me?" Evan pressed the elevator button again.

"Los. Angeles. Do. You. Like. It?" She furrowed her brow like he was an idiot.

"Yeah, it's good I guess." Not that he'd be going back any time soon.

"If I gave you a video tape, do you think you could get it in front of James January?" She pulled out a VHS—an actual, honest to goodness video cassette—and waved it toward him. "It's a few years old now, and a little bit racy but—"

Ding!

Evan couldn't get on the elevator fast enough.

Eighteen minutes.

The doors opened on the fourth floor, and he pushed through the ICU's swinging doors. He ignored every sign asking him to check in at the nurses' station and marched straight to room 413.

"Gramps? Hey—" Evan pulled back the curtain and stopped cold.

His grandfather lay in the bed, covers tucked to his chin. Around him machines beeped and rattled, and a purple bruise floated along the entire right side of his face. One leg stayed buried under the crisp white sheets, but the other poked out, revealing the heavy cast that covered him to the knee.

"Gramps?" Evan inched closer, but Gramps didn't stir.

Where was his father? Evan had tried to call him from the airport to say he'd made it, to tell him Matt was driving him straight to the hospital, but no answer. Instead, Evan left his dad a terse voice mail and spent the rest of the drive to Peoria staring out the window at cornfields.

Fifteen minutes.

He pulled a chair to the bedside and forced his eyes to stay on the unmarred side of his grandfather's face. Gramps had fallen getting off the bus at the Senior Village. One minute he was on his way to poker with "his boys" and the next he'd been flat on his face, unconscious and broken.

"I'm sorry," Evan said. "I should have been here to take you. It was all for nothing anyway. Dad was right." The words burned like acid on his tongue. "But if you wake up—when you wake up—I'll take you. It won't be a problem." He leaned in to brush a speck of lint from his grandfather's cheek. "Just wake up, okay?"

He wanted it to be like the movies. He wanted Gramps to hear him and come fluttering back from wherever he'd gone.

Except he didn't. He lay there, silent, his chest moving with the rhythm of the machines.

Ten minutes.

More lint. Except the hardened yellow fleck wouldn't budge from the corner of Gramps's mouth. Evan leaned in further. Wait. Not lint. *Please don't be something disgusting.*

Gramps eyes flew open. "Here's Johnny!"

Evan fumbled backwards, groping at anything he could find.

"Don't pull out my catheter!"

Evan's butt hit the floor as he let go, and a lightning bolt of pain struck his left leg. "Shit."

"Evan? Evan?" The hospital bed began moving. Gramps peered over at him from the side. "I was only messing with you. Didn't think you'd pee your pants over it."

He tried to breathe through the pain, but all he saw were the proverbial stars. "Jesus, Gramps. I thought you were in a coma or something."

"No. I was just out for a bit, but they found all my marbles. Just got a broken ankle."

"Dad?" His father's voice entered the room, but from this angle all Evan could see were his work boots. "They were out of pepperoni slices so I got one mushroom, one sausage. I thought Evan would be here by now."

Evan winced at his dad's tone. He didn't have to say the next words—Evan already knew what they would be. *Must think he's too important to come home.*

"Oh, he's here alright." Gramps jerked a finger toward the floor. "Caught the kid trying to clean the mustard off my face, so I gave him a little scare."

Mustard. Of course.

Evan hobbled to a standing position. "Hey, Dad." He gave a quick wave and flopped back into the chair. He might have come home, but he wasn't quite ready to clear the air. Not yet. Parents were supposed to encourage their kids, push them toward their dreams. Evan's dad? Not so much. He'd held Evan's dreams in his fist, tightening his grip with every dig. *Why would you want to do that?* he'd asked. *Waste of time*, he'd said. *Not for people like us.*

"Are you okay?" his dad asked.

He winced as he nodded. "Just twisted something I think."

"I'm calling the nurse." Gramps pressed the call button before anyone could protest. "Give me the sausage. I don't want any of that fungus stuff." He took the slice of pizza and folded it in half. "Now, what's this about not going back?"

Evan untied his shoe and pulled up his jeans. Everything felt too tight. And not only because of the massive swelling in his ankle. His lungs felt too tight. His lips. How much did his father know about what happened? He definitely wasn't up for explaining it all right now. Or maybe ever.

"Just seeing if you were dead or not," Evan said.

Gramps squinted at him between bites of pizza. Clearly, he wasn't buying it. Evan gave his head a tiny shake.

"Mr. Abramson? What do you—did the doctor clear you to eat pizza?" The nurse stopped in the doorway and adjusted his stethoscope.

"Sure did. And the bratwurst I ate earlier." Gramps sounded so sure of himself, Evan almost believed—only for a half second—that the old man was telling the truth.

The nurse frowned. "What do you need?"

"My grandson here fell. He needs someone to look at his ankle. You got any other nurses on duty? Maybe a pretty one, blonde? You've had your fill of brunette nurses for a while, haven't you kid?"

Why weren't visiting hours over yet? "I'm okay, really."

"Let me see." The nurse came around the bed and stopped short when he saw Evan's ankle. He poked it with one finger, and Evan gasped with the heat of the pain.

"Wow. That's swollen."

"Yeah."

"I'm going to get a wheelchair and send you down to the ER. You need an X-ray."

"Send a blonde one. Of the female variety!" Gramps called after him.

But much to his grandfather's disappointment, the same guy came back with a blue-backed wheelchair. "Hop in."

"I'm fine. Really."

"Get in."

His ankle did hurt like a bitch. Maybe in the ER they'd give him enough pain meds to knock him out until this *So Late It's Early* business ended. Which, at the rate things were going, would be pretty soon.

He slid from one chair to the other. "This is your fault, old man."

Gramps waved him off. "If you'd left my mustard alone—"

"Alright you two," Evan's dad said.

"Don, you stay here with your dad," the nurse said to Evan's father. "We'll extend visiting hours for you—just this once—until this one's out of X-ray."

Evan leaned back in the wheelchair as the nurse pushed him toward the staff elevator. Every time he thought things couldn't get weirder, they did.

"So you said the *L* word and she freaked, huh?" The nurse pushed the elevator button as they waited. "Happened to me once. Sucks."

When did all these people start watching So Late It's Early? When he'd announced he was leaving home to do an internship on the show, the most common response had been a blank stare. Followed closely by questions about late-night infomercials.

"It was just a bit," Evan said. "For the show. You know, 'don't believe everything you see on TV' and all that."

His phone vibrated, and Evan twisted until he could free it from his pocket without putting pressure on the ankle.

Clint: **How's your grandpa?**

Evan: **An asshole. But I think it's going to be fine. Thanks for checking.**

He started to slip the phone back into his pocket, but another message came through.

Clint: **Glad to hear it. Check this out.**

Evan stared at the video Clint had attached. He had no idea what it was, but the still on the screen told him *who* it was—and he wasn't sure he could face even more pain right now.

"Oh. That's her, right? Go on, hit play." The nurse was practically breathing down his neck.

"Maybe I'll watch it later."

The man reached over and hit play.

Evan was certain this was some sort of privacy violation. HIPAA or HIPPOS or something like that. Or maybe just a violation of common decency. But once the video started playing, his train of outrage derailed.

Marisol stood on a chair on what looked like a crowded patio. Anyone else would have looked like a crazy person, but she looked commanding. In control. Focused. "When I was a little girl, I lived in a very small village. We did not have electricity or doctors. But we did have a woman who'd become our village's health leader. When I started showing the signs of diabetes—losing weight, being thirsty all the time—she recognized it. Without her, I would not be here today."

The crowd applauded. When they were done, Marisol kept going. Her expression stayed serious but sincere. Her voice kind but sharp as she talked about her life and her work and her goals for Nicaragua. Then the screen cut to black.

Evan stared for three full seconds before he hit play and watched it all over again. This was her presentation. The one she was supposed to do for James. The one she'd worked so hard on. He had no clue why she was giving it from the top of a chair on a patio, but it didn't matter. If the rest of it had looked like that clip, she'd nailed it. Marisol didn't need James's help. If anything, the host could take a pointer or two from her.

Evan: **Tell her I said good job.**

A paltry response, but it would have to suffice.

Clint: **She doesn't know about the show last night.**

Evan: **Good.**

Clint: **I guess that means don't tell her?**

"What? You have to tell her," the nurse said. "How will she know how you feel if you don't tell her?" He swiped the phone from Evan's hand.

"Are you serious right now? Give me my phone."

"Just. One. Second." He handed it back with a wink and a smug smile. "You're welcome."

Evan looked at the screen. **Tell her everything.** "Awesome. Thanks." He hoped the sarcasm was thick enough to cover that tiny hole where actual hope had spouted out.

The nurse looked all too smug. "X-ray is this way. Don't be surprised if you have to sign a few casts on the way."

An hour later, Evan had signed two arm casts, one doctor's prescription pad, and a cafeteria worker's apron. He also had an aircast of his own and an appointment to come back in a week for another X-ray. If there was ever any question of whether he was back in Peoria to stay, it had been answered loud and clear.

"Here's your stuff. Someone called your dad. He's on his way down." A new nurse smiled and handed him a plastic bag of his belongings. "Sorry about things with that girl. You were too good for her anyway."

In what world was he—a random kid from Illinois who played make-believe with camera equipment—better than someone who'd overcome tragedies and chronic illness and still found a way to save other people's lives? He loved making up stories and seeing them come to life through the camera. But it wasn't even in the same ballpark as what Marisol did every day.

"Thanks." He dug through the bag in search of his phone. Maybe there'd be an update from Clint. Or even from Marisol.

No, he wouldn't let himself hope. But as soon as the screen showed no waiting messages, disappointment settled into his gut. She hadn't called. Clint had told her "everything" and that wasn't enough.

"Both of you now, huh?" His dad walked in with his hands in his pockets, and the lines around his eyes looked deeper than Evan remembered. "You were always two peas in a pod."

"Huh?"

"You and Dad. Both broke your ankles. If I didn't know better, I'd think you did it on purpose."

Evan nodded. He didn't know how to deal with this situation. Whether he should apologize or keep up his righteous indignation. Whether he should acknowledge what they both seemed to be thinking—the last time they walked together through these doors, they'd been irretrievably broken.

"You hungry?" his dad asked.

"Sure." Evan shoved his wallet in his back pocket. And his phone. The flash drive full of *So Late* clips was all that remained in the plastic bag. The flash drive he'd been carrying around for God knows how long. *Stupid.* "Can you wheel me that way?" He pointed to the trash cans.

No way anyone would find it in the Peoria General Hospital trash can and look at the contents. Not that it would matter. By the time they could do anything with it, the show would be long gone. Time to let it go.

"This too? Fell out of your wallet." His dad handed him a pink slip of paper.

Evan didn't have to unfold it to know it had Marisol's phone number on it. But he did anyway. Her loopy, sloppy numbers appeared at the top and a big smudge from the mojito she'd been drinking at the bottom. "Yeah."

"How about the Rib House for dinner? Celebrate your return home?"

Celebrating was the last thing he wanted to do. Evan reached out and dangled the paper and the plastic bag over the trash can.

"Sure." He let go, and as soon as the flash of pink disappeared, an idea struck him straight in the chest. If he hadn't already been in a wheelchair, he would have fallen over with the weight of it.

• • •

Marisol stepped down from her chair to the thunder of applause. Maybe it was the unlimited mimosas. Maybe it was the thrill of being outside in the California sunshine. Or maybe it was her. The presentation had gone off without a hitch. She didn't need the posters or the PowerPoint slides. She needed her knowledge, experience, and storytelling abilities. Everything else fell into place. Including an audience who couldn't stop asking her questions.

"I have a question about finding community health advocates."

"How much experience do you require for your advocates?"

"Can I get another mimosa?"

"I am very sorry," Marisol said. "I have to go to a meeting at this very moment. But if you email me with your questions, I promise to answer them as soon as I can."

Amid the chaos of the rats and the blackmail, she hadn't had time to eat. And now with her final interview about to start—she glanced at the clock—in six minutes, the woozy feel of low blood sugar was creeping in.

She sprinted over to bar. "Orange juice please."

"No champagne?"

"No, only the juice." Not that she didn't feel like celebrating. She wanted to dance on the bar with her fifty newest friends. Never in a hundred years would she have imagined feeling this good about her presentation. Of course, never in a hundred years would she have imagined being sabotaged by genetically modified rats and giving her presentation among free-flowing mimosas either.

"One OJ." The bartender winked at her.

Marisol downed the juice in three swallows. "Thank you."

"No problem. Best tips I've got in six months."

"Hey. There you are." Clint looked like a kid about to sink his teeth into a birthday cake. Excited, crazed, and a little bit nervous. "Great job. Do you have a minute?"

She grabbed her laptop bag. "I have to go to my interview. But thank you for everything."

"I need three minutes? Five tops."

"My interview starts in two minutes. I will find you after, yes? Meet you in the bar." She didn't wait to hear his response. Luckily, for once, the interview room was stationed nearby, and she ducked in exactly as the clock struck three.

"Hello. I am Marisol Gutierrez. Very nice to…" Her voice faded as she took in the scene in front of her. "Very nice to meet you."

A plump, balding man in a red tie sat at the end of the table. Light streamed in through the windows behind him, illuminating the floral wallpaper along the walls—and the three celebrity gossip magazines spread out in front of him.

"I was starting to worry you wouldn't show." He crossed his arms in front of his chest. "Which would be very disappointing, because I have *so* very many questions."

The excitement and confidence she'd built during the

presentation began leaking out. She wanted to slide to the floor and give up altogether.

No. Not today. Mentally, she plugged the leak and took a seat. "As you know, I was giving a presentation."

He knew because he had been there. All three of the interviewers had been there in the back with their score sheets, sipping mimosas with the rest of them.

"Hmmm."

She fought the urge to ask what he thought of her presentation, but keeping a lid on it got harder every time she glanced at the table and saw those headlines staring back at her. The pictures of her running with Clint. Shaking hands with James January. Kissing Evan.

"How long ago did you audition to be on the show, Ms. Gutierrez?"

"I do not understand."

"The *So Late It's Early Show*. How long ago did you audition?"

"There was no audition."

"As a grant finalist and scholarship recipient, the Della Simmons Foundation paid for your plane tickets, hotel, and conference fees. If you were simply using our funds to further your acting career—"

"I was not. I did not. I was on the show by accident."

"Accident or not, collecting a paycheck from an outside source while you're here on scholarship is a serious violation of the rules."

"Excuse me?"

"It's all about professionalism, Ms. Gutierrez. I'm just trying to ascertain why exactly you're here."

She glanced at the magazines again, feeling her insides twist over on themselves. The show had screwed her over, but that didn't mean she had to let the Pubes do it too.

"I am here to learn about new advancements in public health. I am here because the organization I work for saves people's lives. I am here because your organization recognized that and asked us to come. I am here because *Ahora* deserves the grant."

Marisol folded her hands in her lap and looked him straight in the eye, refusing to see—even for a second—those photos of who he wanted her to be.

"And how do you think the people you—quote—save will feel when they hear you've been sleeping with American television stars?"

Time stilled. That rage clawed its way right back up her throat, and when she opened her mouth, Marisol wasn't sure what would come out. That she hadn't slept with anyone since she set foot on American soil? And why should it matter if she had? That this conference was a complete joke? Exhibit A: the applause that horrible dance fighting movie had received.

"I do not see how my sex life is any of your concern."

"You don't see how sleeping your way to the top might be a concern for some people?"

His smirk. God, that smug smirk was too much for her to handle.

"No. I do not. I do not see how any of this"—she waved her hand at the mess of glossy magazines on the table—"matters. I have been at the conference this whole week. I attended all of my interviews, even though they were poorly organized. And I did not complain when someone—from a certain organization that hates fat children—let genetically modified rats loose in my presentation room. No. Instead, I took what I had and made the best I could with it. Which is exactly what people in public health have to do. All the time we scramble for the scraps others leave behind and turn them into a full meal. Which you would know if you ever, even for one day, did the kind of work that I do."

Stilled silence filled the room.

Finally, the man cleared his throat. "I think I've heard enough."

Marisol set her jaw. She wasn't getting this grant. That much should have been clear from the moment she stepped into this hotel. But she also wasn't leaving this chair without saying one more thing. "I will make sure everyone knows exactly what the Della Simmons Foundation stands for." She pointed at the magazines. "Everyone."

She flew out of the room, her laptop bag flopping against her back. Tears gathered in the corners of her eyes, but she wouldn't let them fall. Not here. Not now, while anyone from the conference could see she'd been defeated. Anyone like—

Pube One's smile bubbled with artificial sweetness. "I'm so sorry to hear about those rumors. You don't think it could be someone from here spreading them, do you?"

Marisol had no doubt who was spreading the rumors around the conference.

"Anyway, I guess it doesn't matter much now. Can you autograph this for me?" she held out one of the magazines.

Marisol could tell the woman expected her to lose it. To put the final nail in her coffin right there in the hotel lobby in front of fifty sets of curious eyes.

"Sure." Marisol put on a sticky sweet smile of her own. "Do you have a pen?"

Pube One's eyes widened a fraction of an inch, but she produced a pen from her bag and held it out. Marisol snatched it and started scrawling, her words big enough to take up the entire cover of the magazine.

Fuck you. (I wrote it in English because
I know your Portuguese is not good.)

She shoved the magazine back at the woman and stormed across the lobby. She'd stop in at the bar, see whatever it was Clint needed to tell her, and shut herself into her room until Tuesday. She'd use the time between now and then to order room service and think of ways to tell her family what she'd done.

She found Clint at a tiny table in the corner, surrounded by vacationers and business men. All too caught up in their phones and their drinks to notice her approach.

"Clint?" She forced out the single syllable, unsure she could manage more without breaking.

"Hey. She's here. I've got to go." Clint hung up and stuffed his phone into his suit pocket like it was contraband and she was the police. "Wow. That didn't take long. I guess you…" His Adam's apple bobbed as he gulped the words back down.

"What did you want to tell me?"

"Nothing. Never mind. I figured it out."

Marisol could tell there was something more. But she couldn't bring herself to care. Not now. She stuck out her hand. "It was very nice to meet you. Good luck with everything."

"Good luck? What? There are still a few days left of this thing."

"Not for me." Her voice cracked. If she didn't get upstairs soon, there was going to be a five-alarm sobbing emergency right here in the bar.

"What do you mean?"

Marisol shook her head. The words stuck in her throat, and her skin went hot.

"That bad, huh?"

"Worse."

"Come on." Clint wrapped an arm around her shoulders. "We're getting out of here."

"Where?"

He nudged her toward a back exit. "Skydiving."

Maybe she'd misheard him. She *was* sniffling awfully loud. "Did you say—"

"Trust me. It's a patented McIntyre solution for all of life's ills."

DAY ELEVEN

The hours had blurred together as Evan sat in front of his computer. Ten o'clock, then eleven, then midnight. Soon it was ten o'clock again, and the sun beat through his bedroom window. Every so often doubt crept into his sleep-deprived creative haze. Maybe with the benefit of a nap and without the benefit of narcotics he'd see this had been a terrible idea.

But maybe not.

It was that *maybe not* that kept him moving, editing, dubbing.

"Evan?" His dad's voice came through a crack in the door. "You awake?"

He didn't look up from the screen. "Come in."

"I'm going to get Gramps from the hospital. Do you want to— have you slept at all?"

"I will. As soon as I finish this."

"Evan." His dad ambled over and sat on his bed. "You need to rest."

"I will."

"What are you doing?"

How could he explain the last week and a half? Especially to his father who, by all accounts, hated television and Los Angeles and anything except manual labor and booze. "TV stuff. I have to finish this. I'm on a deadline."

"Gramps said you weren't going back to LA?"

"I'm not." Evan took a deep breath. "I just have to do this one more thing. Then I'm done with it okay? You were right. It was a stupid idea. But I have to finish this."

"We'll talk more about this later." His dad shook his head as he slipped out of the room.

Evan barely noticed. As soon as he'd fished the flash drive out of the hospital garbage, it became a compulsion. He'd loaded the footage onto his computer, pulled every picture and video from the *Ahora* website, and started sending the emails.

Julia. James. Andrew. Even Penny.

Marisol's mom, whose email address was listed on the *Ahora* website.

For a full thirty minutes he'd doubted himself, typing and retyping the email to a woman he'd never met. Trying to explain everything that had happened without sounding like a Nigerian prince on the eve of coming into his trust fund. And then, finally, he hit send.

The response came back almost immediately.

> **Evan,**
>
> **My son told me about the show. I'm not sure what to think, but I know my daughter. She wouldn't have agreed to help you if she didn't trust you. So I'm going to trust you too. Here are the things you asked for. You should email my son as well. He's in the States and may be able to help more from there. Technology isn't my strong suit.**
>
> **Melinda**

Attached was a link that took him to a cloud drive. And once he put in the password Melinda had provided, Evan was up to his ears in photos and videos of *Ahora's* work. He'd spent way too long combing through them, watching videos of Marisol grinning at the camera as she hiked through miles and miles of green. Making faces at little kids seconds before she stabbed them with vaccines. Helping an elderly woman onto a makeshift exam table.

The charts and graphs Marisol had him make into fancy posters were there, as well as the organization's annual reports for the last ten years. Evan took it all in, reading until his eyes felt like they'd bleed. Then he grabbed a drink of water and read some more.

As soon as his dad left the room, he caved and took Melinda's advice. He needed more pointed footage. He needed someone who could talk about *Ahora* and its work, someone who could do it directly into the camera and tie everything together.

Marisol would have been the obvious choice, but she wasn't answering her phone. So Evan said a prayer and typed out his email to her brother.

> **Felipe,**
>
> **I'm sure by now you've heard what's going on in Los Angeles. Can you find ten minutes to do an interview with me? Can be done via Skype. I've attached the list of questions. Please let me know ASAP.**
>
> **Evan**

The computer dinged immediately with an automatic reply.

> **I am in Los Angeles and away from my inbox. I will return soon.**

Evan refused to panic. He'd find a way to make it work, even if he had to record himself reading from *Ahora's* annual reports. There had to be a way.

"Here's Johnny!" Gramps rolled into Evan's room without bothering to knock. There was barely enough room for their two wheelchairs in the bedroom, much less for of all the memories that being there, surrounded by all his childhood belongings, brought out.

"Gramps, I'm in the middle of something."

"I heard. Your dad thinks you're having a nervous breakdown."

Evan hit pause on the playback. "I'm not. I swear."

"You sure?" Gramps wheeled a little farther into the room, narrowly avoiding knocking his broken leg against the desk.

Evan slumped in his chair. "No."

"Let's see it then. I'll tell you if you've lost it."

"Gramps, no. It's not done yet."

"I don't care. I'm old. I don't got time to wait for things to be done anymore."

Evan's finger hovered over the play button. "It's a short documentary—"

"Don't tell me what it's about. Let me see it. Show don't tell. Didn't you learn anything out there in California?" He reached out and turned off the lights.

"Okay, but I'm going to go back in and—"

"Stop talking, kid." Gramps clicked the mouse.

Evan's heart took off at seventy miles an hour as light music played from the speakers. The title screen faded in.

LAURIE ABRAMSON PRODUCTIONS PRESENTS AHORA:
COMMUNITY HEALTH FOR NOW AND FOR THE FUTURE.

Evan grabbed a notebook. If he was going to watch, he was going to make note of every flaw he could find. It needed to be perfect. Marisol deserved for it to be perfect.

Twenty minutes later, Gramps finally stirred. He sat back in his wheelchair and flipped the light back on.

"It's a rough cut. But I've got some notes on how to fix it." Evan waved the notebook.

"So that's the girl, huh? The real girl, not the one on TV who makes you act like an idiot."

Evan shook his head. "Same girl. And I act like an idiot all on my own."

"So why are you doing this here instead of there? And don't give me any of that bologna about breaking your leg. They'll let you on a plane with a cast. Especially with a sissy cast like that one."

"There's an entry fee for the documentary contest, assuming they'll let me put in a late entry."

"And?"

"And once I pay that, I'm broke. So it's contest entry or plane tickets, not both."

"Laurie Abramson Productions, huh? She'd be proud of ya, kid."

Evan kept his eyes on the computer screen, feeling too much to look his grandfather in the eye. But he knew Gramps was right. His mother would definitely be proud. "Thanks."

Gramps wheeled himself into the hall, slapping Evan's desk on his way out. "Call me when you get there, yeah? And I still want those head shooter things."

"Head shooter things?" Evan called after him. Maybe the head injury was worse than they thought. "Gramps, I told you…" A check poked out from the edge of his keyboard.

Pay to the Order of Evan Abramson.
Memo: Laurie Abramson Productions & Head Shooters

"You crazy old bat," Evan whispered.

Gramps's voice echoed through the hall. "I want one of them producer credits."

. . .

She didn't know how Clint had convinced her to do this. Obviously, she'd been out of her mind. "I can meet you when it is over. I think that is a better idea."

"Nope." He didn't budge from her hotel room doorway.

"I think it is better if I stay here."

"When have I ever steered you wrong? I was right about the skydiving, and I'm right about this. Besides, we discussed this."

And they had. At length.

Somehow, last night—as they stood in line at the weird indoor skydiving cage—he'd convinced her to attend the afternoon awards ceremony. He'd started by dangling hope in front of her. "You never know," he'd said. "People loved your presentation."

When she reminded him about the final interview, he'd moved on to a different tactic.

"We both know the Pubes are going to win, so let's go in there and drink our body weight in expensive wine. Then waltz out of there like we don't need their money."

"But I do need their money."

Around them, kids stared at the wind tunnel contraption, pointing at the people flying around inside. People whose faces were so contorted by the rush of air that they looked like hound dogs with jowls flying in the breeze.

"Fine," Clint said. "We'll waltz out of there like I've been disqualified from their money and like you don't want it. And on our way out, we'll swipe one of those bottles of wine and take it with us on one of those celebrity home tours."

Marisol couldn't stand the thought of showing up at some poor celebrity's house like a glorified peeping Tom. Not after everything. "How about a movie?" she asked.

"Done."

Then she'd donned the jumpsuit and stepped into the cage. And exactly as Clint had promised, the rush of the wind tunnel and the weightlessness of flying—even just ten feet above the ground—had been enough to make her forget everything. At least for a precious few minutes.

But now, with only ten minutes before the start of the awards ceremony, not even the allure of sitting in a darkened theater with sat a bottle of wine and a box of snacks seemed like a good enough reason spend an hour or two in a banquet hall eating limp salad and feeling like the world was caving in. Still, she'd promised Clint. So she tucked in her shirt, threw on a cardigan, and followed him down to the banquet hall.

"Marisol! I was hoping you'd be here." A woman she recognized from yesterday's presentation pulled up a chair. "I'm Claudia Shelby."

"Yes, I remember. Nice to see you." She hoped her smile looked more welcoming than it felt.

"I'd love to pick your brain about a few things, but I didn't catch your email."

Marisol pulled a business card from her pocket. "Email me anytime."

"Great. I'm with Safe Children First—I don't know if I mentioned that. I'd love to talk about ways we can work together."

Marisol's lungs stuttered. Safe Children First? She'd seen their name on all the conference sponsorship forms. And once upon a time, her mother had put them on a list of "dream organizations" she'd hoped to work with. "Yes, I would love to work together. Maybe I can get your email too?"

The woman handed off a business card before she moved on to her table, and Clint gave Marisol a light nudge with his elbow. "See?"

She nodded, letting a spark of excitement flicker.

Only to have it stomped out by the appearance of Puble-Dee and Puble-Dumb. "So good to see you both," one of them said. So fake, so prim, so proper. It made Marisol want to scream.

"You too," she said.

"How do you feel? Bless your heart. You've had a lot going on this week." Pube One put a hand over her heart. "No wonder you look so tired."

Marisol stared at the table setting, focusing all her energy on the vase of sprawling white flowers in the center. A place card protruded from the center of it, announcing this was the table of the Della Simmons Grant Finalists.

No escape.

Clint squeezed her elbow.

She nodded, wishing for once she hadn't murdered her cell phone. At least it would have given her something to stare at while she pretended not to notice the horrible women beside her. Instead, she let her gaze fall around the bustling room. The end of the conference meant everyone talked a little louder, drank an extra glass of wine, let their shirts stay untucked. One man smacked another so hard on the back he spilled red wine all over the tablecloth. They both let out a hearty laugh and refilled their glasses as if nothing had happened. These were the versions of her fellow conference goers she wanted to know. The ones who got messy and laughed about it and moved on. The ones who spent more time looking at one another than monitoring their own behavior for any signs of imperfection.

She turned to Clint. "If I ever run a conference, I will make everyone do something very embarrassing on the first day. Then they will all relax and be themselves."

"Like what?"

"Maybe they will have to take part in a talent show." She smiled as she remembered building that purple gum version of the Statue of Liberty. "Or do an obstacle course."

"I'd start with drinking games. You know all those horrible ones you play in college. Never Have I Ever. Beer pong." Clint rubbed his beard. "Yeah, beer pong. My conference would start with beer pong. It would be epic."

"You'd both be walking liabilities," Pube Two said—in a pageant girl voice that would make Miss Universe jealous. "Good thing you aren't in charge."

Marisol allowed herself two seconds to channel all her disdain into a glare, then forced her voice to match the Pube Two's Miss Congeniality tone. "Good thing."

"Welcome everyone to the closing ceremony of our little conference." Scorpion Lady's voice came through the speakers and cut through the crowd. "Well, the first of our closing activities, I guess. Tomorrow we'll have the final screening of our documentaries followed by the award for best film. Please stop by. All of our films will be shown one final time tomorrow afternoon, so if you didn't get the chance to see them in the evenings this week, make it a point tomorrow. We have some really special stories out there."

Do not roll your eyes. Do not roll your eyes.

Too late.

Across the table, the Pubes tried a little too hard to ignore her. Behind them, a flash of red hair caught Marisol's eye—reminding her of Annie—and a pang of guilt hit. She still hadn't answered her friend's questions. Or her brother's. Her mom had stayed eerily silent on the whole matter. Which meant either she was furious or her Internet access was down again.

Tonight, she promised. After the Pubes officially won the money and she had time to clear her head, she'd sit down and explain everything. It would be easier over email anyway. She wouldn't have to deal with interruptions or questions. No disappointed looks from Felipe.

"Please welcome our first speaker," Scorpion Lady droned on. "Legendary documentary filmmaker Easton Sullivan."

Polite applause lingered as the man lumbered from one end of the room to the other. And as Marisol's gaze followed him, she caught sight of the redhead again. If she didn't know better, she'd almost be fooled into—

"Annie?" She clamped a hand over her mouth, cutting off the rest of her thoughts before the clapping died out.

No, not possible.

The girl gave a little wave and pushed the mass of curls out of her face.

Yes, very possible.

Marisol crept away from her table, heart and mind running wild. Annie—her very best friend—had come all the way across the United States to see her. Something was very wrong.

Especially given the glare of the guy standing beside her.

Felipe.

"Hi." She grabbed them both around the shoulders and ducked into a service hallway. She ignored the sidelong stares from waitstaff as she plastered on a smile. "What are you two doing here?"

A long pause, broken only by the clattering of dishes, sunk into the space between them.

Finally, Annie spoke up. "We thought you could use a friendly face. Or two." She elbowed Felipe in the side.

"*Sí.*"

One friendly face. One unreadable. Her brother always kept his emotions on lockdown, but usually Marisol could parse them out. He'd give something away in his posture or in the slightest change in his tone. But not this time. He'd become a brick wall.

Or a ticking bomb.

"I need to go back in there. They will notice if I am gone." The world had officially spun off its axis. She was choosing time with the Pubes over her family. "I will find you after the ceremony, yes?"

Felipe stayed mum.

Annie wrapped her in a hug. "Good luck."

Marisol knew she should warn them. Let them down now, before they got their hopes up about *Ahora* winning the grant. Dull the sting of her failure. "Thank you," she said before sneaking back to her table.

"You found them." Clint's eyes glinted.

Marisol's brain threatened a complete revolt as she slid into her seat. "You knew they were coming?" she whispered.

He shrugged.

"And now, our biggest award of the afternoon. The Della Simmons Community Improvement Grant. I'm sure you've had the pleasure of meeting some of our finalists this week, during their presentations and then later at the hotel bar."

Light laughter filled the room as the waitstaff cleared salad plates and brought out the main course. At least she could eat her feelings once the Pubes walked up there for their stupid acceptance speech.

The filmmaker's voice carried over the speakers. "Each of these people—and the organizations they represent—enrich people's lives in more ways than most of us could ever imagine. From building wheelchair ramps in Appalachia to teaching fitness to Brazil's most vulnerable children to bringing medical care to the most remote parts of Nicaragua, each of these people deserves a round of applause."

Marisol clapped along with everyone else, but the platitudes were only that: hollow nods to the work she'd done. The work her mother had done. The work Felipe had done.

Their mother must have called him—begged him to fly out to California and rescue *Ahora* from Marisol's mess. She wanted to feel indignant, to be monstrously offended that her mother had suddenly done an about-face on this whole "I believe in you" nonsense. Except she needed to be rescued.

The first day in Los Angeles she'd pulled a thread that led to one snag after another after another. And now she sat here, in this stuffy room, trying to smile as she waited for the affirmation she'd secretly known was coming all along: she couldn't do this.

She wasn't professional enough. Polished enough. Well-versed in spreadsheets enough.

She wasn't enough.

"You okay?" Clint whispered.

"How did you know my brother was here?"

His eyes shifted to the filmmaker onstage—and his laborious speech. "Your brother is here?"

"Clint."

He took a long swig of water. "What?"

"May I have the envelope please?" Onstage, the man waved a pale blue envelope around while the more tipsy of the conference bunch drummed on their tables. "Oh. I already had it right here." He laughed at his own joke. Way too hard.

From the corner of her eye, Marisol caught Felipe and Annie shuffling along the back wall. She sent out one last prayer—more of a grovel really. Maybe someone had seen the light after watching the Pube's horrible movie. Maybe someone had been so moved by Marisol's presentation they'd overcome the rabid hatred the last interviewer seemed to hold. Maybe, just this once, something about this damn trip would go as scripted.

"And the winner of the Della Simmons grant, worth twenty thousand dollars, is…"

More fake drumrolls. More pleading with the universe.

"Appalachia Together!"

Applause erupted, and beside her Clint froze.

"You won," she whispered.

"Whaaaa…"

"Are you having a stroke? You won. Go." She clapped along with everyone else, feeling as dumbfounded as Clint looked. But lighter and less rage-filled than she had only a few moments ago.

"They said we were disqualified," he said.

"You need to go up there." She elbowed him. Her heart pounded as the applause faded, but, bit by bit, a smile crept across her face.

Clint jerked out an arm, bracing himself on the table to stand. "I can't believe it. They said we were disqualified."

"You were supposed to be disqualified." Pube One glared at Pube Two.

"Go," Marisol said. "Before they take away your money and give it to the Pubes."

The applause was on its last breaths now, and people were starting to look at them sideways.

"What did you call us?" Pube One asked.

Marisol ignored her. "Go." She elbowed Clint again.

"Okay. Okay." He shook himself off—returning to the shiny, composed, supermodel version of himself—and took a single step.

Plates clattered. A pitcher of water landed on its side. A basket of bread tumbled onto the floor.

Marisol pushed her chair back, missing most of the tidal wave streaming from the overturned pitcher. Clint wasn't so lucky. The water spread over his pants in the worst possible way.

The room fell silent.

"I tucked the table cloth into my pants," he whispered. "I do that when I get nervous."

"Just. Go." Marisol held her hands to her mouth, keeping in whatever else might come out. At this point her emotions were riding on overload, and she had no clue what might escape. An earthquake-inducing sob? A giant hee-haw?

Clint grabbed his suit jacket from the back of his chair and tied it around his waist like a weird kilt. The applause started again, and Marisol joined in. Clint deserved this, probably more than any of them.

She gave him a tiny nod as he started his acceptance speech and slipped out. If anyone asked, she could say she needed to wring out her skirt in the bathroom. Which was true. Also true: a serious need to lock herself in a stall and hang her head in shame. Maybe after a few minutes, she'd splash some cool water on her face and come away refreshed and ready to face her brother.

She put her hand on the knob as she double-checked it was the women's restroom.

"Mari, wait." Annie's voice echoed through the empty hallway.

Felipe's followed, lower and in Spanish, but otherwise carrying the same weight of worry as Annie's tone. "Where are you going?"

She stared straight ahead and pushed open the door. "Be right back."

Two seconds. That's how much peace and quiet she managed to steal in her stall before the bathroom door swung open again.

"Mari?"

Maybe she could pick up her feet and pretend she wasn't there. Or climb through the tiny window near the ceiling. Or through the ceiling vents like in all those movies. "*Sí.*"

"You okay?" Annie asked.

"Only need to wring out my skirt. Someone spilled water."

"Yeah, I saw." Annie's red curls appeared under the stall, followed by her face.

"What are you doing?"

"Seeing if you're okay."

"I think you are seeing more than that, no?"

"You're standing against the wall, fully clothed, with a wad of toilet paper in your hand."

Marisol sighed and unlocked the door. "Your head is going to fall off if you stay like that."

And then Annie had her wrapped in a bear hug. "I missed you so much!"

"Can. Not. Breathe."

"Sorry, sorry." Annie released her death grip. "I'm sorry about the grant. They were stupid not to pick you."

"No, they weren't." Marisol wiped her eyes with the wad of tissue. "Is Felipe still out there?"

"Probably."

"And he knows everything?" Her voice cracked.

"Well, you know Felipe. He always thinks he knows everything.

But I think we're both a little lost on what's going on here. He got this phone call—"

"Of course." She'd been right. Her mom had finally caved and called him to swoop in and fix everything. Too bad she'd been a little too late.

"Come on," Marisol said. "I want to get this over with." She grabbed Annie's hand and tugged her toward the door.

"Wait." Annie planted her feet. "Real girl talk before we go out there. This Evan guy? This is the real thing isn't it?"

"Evan?" Why was Annie asking about this now, with everything going on outside the bathroom door?

"Yeah. Not just for TV, right?"

Marisol bit the inside of her cheek. For a while, it had felt more like the "real thing" than anything she'd experienced. At home, all of her flings had a two-week shelf life. Maybe a week or two more if they were stuck together on a brigade. But even then, she'd usually be bored and itching for the guy to get the hell out of Nicaragua by the second week. *That must be it. We never made it to two weeks.*

"It was only for television," Marisol said.

Annie crossed her arms and leaned against the sink. "Are you sure?"

"Yes."

"Well, you might need to tell him that." Annie pulled open the bathroom door. "Because his emails were *definitely* not only for television."

"Emails?" Marisol's feet stuttered, and she stopped in the doorway. There, ten feet down the hallway, Felipe stood with his arms across his chest looking mildly amused as he spoke with a guy standing on crutches.

A guy with stray blond curls and a certain perpetually rumpled look.

Evan.

• • •

Everything hurt. His head—a side effect of too little sleep and too much crazy. His armpits—a side effect of using the ancient crutches he'd found in the attic. His broken ankle—a side effect of, well, no side effects. He'd opted for a hefty dose of over-the-counter stuff so he could be coherent enough for what he was about to do. But Evan was starting to wish he wasn't so coherent.

"You'd just have to narrate a few things. Tell a couple of stories about what's being shown on the screen."

Felipe's forehead wrinkled. "Where did you get this video?"

"I made it. Well, I parsed it together from a bunch of places. Some footage from the show, the stuff your mom sent me, a couple of things from Marisol."

"So Marisol knows?"

"No." Evan felt like he was being interrogated. Like maybe he should ask to have a lawyer present or to at least have his rights read. He shifted on the crutches. "Not yet. I wanted it to be a surprise."

Felipe shook his head. "I think it is best if she knows."

"Evan?"

His chest tightened. He'd know that voice anywhere. Especially after listening to it on repeat for hours on end. Suddenly he was hyperaware of the fact that he probably looked—and smelled— like a hobo.

"Hey," he said. "I was looking—"

"What happened to your leg?" Marisol kept a safe distance. Way too safe.

"My grandpa decided to play dead."

She cocked an eyebrow, but beneath that sheath of skepticism he saw her lips twitch up at the corners. "Your grandpa?"

"It's a long story."

Her expression went slack again. "Why are you here? I am not going back on the show."

The show. The gauntlet was about to come down, and he wouldn't be there with them. Wouldn't be there to sit on the stained couch and participate in the world's worst countdown. Wouldn't be there to see if busting his ass over the last week and a half had made any difference. He tried to tell himself it didn't matter. That the news would find its way to him one way or another—probably multiple ways. But still it stung.

"I wanted to talk to you, but you weren't answering your phone."

"I threw it away."

"Because you don't want to talk to me?"

Annie and Felipe were suddenly fascinated by a painting of the Los Angeles skyline. Marisol stared at her feet, then ducked back into the bathroom.

Evan blew out a breath. He'd prepared himself for this moment, or at least he'd tried. Somehow it was more painful than he'd imagined. And he'd imagined it to be somewhere between stigmata and spontaneous combustion.

It was all the confirmation he needed. He'd have to make the video without Felipe's help. He'd just cross his fingers that two years of high school Spanish had given him enough to stumble through the information.

"These are for Marisol." He handed Felipe a pair of tickets. "It's a special taping, so she can take whoever she wants. When they do the contestant interviews make sure she says the words 'giant banana hammock.'" He rolled his eyes. "Sorry, I didn't pick the password."

Evan started to hobble away, hoping to hear Marisol call out for him to wait. But the sound of his crutches rubbing against the hotel carpet was the only thing that followed.

One more errand and he could get out of here.

He pushed his way through the crowd until he found the person he was looking for: Easton Sullivan. The man was a small potatoes documentary producer who thought he was big potatoes. According to the conference website, he was also the film festival's biggest sponsor.

"Mr. Sullivan?" Evan balanced perilously on his crutches and stuck out a hand. "I'm a big fan. Your piece on the hazards of jump rope was very thought-provoking."

The man straightened his jacket. "Ah yes. *Amusement or Assassin: Jump Rope in Jeopardy.* One of my favorites as well."

Not only did he have an inflated sense of the size of his potatoes, but Easton Sullivan loved alliteration.

"If you have a minute, I wanted to ask you about the documentary festival tomorrow."

"Are you with the press?" Easton ran a hand through his—mostly nonexistent—hair. "Variety? ScreenDaily? Filmmaker?"

"Uh, no." He was standing there on crutches in a crusty T-shirt. In what world did he look like a journalist? "I wanted to see about putting in a late entry."

Easton's shoulders sagged. "I'm sorry, son. No can do. The last deadline passed two days ago. If you'll excuse me—"

"Please. I know you have room in the schedule. I looked online. It's..." He remembered how silent Marisol had fallen when he asked about her phone. "It's important."

"Lots of things are important. Death and taxes and all that. Doesn't mean I can break the rules."

Evan refused to let himself correct the death and taxes line. "I'm only asking you to bend them. Please. I'll pay the late entry fee. It's not a problem."

"We've already printed the schedules. Again, I'm very sorry." The man started to shuffle away.

Time to bring out the big guns.

He cleared his throat and tried to sound more like a member of the mafia and less like a mid-pubescent Peter Brady. "I'm sure your mother is going to be very disappointed."

"Excuse me?"

"Your mother." Evan pulled out his phone, and a few swipes later the woman's face appeared onscreen. Right beside James January and her twin granddaughters. "Betty. She's really something. I'd hate to tell her she can't be on the show anymore." The thought of not having Betty clomping along the stage of *So Late* hurt Evan's heart. But Easton Sullivan didn't need to know that.

Evan had made the connection his first week at the show, when Betty showed up with a complete photo album and list of her son's accomplishments—in case she needed to "throw some weight around" to get a seat. Little did she know she'd have her pick of seats. Every day.

"How did you get that picture of her?"

"I'm the one who gets her out of the audience every afternoon and helps her to the stage—with the assistance of your daughters, of course."

"Old bat. All she does is complain about James January—rightfully so; that whole studio is a shit show. But she won't stop going." Eston leaned in closer to look at the photo, his nostrils flaring.

Either it's working or he's going to tear my arms off and beat me with them.

Evan shrugged and adjusted his crutches as if he were about to walk away. *Please don't make me walk away.* "To be fair, all she does is complain about you too. But I think that's just her way of showing love. Anyway, too bad she won't be able to be on the show anymore."

"I thought the show was getting cancelled."

"Maybe. Maybe not. You know how the executives are. One minute they love you—"

"The next they're ready to serve you your balls on a silver platter."

"Exactly. Well, nice to meet you."

Easton Sullivan's balding head turned a shade of red never before seen with the human eye. "Fine."

"Fine?"

"Fine. Our entries are sparse anyway. You can have the two o'clock spot." He jotted a note on the notepad in front of him. "But you have to pay the late entry fee."

"Absolutely."

"And you'll let my mother keep going on that stupid show."

"For as long as it's on the air, Betty will have a place in the audience."

"Where is it?" Easton stuck out a chubby paw.

Evan glanced over his shoulder. "Where is what?"

"Your movie. The thing you just blackmailed me over."

"Oh, right. It's not done yet. I'll have it to you tomorrow morning, I promise. First thing."

The man rolled his eyes. "I'm going to regret this, aren't I?"

Maybe. Probably. "Absolutely not."

Evan made plans to drop off the video at ten the next morning and hobbled toward the door. The rolling tides of adrenaline that had plagued him all day—brought about by hope and fear and hope again—had officially subsided. At that moment, he would have promised Betty her own late-night talk show if it meant he'd have an extra day to work on this film. And a pain medication-fueled nap.

Instead, he grabbed a cup of coffee on his way out the door. Maybe with a little more caffeine he could at least make it to the studio to grab the footage he'd asked for. Assuming Julia hadn't burned the entire place to the ground in a fit of cancellation rage.

"Evan?" Felipe still held the *Who's Got the Coconut* tickets in his hand.

He blew out a long breath. Not only had Marisol made it clear she didn't want to talk to him, but she'd spurned the tickets. How had he messed this up so bad?

"What's up?"

"These are real?" Felipe waved the tickets.

"Yeah. It was part of the deal. She did the show, she got the tickets."

"But she quit the show, yes?"

Evan nodded. "Doesn't matter. I've never seen anyone who loved that show so much." His mom had loved that stupid show that much.

"Okay. I will do it."

"Do it?"

"Help with the movie."

Evan nearly choked on his coffee. "Seriously? Great. I need to go to the studio. Can you come to the studio? Are you free right now or…" The wave of adrenaline came crashing back.

Felipe glanced over his shoulder where Annie and Marisol huddled together, obviously pretending not to look at them. "Give us five minutes."

• • •

Marisol braced herself against the doorframe, trying to keep herself upright while simultaneously not looking out the window. Because every time the car jerked, she ended up closer to Evan, but looking out the window meant facing the terror of Annie's driving.

"Are you sure you have a license?" Evan asked from the backseat.

"It's fine. I'm a little rusty, that's all." Annie yanked the car into the next lane. "Plus, LA is notorious for horrible traffic."

"Maybe I should drive then?" he asked.

"You have a broken leg, and you have not slept for days." Marisol focused all her attention on the headrest in front of her. She still wasn't sure how she'd ended up like this—crammed in the backseat of Evan's car with her best friend at the wheel and her brother in the front, looking like he was about to vomit. But her life seemed to get stranger by the minute, and all she could do was hold on for the ride.

Literally.

The weirdest part of all was Felipe's insistence on going to the set of *So Late It's Early*. There had been no talking him out of it when he'd come back from whatever chat he'd had with Evan. Instead, he'd tucked a few pieces of stray paper into his back pocket and slipped his hand into Annie's before whispering something in her ear.

"Come on," he'd said to Marisol. "Evan is going to take us to the studio."

"Why?" Every time she set foot on the set, something went wrong. If she'd learned anything, it was that the universe was screaming at her to pack up her bags and go home.

Apparently, her brother preferred to taunt it.

"We are going to have to explain all of this mess to *Ahora's* donors. And probably a few of our NGOs. Since you do not want to tell me anything, I guess I will have to go there and find out for myself."

"What do you want to know?" she'd asked. She wasn't sure how much he already knew—obviously a lot—but she'd spill it all if it meant she didn't have to go back there.

"Too late." He turned and pulled Annie along with him. "*Vamos.*"

Now her brother didn't trust her, but it didn't matter because his girlfriend was going to kill them all in a fiery crash.

"Marisol?" Evan asked, his voice hushed.

"You have insurance, yes?" She wouldn't look at him. Just the thought of looking at him made her resolve slip a little.

"I heard that!" Annie met her eyes in the rearview mirror. "It's fine, I swear."

"Marisol?" It was almost a whisper this time.

His eyes were bloodshot and tired, like they had been after their marathon day of writing and filming. His shirt had taken a dive from rumpled to full-on wrinkled, and his scruff situation was about to become a beard situation.

Damn it. She'd looked. "What?"

"Have you seen the paint and crank segment?"

"I have not seen any of them." And she didn't want to. Ever.

A phone appeared in her field of vision, accompanied by a set of headphones. "Just hit play."

Her stupid, traitorous finger pressed the little triangle before her brain could protest. And then she was lost in it. Everything on-screen looked exactly like she'd imagined it would that day— but better. With some distance, it was more ridiculous. More funny. More everything.

Something she hadn't imagined was there too. In spades—super obvious, megaphone-style spades. The way Evan looked at her—not the fake, lovesick look either. And the way she looked at him.

She hit the replay button, and on the second viewing she saw what every member of the public had fixated on. The camera had caught every single glance between them. Those unspoken conversations about what was happening onstage and a few stolen looks that suggested what was happening offstage.

"We're here." Annie pulled the headphones from her ears. "You okay?"

Marisol nodded. She'd been so lost in the video that she hadn't stopped to worry about the terror of Annie's driving. Or noticed they'd arrived at the studio. She handed the phone back to Evan. "Very funny."

He glanced at the screen. "We have about ten minutes before the show starts. Can someone get my crutches out of the trunk?"

Together, the four of them hobbled inside. Marisol expected at least a dash of resistance. After all, the show was about to start and the intern was dragging three—well, two—strangers in behind him. But the security guards and staff only nodded as they walked into the studio. It buzzed with preshow excitement, and almost every seat in the house was filled.

"You guys can sit there." Evan used a crutch to point to two empty seats at the edge of the front row. "Uh, Felipe, I better take you backstage. For that thing…"

"No one is going to be able to answer your questions right now, 'Lipe." Marisol tried to keep her voice to a whisper. Already they'd attracted the attention of every audience member in a ten-foot radius. The last thing she wanted was for Felipe to make it worse.

Evan cleared his throat. "Well, there are only two seats, so I'll take him back and see who we can find."

The two of them disappeared into a side door before Marisol could protest further.

"Down in the front!"

Marisol turned.

Ted the Man Baby.

She never thought she'd be grateful to see an adult man wearing a diaper and nothing else. She marched up the aisle and to his seat. "Where is your flask?"

"Right here, baby." He pulled it out from his diaper and wiggled it between two chubby fingers.

She snatched the flask from his hand and unscrewed the cap. "What is this?" She almost didn't care. If it could numb all of these feelings—or some of these feelings—until she could get out of this place, she'd drink it all.

"You don't wanna do that, sweet cheeks."

"I think I can handle it." She lifted the flask to her lips, closed her eyes, and prayed Ted wasn't addicted to something horrible, like baby food-flavored vodka. Or nail polish remover.

He wasn't.

And what was in the flask wasn't going to numb anything anytime soon.

"Iced tea?" She wiped her lips and shoved the flask toward him.

His eyes widened and his eyebrows went so high they nearly touched the bonnet he wore. "Shhh. I've got a reputation to uphold. I'm sure you know what that's like."

Marisol slipped back to her seat.

Where Penny waited.

"Julia wants to talk to you," she said. "Now." Penny's face filled with desperation—a look so removed from her usual unmasked contempt that Marisol couldn't protest.

She left Annie behind and followed Penny backstage. Everywhere she turned, monitors glowed with James's opening monologue, but there was no one around to watch it. The studio had become a ghost town, haunted by the awkward silence falling between their footsteps

"Did you know it is tea?" Marisol asked when she couldn't take it anymore.

"What are you talking about?" Penny asked.

"The thing with the baby and the flask. Tea."

"Yeah, I know. Everybody knows. Ted's been sober for like eight years now or something."

"Oh." Marisol stopped in the hallway. They'd come to a dead end, and the only option was to turn back or go straight into the doorway ahead of them. "Why are we back here?"

Penny shrugged. "Nobody tells me anything. Well, unless they're telling me to bring them coffee or sweep the stage or escort the guests to the green room. Whatever." She rolled her eyes, again, and twisted the door knob.

"Penny?" Marisol asked.

"What?"

She tried to find the words. This wasn't how she'd planned to confront Penny, but now that she'd started she wasn't sure she could stop. "Why did you post all those photos? Why did you make it look like the sketches were about me and Evan?"

"Because they were about you and Evan?"

"No. They were about fake people."

Penny shook her head. "Not really. I mean, the sketches were always about the fake people, but the social media stuff—the stuff people really latched on to—that was about you and Evan."

"Well, the real me did not appreciate the rumors. Sex tapes? Pornography? A green card marriage?"

Penny held up her hands. "I didn't have anything to do with that. I posted the pictures, and everything took off."

"Nothing to do with it?"

"Okay, maybe once the paparazzi got interested, I tipped them off about you guys filming a sketch in the parking lot. I'm sorry. But I didn't spread any of the rumors, I swear. It's just, I worked so hard to get an internship—any internship—and then when I finally did, everything started to fall apart."

Marisol sighed. She knew what it was like to hold something together that kept threatening to crumble in her hands. "Okay. Thank you for telling me."

Penny pushed open the door, revealing Julia on the green room couch.

Mascara smears stained both her cheeks, and she sniffed between orders into her headset. "Cut to commercial." *Sniff.* "I'm working on it." *Sniff.*

Marisol froze. This was more frightening than anything else she'd considered. Where was the fire-breathing dragon? Where was the one person who would set James back in line when he got too… James-like?

"Julia?"

"Oh, God. Good. There you are."

Marisol's fear level skyrocketed to standing-on-the-edge-of-a-cliff levels. "Are you okay?"

"No. Well, I wasn't. Then I saw you sitting in the audience, and I figured it out."

Marisol glanced over her shoulder at Penny, who shrugged.

"Figured what out?"

"Who to put on as our celebrity guest."

And now Marisol was plummeting from the cliff to the jagged rocks below. "No."

"Please. Let us do one last Marivan segment. Everything's a mess. Tonight's our last show and we don't have any guests. If I don't figure something out, James is going to murder stray kittens or something onstage."

"Kittens?"

"Well, it's either that or try his new standup routine. I think the kittens would be less painful, personally."

Marisol dragged in a deep breath and tried to let all of this information sink in. "The show got cancelled?"

She nodded.

"Does Evan know?"

"I don't think so. He had to go home. His grandpa got sick. He emailed about your documentary thing this morning, but I didn't have the heart to tell him." *Sniff.* "God, do you know how hard it is for a woman to get even a writing job in late-night? Much less a head writer job? Then producer? And I blew it. I blew it so fucking hard."

"Evan is here," Penny said. "And I don't think we're supposed to mention *that thing.*"

Julia ran her hands through her hair, making it stand straight up. "Oh shit, right. Never mind. Ignore me. I don't know what I'm talking about. Except I really need you to go on the show. I don't want to be known as the producer that let James tell jokes for an entire hour."

"What is the documentary thing?" Marisol asked.

Julia barked a few more orders into her headset and turned

back to Marisol. "The documentary thing is nothing. Can you please go on the show? Please?"

No way. Absolutely not. No more television shows. No more seeing her private moments splayed all over magazines. "Tell me what the documentary thing is."

"Marisol—"

"Do you want me to go on your show or no?"

"Evan is making a documentary. About you."

"About *Ahora*," Penny said. "For some film contest or something. Said you could win a lot of money to help people. Or whatever," she added. "I think that's what he's doing right now, actually. He brought in this guy to translate a bunch of stuff to English or something."

Felipe.

"He's way hot. If you're not going to make up with Evan, you should check that guy out." Penny raised her eyebrows.

"He is my brother."

"Oops."

Marisol turned to Julia, praying it was too late to go onstage. Because she wanted to march to whatever part of the studio Evan and Felipe were in and demand some real answers. Demand blood. Maybe she'd be the one killing kittens instead of James by the time this was all over.

"Okay. She's a go," Julia said into the headset as she wiped the mascara from her cheeks. "But I've got another idea. Stall a few minutes. Do not, I repeat, *do not* let James tell the joke about the size of the President's penis again. Marisol, just wait here. We'll send someone back to slap some lipstick on you."

And then she was gone, dragon lady persona firmly back in place.

"He is really making a documentary? How?" Marisol asked.

Penny fidgeted with her phone. Then her headset. Her phone again. "I should go."

"Penny, please."

"Fine." She slunk down onto the couch. "Not like they can

fire me now, can they?" She swiped her fingers across the phone. "So after James and Julia made him proclaim his love for you on national television—"

"What?"

"The show with the phone booth thing?"

"My hotel plays a show about cousins, not this one."

"Oh. Right. Okay, well James and Julia told him to say he loved you on the show. They thought it would increase the buzz or whatever. Evan got really pissed about it, but he did it anyway. He said he would only do it if James made sure you got to be a contestant on *Who's Got the Coconut*, but..."

"But what?"

"I think he does love you. It's like one of those things, where you just know. Maybe you don't actually love them yet, but you know you're going to."

She didn't.

Or maybe she did, now that Penny had said it aloud.

• • •

The editing room had been off-limits his entire time at the show. The sign on the door read NO INTERNS ALLOWED, and at orientation someone had threatened to chop off the fingers of anyone who touched the editing equipment. But today he'd dragged a perfect stranger into the room, expecting a battle.

Didn't matter. At this point, he had nothing to lose.

"Hey," Evan poked in his head. "James said—"

"Yeah, okay." The guy in front of the monitor barely looked up. "Just stay in the back and stay out of my hair. Don't make a bunch of noise."

"That was easy." *Too easy.* He hadn't even had to tell the guy that James had given him permission—which was technically true. His email did say he'd help in "any way he could." But there wasn't time to worry about it. They had an hour. Maybe an hour and a half, depending on how things were going onstage. "Come on."

A half dozen or so clicks later, he jammed the flash drive into a computer and pulled up his creation. On the wall, a row of monitors played the show taping less than a hundred feet away. Evan muted them and pointed back to the computer screen. "This is just a rough cut. It needs some smoothing out, but you'll be able to get the basic idea. And once I have your parts, it will be a lot smoother."

They listened through the headphones as the music played and the images came up on the screen. *Ahora* headquarters. Their clinic in Managua. A group of people going out on a brigade. A video of a little girl. Charts. Graphs. Another video of children playing outside, with Marisol at the center of their game.

By now, Evan had spent so much time on the movie, he could see the entire twenty-five minutes on the backs of his eyelids—not that he'd actually seen the backs of his eyelids recently.

When it was over, Felipe pulled off his headphones but stayed silent.

"The first thing I think we should do is subtitle those videos in English," Evan said.

More silence.

Evan swallowed hard. Why wasn't Felipe saying anything? "I know it doesn't fit the typical documentary style—it's more like an infomercial for *Ahora*, I guess. But it still tells a story."

Felipe nodded. "It does. Very well."

Evan exhaled. "So the subtitles…"

A few minutes in, they were lost in the process of subtitling and recording Felipe's voiceovers. So much so that Evan didn't hear the door open twenty minutes later.

"The rumors are true." Julia crossed her arms. "You *are* here."

"I, uh, just got back." He hobbled upright. "Broke my leg and everything. See?" He'd walked into the editing room ready to punch his way to the equipment if need be. But now that Julia was here, it was like his balls had crawled up inside of him and resolved to die a quick, painful death. "We were—"

"Using the equipment without authorization? In a room where

you aren't allowed? With a member of the public? Does that about sum it up?"

"Yeah, but—"

"Are you done with that?" She nodded toward his computer screen.

"Almost."

"Then hit save and hand it over."

"What? Come on Julia. You know how important this is. Give me ten more minutes, then I'll get out of here. Please."

"Three. Final offer."

"I need at least five."

"If you want to waste your three minutes trying to negotiate—"

"Okay, fine." He flipped around and scrambled to put on the finishing touches. It wasn't perfect. Far from it. Even amateur critics would see the flaws from a dozen miles away. But it was something where before there had been nothing. And it had heart.

"There." He uploaded a backup to his email, just in case, and ejected the flash drive. "We're done."

Julia held out her hand.

"Come on, Julia. You know how important this is."

She didn't budge.

"You're basically stealing vaccines from babies right now, you know that right?"

"Evan, if you don't give that flash drive to me right now, I swear I will make you regret it."

Absolutely not. No way. No how. At this point he'd cram it between his ass cheeks if he had to—or maybe that was the zero-sleep, throbbing-ankle, too-much-stress talking.

"Is that Marisol?" Felipe pointed at one of the televisions on the far wall.

It was. She sat primly on the edge of the armchair, looking as beautiful as ever. No one at home would know she'd had anything but the most pleasant of days.

"Got it." Julia plucked the drive from his half limp hand and

strutted toward the door. "He goes back to the audience. You"—
she pointed at Evan—"come with me."

If there had been no arguing with her before, there definitely
wasn't now. Not when she had the video in her pocket. She gave
Felipe instructions on how to find his way out, and then Evan
followed her, his crutches clacking behind in the empty halls.

Too empty.

The notice.

It must have come before the taping. And the news couldn't
have been good, not if the halls were this barren. No wonder Julia
was acting like some bear-porcupine hybrid. Because they'd failed.

He'd failed.

"Julia—"

"Shhh. Can't you keep those things quiet?"

"Sorry, next time I'll try to break a less noisy bone."

"Stay here for a minute, okay?" she whispered. "Don't talk to
anyone. Or touch anything. Or break any more bones. Okay? Just
stand here until I get back."

"Where are you going with the video?"

"Just. Stay. Here." Her expression softened at the edges.
"Please, Evan."

"Fine."

She left him in the shadows of the studio seats, tucked far
enough away that no one—not the audience, not James or Marisol—
could see him. But he could see them both perfectly.

"Well, now. That's quite a story," James said. "Is this one of
those schemes where you get people to go to parties and con them
into buying sex toys from you?"

The audience laughed.

Marisol did too. "You can do that?"

"In America, anything is possible. If you want to be a sex toys
salesperson anyway."

"No one at *Ahora* is selling sex toys. I promise."

"Well, I hear we have some video proof to the contrary." James
winked, then stage-whispered, "Don't worry it's not really sex toys."

He raised his voice again. "Or is it? Let's take a look." Every head in the studio—including Evan's—focused on the giant, double-sided television hanging overhead.

A few familiar notes played over the sound system.

His video.

His unfinished, imperfect video was being played on national television. And he hadn't had a chance to explain it to Marisol. He'd wanted it to be a surprise, but maybe not *this big* of a surprise.

Someone had started it in the middle, cherry-picking a few precious minutes where Marisol weighed an infant, then took its temperature. But Evan didn't watch it. He watched Marisol watch the film. Took in every tilt of her chin. Every furrowed brow. Every tiny smile. And when the lights came up and the screen went black, he knew that even if everyone else in the world hated it, the one person who mattered didn't.

"Well, I don't know about you," James said. "But I'd buy vibrators from those people any day of the week."

The audience laughed, and the sound filled all the space around Evan's tiny nook.

This. When he was back home in Illinois, working at whatever buzzkill job he'd get, this is how he'd remember *So Late It's Early.* This cocoon of weirdness and laughter no one could escape, no matter how hard they tried.

"And this video is going to have its world premiere at a big film festival tomorrow, is that right?" James asked.

"I am not sure," Marisol said. "This is the first time I have seen it." She put on a stage whisper of her own. "I was worried it would be about vibrators."

The cocoon grew thicker.

"Well, let's find someone who can give us some answers then. Where is he?" James shaded his eyes from the spotlights.

In the back, someone began chanting—someone who sounded suspiciously like Ted the Man Baby. "Mar-i-van. Mar-i-van." Before long, it sounded like most of the audience had joined him.

Julia appeared at his side. "Are you going to go or do you need me to carry you out there?"

He went.

Because Marisol was there, and—even if only for a few minutes—he'd be there too.

After a crutch-assisted journey entirely too long for late-night television, he made it to the stage. Behind him, the fake Los Angeles skyline glowed, and hundreds of crumbled papers still covered James's desk—papers the interns had to clean up every night and replace every morning. How had he grown to actually like this weird little show? If they'd only had more time. A few more weeks to work out the kinks and bumps. To get James to quit cussing all the time.

"Well, are you going to sit your ass down or not? You want me to bring Betty out here so you can borrow her walker?" James asked.

"No, that's okay." Why couldn't he be as collected as Marisol in front of the camera? "I'll just..." He tried to find a way to lean his crutches on the couch, not hit anyone, and not fall on his face.

Marisol stood. "Here."

With a long look, he tried to telegraph all the things he wanted to say—those things he wouldn't be able to say on television—in her direction. He balanced on his good leg and held out a crutch.

Except she didn't take it.

"Um, can you..." His balance faltered, and for a half second he pictured himself lying face down on the stage, blood gushing from his nose.

But then he steadied.

Because Marisol's arm slipped around his waist.

"Thank you," she murmured, one heartbeat before she pressed her lips to his.

The audience roared behind them.

DAY TWELVE

In the span of two hours, her hotel room went from tropical storm to the after effects of a category five hurricane. Makeup littered the bathroom counter. The smell of hairspray and soap hung thick in the air, and her suitcase lay open on the floor, completely devoid of its contents.

Because they'd been strewn across her bed.

"Are you sure this will be okay?" She looked again at her reflection. The blue dress was dry now, and just as pretty as it had been that night at the dim sum restaurant. But the thought of wearing it downstairs, of mixing a piece of the show with the conference, made her chest tight.

"You look great, Mari. I promise. Just a couple more touches." Annie pinned a piece of Marisol's hair behind her ear, giving her an old-Hollywood style. "Perfect."

"Thank you. For this. For coming."

Annie pulled back and looked her straight in the eye. "Of course. But next time you become a television star, clue me in so I can ride on your coattails, okay?"

A knock sounded at the door.

"Don't move," Annie ordered. "I need to spray you one more time."

Marisol sat perfectly still while her friend answered the door. Inside, her heart pounded at the speed of sound. But for once it wasn't accompanied by earth-shattering nerves or ten metric tons of pressure to succeed. It was simply anticipation.

"Wow." Evan stepped around the entryway. "You look amazing."

"You too." Tuxedo, bow tie, perfectly pruned five o'clock

shadow. It took every bit of her waning willpower not to jump up and pull his face to hers again. There had been no more kissing after that moment on camera, but she'd thought about it. A lot.

"Do. Not. Move," Annie said. "Evan, hobble on back. Mari, cover your eyes."

A cloud of hairspray descended, and when it was safe to open her eyes, Marisol found Annie standing back to admire her work. "You're perfect," she finally said. "Meet you guys in front of the elevators? Twenty minutes? Hopefully your brother is packing our suitcases."

Marisol wrapped her arms around Annie's shoulders one more time. "Thank you again. I wish you could stay longer."

"Me too. Call me after you guys win big, okay?"

Marisol nodded and squeezed her friend a little tighter, trying to absorb everything about this moment.

"If I leave you two alone, you better not mess up that hair," Annie whispered.

"No promises," she whispered back. "Look at him."

"Mari—"

"Okay, okay. I promise."

Then it was just Marisol and Evan. No cameras. No sets. No one stealthily snapping photos while pretending to search for cell service. And suddenly she felt shy and awkward. Like she didn't know what to do with her hands. Like she might have a glob of spinach in her teeth—even though she'd brushed her teeth twice since lunch.

"I brought you something." Evan took a few steps closer, wincing every time the crutches hit the ground. "It's in this bag."

"Here." Marisol slipped her arm under his shoulder and helped him sit on the bed. The movement was instinctual at this point— years of brigades and nursing had seen to that. But the way his closeness made her feel was something brand new.

"It's all the footage from the show. The finished versions and the outtakes. Plus, a few copies of the film. Your mom asked for them." He handed over a bag full of DVDs. "I shared it with her on the cloud, but she said this was better."

"Her Internet does not always work."

"Did you call her?"

Marisol nodded. She'd spent more than an hour on the phone with her mom that morning, explaining everything. The Pubes, Clint, the show, the documentary. Not so surprisingly, her mom had already gleaned most of it from conversations with Evan and Felipe. Surprisingly, she'd seemed okay with it all. Even more surprisingly, she'd said she managed to watch a clip of the show.

"Of course I like it," she'd said. "It has you written all over it."

"How is your back?" Marisol asked.

"Will be okay. How is your heart?"

In pieces. But also whole. "I am worried about the brigades."

Her mom laughed, and for a minute Marisol wondered if her mom had dipped a little too deeply into the pain meds. "Mari, the brigades are going to be fine. Hold on a second." The shuffling of paper filled the line.

"Mom?"

"Hold on." More shuffling. "As of 11:38 this morning, *Ahora* added 214 new donors to our list. And I bet, if I looked at it now, it would be even more."

"*¿Verdad?*"

Her mom began rattling off names and cities and dollar amounts, one after the other. "Ted the Baby. Los Angeles, California. One hundred dollars. I guess we need to find a way to make people use their real names?"

Marisol laughed. "That might be his real name."

"Clint McIntyre. Deer Hollow, West Virginia. Fifty dollars. Donald Abramson. Peoria, Illinois. Five hundred dollars."

"That must be Evan's grandfather. They are very close."

"Here's the best one. Are you sitting down?"

"Yes."

"The *So Late It's Early Show*, Gone but Not Forgotten, USA."

Marisol grinned. Definitely not forgotten. Too weird to be forgotten. "That was nice."

"Ten thousand dollars."

It had taken Marisol ten minutes to recover. In all, they'd received enough to make up almost all of the lost grant money, and the donations were still pouring in. By the time she'd hung up the phone, Marisol felt like she finally understood what the universe had been trying to tell her all along.

That she'd find a way. Her way.

"Evan?"

"I also brought you this. You might not want it, but I thought it would make a good souvenir." He handed her a glossy magazine cover.

In Last Show, James January Finally Does Something Right.

Below the headline was a picture of Marisol and Evan wrapped in a kiss while James clapped from his messy desk.

Marisol knew exactly where this magazine cover would go. In a frame, right in the middle of her living room so everyone could see it. And maybe another copy for her bedroom. And one for *Ahora* headquarters. And one for—

"You want me to get rid of it? I mean I know the magazines aren't your favorite."

She grinned up at him. "You're my favorite."

And then, despite all her promises to Annie, they were kissing. And kissing. And kissing.

His mouth felt hungrier than all the other times they'd kissed, and she knew hers was too. The clock was ticking louder on the time they had left, and everything else faded into the background.

"Marisol?" He pressed his forehead to hers, pulling her top lip between his. Then the bottom. Then another full, desperate kiss that made her forget everything but the way his hands fit perfectly against her face.

"*¿Sí?*"

"I forgot." His fingers skimmed the neckline of her dress,

moving ever so slowly, making small swirls along her skin. Which was all it took for this dress to go from her favorite piece of clothing to her worst enemy.

He tugged at the zipper, but only made it an inch before the knock sounded at the door.

"Mari." Annie's voice came from under the door. "We're late."

Evan groaned. "Make her go away."

Marisol didn't know whether she wanted to laugh or cry. "*Uno momento, por favor*," she called out. "Fix please." She straightened her dress and turned around.

"This has to count as cruel and unusual punishment." He pulled the zipper down, just a little more, and kissed the back of her neck. And her shoulder. And the ridge of her spine.

"Mari. If you are messing up that hair!" Annie called.

Evan pulled the zipper up and pushed her toward the door. "She means business."

"You have no idea." Marisol pulled open the door. "Look, I didn't mess it up. Too much…" Her words faded as she took in the sheer amount of people on the other side of the door. Annie. Felipe. Julia. Penny. James January. Sammy Samuelson.

"Sammy Samuelson?!" Her brain shuttered and shut off. The host of *Who's Got the Coconut* was at her door.

So she slammed it shut.

"Evan. Evan! Sammy Samuelson is out there." Her heart seemed to be beating in her throat, and nothing was making sense.

"Yep, and I assume you want to hear what he has to say." Evan pulled the door back open, and Marisol took a deep breath.

"Right. Oh. I am very sorry. Nice to meet you." She extended a hand toward the game show host—who had the courtesy to pretend she hadn't just had a complete mental breakdown at the sight of his face.

"I thought it would be nice to meet you tomorrow before the show," Sammy said. "I hope that's okay. I know your appearance is going to give our special celebrity segment a great boost. We really appreciate you coming out on a Sunday."

She must have been hallucinating. Or maybe the part of her brain that understood English had packed up and gone home for the day. "My appearance?"

"You still haven't told her?" James asked. "My God, kids these days."

Marisol stared at Evan. "Told me what?"

"I was going to, but then you bozos showed up." Evan pulled a piece of paper from the inside pocket of his tuxedo jacket. "Marisol Gutierrez, tomorrow all your dreams—"

"Nobody does it right," Samuelson said. He cleared his throat, and the voice that emerged was the same one she'd been listening to for years. "Marisol Gutierrez, tomorrow all your dreams can come true. If you can find out WHO'S. GOT. THE COCONUT!"

The room went hazy at the edges. Her knees shook. And her tongue felt three sizes too big for her mouth.

"Mari?"

"Marisol?"

"Is she okay?"

"Her blood sugar. Mari, when was the last time you checked your blood sugar?" Felipe asked.

"She just checked it," Annie answered. "Was it low then? High? Mari?"

She swallowed hard and leaned against the wall for support. "It was fine. I am fine." Her vision cleared and everything shifted back into place. "This is the problem when everyone in your family is a doctor," she explained. "You cannot even faint from excitement without someone trying to stick you with a needle."

Everyone chuckled, and Evan helped her stand upright.

"You ready then?" Annie asked, tucking a bobby pin back into Marisol's hair.

"Depends. I want to make sure we get there too late to see any part of"—James pulled a pink piece of paper from his back pocket—"*Foreskins of Our Forefathers*. I don't need to know anything about George Washington's foreskin status, thank you very much."

Marisol shut the door behind the crowd, watching them

meander their way toward the elevator doors. The sounds of laughter and dirty jokes trailed behind them. Most people would say they were a little too loud and little too brash for their long dresses and dark tuxedos.

To Marisol, they were perfect.

"Ready?" Evan asked.

"Ready."

DAY THIRTEEN

Over the last twenty-four hours, the studio had begun to shutter. Someone packed away the paintings and knickknacks from the set. Soon someone would entomb James's desk in bubble wrap to await its next host—a host who, Evan suspected, would be unlikely to cover it with crumpled pages each day. And someone else had begun to cart out boxes of props.

That last someone was Penny.

"Wait." Evan hobbled his way through the door. "Do you have to take this stuff right now?"

"Unless you're planning to haul it all out on one leg."

"I'm sorry you got stuck doing all my work again."

"I know. I just like to remind you." She gave him a haughty grin. "What do you want? Everybody's taken something so far. James took three plastic skeletons. I think Julia took a pair of shoes or something. I, on the other hand, am now the proud owner of an entire box of fake turds."

"Nice."

"I can't wait for Christmas."

"I need a costume." He lowered himself into the closest chair.

"Oh. I didn't expect you to be into kinky stuff."

"For *Who's Got the Coconut*."

"Not as fun." She kicked a box toward him. "There's some stuff in here. I think most of the clothes are still in the back corner. Take your pick. I'll be back an hour or two."

"Where are you going?"

"I've got a date. And then James needs me to sign some paperwork for the tour."

"Tour?" Evan asked, but she was already gone. He lowered himself into a nearby chair and tried to take it all in. To memorize every bizarre detail about this place. Because he feared that in a few weeks or months, no one would believe the things that had happened here. Including him.

"There you are." James stepped into the room, hands in his pockets. "I've been waiting around for you to show up."

"Sorry, traffic."

James waved him off. "I'm taking the show on the road. A different city every night. Roaring crowds. A cramped bus filled with your closest coworkers. What do you say?"

"What do I say?"

"Do you want to come along? We'll try to pay you this time. And not in college credit. If you wanted"—James kicked the ground—"we might be able to hire that girl who's always hanging around here. About this tall. Brown hair. Boobs for days."

Evan rolled his eyes. "Are you serious?"

"Yeah, she's got great boobs."

"James."

"Okay, okay. We need some good writers. Writers who'll take chances. You two are a good team. Plus, you know, then you could give it a go."

Time came to a startling halt. Could they really "give it a go"? Maybe this was nothing more than a weird, short-lived connection that wouldn't make it past the next bump in the road. Maybe it would fizzle out a month from now. Or six. A year.

But maybe not. They wouldn't know if they didn't give it a shot. Throw out the existing script and build their own.

Except Marisol loved nursing. Loved *Ahora*. Loved Nicaragua. After watching the pieces of that documentary a million times, Evan would give just about anything for her to talk about him the way she talked about those things. Yes, she was creative and funny and brilliant. But writing jokes on a bus so that upper class Americans could spend too much money on tickets and drinks to see James January? Never going to happen.

But Evan could take the job. He had nowhere to be now. Except home, which was only slightly less appealing than it had been a month ago. "How long is the tour?"

"Still working out the kinks, but I got the call this morning. They're going to start booking slots for the next two weeks. Probably have to play a few small clubs on short notice, but I want to ride the wave of publicity."

"And then?"

"And then we'll see how it goes. Maybe it'll fizzle out after two weeks. Maybe we'll get an installation in Vegas." James flung his arms wide. "I can see it now. James January and Celine Dion. Live at the Bellagio."

"Celine Dion?"

"So you're in," James said, winking. "Perfect, now how do we get ahold of your lady?"

"You can ask Marisol, but I think you're in for a losing battle. But I'm in. On two conditions. Wait, no three conditions."

James crossed his arms across his chest. "I'm listening."

"One: no more nicknames. Two: we have to take the tour to Peoria. We'll fill the seats, I swear." Gramps would have half the senior center in the audience, no doubt.

"I can handle number two. Number one is going to be tougher. What do you think about—"

"Three: you call everyone you know in Hollywood and find Julia a job before we go." He knew he didn't have to say why, not after she'd held this sinking ship together until the very end. She might have been crazy sometimes, but she still managed to pull off what no one else had managed: letting them go out with grace.

"Already done. Did it yesterday in fact. Right along the same time I snagged you this." James pulled a business card out of his pocket. "He's a pompous old bat, but he's an old bat who knows a lot of people."

EASTON SULLIVAN, AWARD-WINNING DOCUMENTARIAN

Followed by a handwritten number and a note on the back.

Evan, I'm running a documentary master class in the spring. There's a seat for you if you want it. No charge. Loved your work.

"Thanks, James." Evan slipped the card into his pocket. Working on *Ahora's* documentary had reignited something inside him—those same flickers of excitement he'd gotten as a kid, when he found a way to tell a story. To string together bits of people's lives into something more. Something that could actually change people's lives.

"I'll get you the paperwork. And"—James glanced into the hall—"how about I let you tell this lovely lady what we discussed?"

"What did you discuss?" Marisol breezed into the room, with a smile thirteen miles wide on her face. "Was it the secret to winning the Big Bank Blowout on *Coconut*? Because I have a theory—"

"I'm sure you do," James said. "I'll let you tell Evan all about it. If you guys decide to ditch that jerkoff Samuelson and his dollar-store toasters, the party invitation still stands."

Marisol ignored his dig at the show. "Thank you for coming last night."

James clapped her on the back. "Sorry you didn't take home the prize."

Her smile didn't falter. "My mother called this morning. Your fans have donated enough for us to go back to four brigades each year until my brother comes home."

"We make quite a team, I'd say." James offered Evan a pointed look and left the room.

"Did you find us costumes?" She'd gone all bug-eyed and crazy with excitement. "We only have two hours before the line starts."

"We don't have to wait in line."

"But that is part of the fun." She winked and sat on his lap, careful to avoid his bad leg.

"We could have more fun in here. I bet there are still a few couches around here somewhere."

"Evan."

"What? I'm just saying, we don't have to go out there in the heat and wait next to all those sweaty people in their old Halloween costumes." He pulled her face to his, tracing the lines of it with his fingers. Then he was tracing other parts of her, etching them into this brain so he could access them when she was gone.

Tomorrow.

Marisol straddled him, hands wrapped around his neck. "But if we do not wait outside, how will I rub it in the peacock's face when I am chosen and he has to stay outside?"

"I'm sure he'll see it on television." He ran a thumb over her lip, and the way her eyelids fluttered closed suggested he was closer to winning than he'd thought. "Besides, we can't do this outside." He let his mouth brush against hers, but just barely, pulling out the moment until she let a whimper escape.

"Evan."

"Hmm?" He didn't move.

She closed the gap, biting his bottom lip a little before she pressed all of herself against him. Her hips moved in circles, and he grabbed her, pulling her as close they could possibly get with all these clothes between them.

"Ahem. I, uh, don't mean to interrupt. Well, I guess I do."

Marisol pulled back but didn't get up. And Evan said a little prayer of thanks, because he didn't want to talk to his boss with a raging boner on display.

"I'm headed out for the afternoon," James said. "Did you have time to discuss… Obviously you weren't doing much talking, so I'll just say it. Marisol, I want you to come work for me. We're taking the show on the road. Think of it like the world's best road-trip, where you share a bathroom with your coworkers. The pay is decent, but not great, and I can—"

"No."

"You didn't let me finish. Evan's coming. You guys can do this"—he pointed to their chair—"any time you want. Okay, maybe not in front of everyone. That would get old."

She glanced at Evan, and for two solid beats his heart stopped. And in those two beats his hopes swelled to bursting.

Then they burst.

"I have to go home. I am flattered though."

James shrugged. "He said you'd say that, but I had to give it a go. Okay, you kids carry on. Don't use the condoms in here though. I think those have been around since Johnny Carson was here." Then he was gone.

"Are you mad?" she asked. "It sounds fun, but—"

Evan kissed her, lightly this time but still hard enough to cut off her words. He didn't want to think about what could come after that "but."

"I'm not mad. But right now"—he scooted her off of his lap—"we have to find costumes pretty damn quick if we're going to show that peacock who's boss."

• • •

The studio was freezing cold, but between nerves and the costume and being wedged into the audience with a hundred other people, Marisol's body was playing a game of temperature ping-pong. Either she was sweating or covered in goose bumps. Sometimes both.

If only they would just call her name.

The show was already two segments in, and no one had so much as uttered her name over the PA system. Instead, a woman dressed as a cowgirl won a new car. And during the family game, a mom, dad, and their two daughters won a thousand dollars, which they promptly lost by betting it on a chance to win a vacation to Costa Rica.

One segment left.

"See the guy over there? The one dressed as the Pillsbury Doughboy?"

Marisol nodded.

"He came to a taping of *So Late* once. Rushed the stage and mooned everyone. Then put his bare ass on James's desk." Evan had been like this the entire time. Laid-back, relaxed. Like being promised a spot on *Who's Got the Coconut* was something he did every day.

"Why aren't you nervous?" she asked.

"Let's see. For starters, you made me dress up as a mermaid. So I already used up all of my potential embarrassment for the day."

"Merman."

"This tail doesn't exactly scream mer*man*." He pointed to the pink sequined tail covering his legs. "But whatever—I'm secure in my masculinity. Plus, you're the one going onstage. Not me. And I took two pain pills this morning."

"You got any more of those pills?" the giant gnome beside them asked. Clint.

Evan rolled his eyes. "You have twenty thousand dollars. Buy your own pain meds, man."

"About that, Marisol—"

"I heard they found your paperwork," she said.

"Weird, right? I guess someone—I think we know who—put it in a box with a bunch of toilet paper? Luckily for me, Thursday night's seafood buffet didn't go so well."

"Congratulations, Clint," she said. "You deserve the money."

The lights flickered overhead, signaling the start to the next segment. Marisol took a deep breath and adjusted the stem on her giant banana costume. This was it.

"Now, let's get down to business." Sammy Samuelson paced the length of the stage. His suit seemed a size too small, and between every segment some poor guy had to rush onstage and powder his forehead. "We've had some wins this afternoon. We've had some losses. But what really need is someone to root for. An underdog, if you will."

A burst of applause.

"Let's bring down this gentleman right here in the center. *Patriot Ninja Fighter* champion, Kevin Clipton."

The spotlight scanned the crowd, and a muscular man wearing a dog collar and a headband with two brown floppy ears lumbered toward the stage. The applause continued as Samuelson made his way toward the other end of the stage. "We need two more people

214

for our special celebrity challenge. Let's see if we have any more in the audience tonight."

He held a hand over his eyes as though he were looking for a ship lost at sea. "Who remembers the 1980s children's show *My Robot Peacock*?" Light applause. "Well, I have it on good authority that he is neither a peacock nor a robot. But that doesn't stop him from dressing like one. Step on up here, Sam Urban!"

There he was. That asshole peacock, with his stupid tail feathers, looking oh-so-smug as he stepped onstage. "He's a celebrity?" she whispered.

"No. That show aired three times in the 80s, then it got cancelled."

"Why?"

"He got arrested. Held a kid down on the set of the show and farted on him."

Marisol blanched.

"And one more," Samuelson announced.

Here it was. The moment she'd been waiting for her entire life. Some little girls dreamed about jobs and weddings and meeting rock stars. Marisol had dreamed of hearing her name over the *Who's Got the Coconut* speakers.

"I think you guys will like this one," Samuelson said. "A living, breathing legend around these parts. Marisol Gutierrez."

"Go." Evan squeezed her hand. "Knock 'em dead."

"Marisol Gutierrez? I know you're out there. I see you in that banana costume."

Every face in the audience turned in her direction, but her muscles refused to move.

"You okay?" Evan whispered.

She shook her head, just a fraction of an inch. How was it that *now*, after all of this, she'd been hit with an epic case of stage fright?

"Look at me." Evan turned her face to his. "You okay?"

No. She was definitely, 100 percent not okay. Everything she'd wanted for so long was right there in front of her. And tomorrow it would all be gone. "Yes. Just nervous."

He kissed her then. Only a peck, but it sent the crowd into a fit of applause.

"Then get up there and kick the peacock's ass."

It was exactly what she needed to hear. Somehow, Evan always knew exactly what she needed to hear.

Marisol pressed her mouth to his—harder this time—and the audience went from fits of applause to full roar. With that long, lingering kiss she tried to convey all the things she wanted to say. Things like *thank you* and *this is real* and maybe, if she really let herself say it, *love*. And when the kiss ended, Marisol launched herself through the crowd and straight to the stage, ready to fight to the death for her place on the champion's throne.

• • •

Evan swiped his key card over the door to *So Late* one last time. By now, almost everything was gone. Only a few boxes waiting to make their final trek to the network's prop graveyard and a few pieces of bulky furniture remained. Once he and Marisol stuffed their costumes into one of those boxes, he'd never be back here again.

He flipped on the lights, and the sound of his crutches on the concrete floors echoed through the hall. "I was going to say you could keep the banana costume if you wanted, but..."

Marisol laughed and shoved a lock of wet hair from her face. A trail of water followed from the door to where she stood, pooling beneath her feet. "No room in my suitcase anyway."

She'd blown away the competition in the first round, slaying the peacock with her ability to complete obstacle courses while calling out the American prices of everyday grocery items. But the final round had ended in dunk tank situation she couldn't survive. Not in a giant banana costume that made it impossible for her to balance on one leg while simultaneously guessing the cost of a new washer and dryer set.

"I'm sorry you didn't win."

"*Ahora* does not need a new washer and dryer anyway."

"Definitely no room in your suitcase for that."

They stood there, him on crutches in his ridiculous mermaid tail and her dripping from her waterlogged banana, and a long silence stretched between them.

This was it. The actual end. Here in this empty studio, they'd say goodbye. He'd start a new chapter in his life. A chapter that didn't involve running scripts back and forth or men dressed in diapers.

One that didn't involve Marisol.

"How about we change and take one last look around?" he asked.

Marisol gave him a small smile, and he could see she felt the end nearing too. "I would like that. Are you okay?"

"I'll be better after you take this off of me."

"Can you get it off yourself?" She grinned.

"You know I can't."

"Interesting." Marisol wandered toward some of the boxes.

"You wouldn't dare." He knew she would. Which was why he loved her.

Shit.

He did love her. Maybe he hadn't known her long enough to know if she was *the one*. Maybe he didn't know every little thing about her life back home. But this version of her—the one who'd dive into a dunk tank dressed as a banana? Who'd force him to walk around in a sequined merman tail all night? He loved her.

"I think pink is a good color for you."

"Marisol."

"*¿Sí?*" All innocence.

"Marisol."

"Okay, fine. But do you have your phone?"

"Yeah."

She stepped away from the boxes and slipped her arms around his waist. He had to duck to avoid getting smacked by the stem of the banana.

"I want to take a picture. Of us," she said.

"You haven't had enough of that?" But already he was fumbling toward his back pocket and pulling out his phone.

"I want a picture of the real us. This one."

"Turn around." Evan held the phone out as far as his orangutan arms would allow and snapped a photo of their faces smashed together. Marisol's surrounded by the yellow foam, and his surrounded by the flowing blond merman wig.

"Will you email it to me?" she asked. "Since my phone…"

He nodded. "I need your email address."

She held out her hand, and he gave her the phone. A few swipes of the screen later he had it back. She unhooked his tail and left him to wiggle it off while she dripped her way toward the bathroom.

"Hey," she called from behind the door. "Please tell your grandfather thank you for the donation. We will send him a letter, but please tell him personally from me."

"What?"

"Your grandfather? Donald Abramson from Peoria, Illinois?" She emerged from behind the door, in her dry jeans and tank top. "Where should I put the banana?"

"Leave it there. *Donald* Abramson? You're sure?"

"Yes. My mother read off some of the names to me. I thought it must be your grandfather?"

Evan's mind spun. "Nope. Not Gramps."

"Oh. I thought because of the city—"

"That's my dad." He sagged on his crutches and let out a sigh. His dad would never apologize. The man had never apologized for anything. Ever. But this was his olive branch, and it was one that extended beyond the two of them. Evan made a silent promise to call him tomorrow.

"Will you tell him I said thank you then?" she asked.

He nodded then pulled off the merman wig. "Ready for the final tour?"

"Do I get to sit on James's desk?"

"If it's still there."

When they made it onto the set, Evan flipped on the lights over the audience seats. It gave the room a backwards glow, illuminating the empty chairs and leaving the stage mostly dark. The furniture still sat in its place, but the usual clutter had disappeared. There was no trace of *So Late* anywhere. Now it was a generic set that could adapt to whatever new show the network decided to try.

"Sit." Marisol pointed to the couch as she propped her feet on the desk and laced her fingers together behind her head. "Mr. Abramson, my producers tell me you have a new job on the way."

A bang-up impression of James.

"You watched the show?"

She smiled. "Last night, after the awards. I put the discs you gave me on my laptop."

"What did you think?"

"You are going to have a lot of fun on your road trip with James." A sadness crept into the edges of her voice before she went back to her official talk show host voice. "Mr. Abramson, before the show, my producers told me you have some unique talents."

Evan leaned back, with one arm stretched over either side of the couch. "Well, according to one Easton Sullivan, I have quite the eye—"

"Nope. Not that talent." She put her feet down and wheeled the desk chair closer to him. "They said you were a very good kisser."

He knew that dopey smile was back, the one that had gotten him into this beautiful mess in the first place. "Your producers told you that?"

Marisol crawled over the arm of the couch and kissed his cheek. "Did I mention I am the producers?"

"You didn't." He pulled her onto his lap, until she had one leg on either side of him. And in the length of one slow, breathless kiss, they were right back where they'd left off earlier. "Did your producers tell you anything else interesting?"

He brushed the hair back from her neck and laid a barely-there kiss. Another behind her ear. Every time his lips met her skin, her hips moved a fraction of an inch. And with every movement his body begged to touch more of her.

"No, I think they left the rest for me to find out." She pulled his mouth to hers.

His hands slid up her back, savoring every inch of her warmth. A part of him let out a few weak-willed warnings: this was a supremely bad idea, it would make tomorrow—when he was still here and she was gone—so much harder, someone could walk in, the doctor had advised him against rigorous activity. But none of those warnings matched the fervor of their bodies pressed together on that couch.

"Evan?" she asked between breaths. "What are the chances that someone is going to come in here?"

"Unlikely. Everyone's at James's party." *How is anyone so perfect?* "But not impossible."

Marisol leaned in so they were forehead to forehead, nose to nose, lip to lip. "I will take the chance, if you will."

"I'm all in."

DAY NINETY-NINE

The Managua airport always made her feel like a rat navigating a maze. Start and stop. Turn around. Start again. Over and over until she found who she was looking for. And today, no matter how hard she tried, Marisol couldn't find the one person she was looking for.

She'd found the man with two screaming toddlers three times.

Four times, she'd circled a lanky teenager surrounded by a half dozen bags.

And more than once, she'd caught the eye of the handsome pilot who'd ducked into the bar.

But Evan? Not once.

Maybe he changed his mind? She pulled out her phone to check for missed messages. But nothing there said he'd missed his connection in Miami. Nothing to say he'd come to his senses and stayed put in the US.

After she left LA, she'd told herself not to email him.

She had.

When he'd responded with tales from the *Not Late Enough to Be Early* tour, she told herself she wouldn't hit reply.

She had.

The first time he'd asked if she wanted to Skype, she told herself she was stringing this along for no good reason.

Still, she'd sat down in front of her laptop and logged on.

And when Evan said the tour was taking a break and asked if she wanted to show him around Managua—help him shoot some footage for a documentary he'd been thinking about making—her heart latched onto the idea and refused to let go.

But now, on her fifth trip around the commotion of the airport,

Marisol's stomach was in knots. What if he slept in footie pajamas with a trapdoor in the back? What if he hated the way she let mail pile up on her kitchen table? What if they'd both changed so much in the last few months that their *thing*—that unnamable pop between them—was a thing of the distant past?

What if their two weeks had been up months ago?

This was a bad idea. Maybe the worst idea. He wasn't coming. Their expiration date had passed, and he'd simply realized it before she had.

"Excuse me? I'm looking for this girl. About this tall, sometimes dresses like a banana?"

She whipped around.

Every *maybe*, every *what if* fell away. He was there. In front of her.

"Evan!"

He swept her into a hug, and she buried her face in his neck. All the old memories—the ones that had become dreamlike in the passing months—were real again. The way he smelled. The feel of his scruff against her cheek. The curl that insisted on performing a one-man revolt.

"I got stuck in customs. Those guys have no sense of humor. All I said was that I was coming here to find a sexy nurse, and—bam—I'm a suspicious person."

She pulled back to look at him. "You did not."

"Yeah, let's go with that." He pressed his forehead to hers, grinning.

Marisol wrapped her arms around his neck. If they'd passed their expiration date, her heart didn't know it yet. The look on Evan's face said his didn't either.

"I missed you," she whispered amid the chaos.

"God, I missed you too."

And when he pressed her lips to hers, there was nothing left to do but hold on. Maybe they'd crash and burn.

Or maybe not.

ACKNOWLEDGMENTS

Being an author is the hardest thing I've ever done, at least voluntarily. But there are people who make it easier. People like my lovely agent, Jess Watterson, who doesn't miss a beat when I spam her with book ideas about Elmo. People like the crew at Diversion Books: Randall, who keeps me from inadvertently committing defamation; Mallory and Nita, who make my life better in a million ways (most of them involving GIFs); Elizabeth, a copyediting boss; and Sarah, who doesn't throttle me when I take too long to turn in proofs.

There are a hundred more people who made this book happen, but I only have room to thank a few. So, extra special thanks to Sarah Glenn Marsh for lending me her expertise and for being such a kind human, Eric Cummings for his countless attempts to explain Dungeons and Dragons (and for the line about dick jokes), and B for coming up with the best game show title of all time. And, of course, thanks to my husband who has read this book more times than anyone (maybe even me). I love you.

Finally, a story. In 2014, I was waiting in the audience holding area at a certain late night talk show. In front of me sat one of the show's interns and a girl who had come to nearly every taping for the last year. Boom, the idea for this book was born. So thank you, Universe, for that serendipitous moment involving robot skeletons, *Veronica Mars*, and me being nosy AF.

AMANDA HEGER is a writer, attorney, and bookworm. She lives in the Midwest with her unruly rescue dogs and a husband who encourages her delusions of grandeur. Amanda strongly believes Amy Poehler is her soul mate, and one of her life goals is to adopt a pig and name it Ron Swineson.

Sign up for her newsletter (**eepurl.com/bM_XXf**) or visit her online (**www.amandaheger.com**).

CPSIA information can be obtained at www.ICGtesting.com
Printed in the USA
BVOW02s0315300916

463713BV00002B/2/P